The King of Hearts

The King of Hearts

St. Clair Publications

ISBN 978-1-935786-12-2

Printed in the United States of America by

St. Clair Publications

P. O. Box 726

Mc Minnville, TN 37111-0726

Cover Design by Kent Hesselbein

The King of Hearts

http://www.kghdesignstudio.com/services.html

The King of Hearts is purely a work of fiction. Any likeness to any person, living or dead is entirely coincidental

"Thank you, Lord Jesus for showing me the path of righteousness; I love you with all of my heart, all of my soul, and all of my mind..."

To My Canadian Princess,
"This is the way it should have happened..."

In Loving Memory of Buddy

"Ich liebe Dich mein kleiner Bud-man"

I would like to extend my deepest appreciation to my daughter, Moriah Tibbetts, for her extensive help on this project. I would also like to thank Stan St. Clair for giving me the opportunity to write this book.

I would like to give special appreciation to Ms. Amy Lignor—*"You are the best friend a person could ever have."*

Many thanks to Maryglenn McCombs, Sheila Bice, Kandice Bice, Ray Boyce, Aunt Mary, and all the citizens of Lubbock for making this book possible. May God bless you.

The King of Hearts

The King Of Hearts

Frank Tibbetts

Edited by Stan St. Clair

and Amy Lignor

"You've got one shot before you die... one word—one **song** *to sum up who you were, and to describe how you felt about your life on this planet to let everyone know that you even existed. Is that the song you'd sing? Or, would you sing something else..."*

The King of Hearts

1

"I was underneath the willow," Tim whispered. Staring up at Jamie, he felt the tear trickle down his cheek, as he slowly made his way up the steps of their beautiful log home in the brilliant-colored hills of Tennessee. The veil of sorrow hung so heavy on his heart that he could barely raise his head as he entered the house.

———

The afternoon breeze was warm and gentle, keeping time with the lazy, late summer days. Jamie's silky, deep brown hair moved ever-so-slightly, as if the breeze was whispering secrets in her ears. The porch swing drifted back and forth as she leisurely pumped her legs like a sleepy child on a swing-set in the park.

Jamie took time to reflect back on the very first time she'd met her uniquely handsome and incredibly talented husband. At least, that's how she'd perceived Tim when he had first entered her world...

———

It was a Friday night many years ago, at a restaurant on the outskirts of Lubbock. Jamie and a friend had stopped in at *The Copper Caboose*; the perfect location to knock back a couple of drinks and unwind from the busy week. The restaurant had a huge bar and karaoke stage, and as the blessed margarita was placed before her, the DJ announced that the next singer to appear would be Tim Cunningham.

People applauded; some even whistled as he stepped onto the stage and lifted the microphone from the stand. The mirrored disco ball above twinkled, creating magical snowflakes that floated around the room like tiny diamond stars.

Jamie remembered that first look like it was yesterday. Dressed in a black, long-sleeved Western shirt with white seams, tucked neatly into a pair of faded Wrangler jeans, Tim Cunningham had been the poster child for sexy. The ringlets of his black, *Harley Davidson* motorcycle boots gleamed in the light as he walked slowly to the front of the stage, closed his eyes, and prepared to sing.

Jamie didn't pay too much attention to Tim until he began his intro. Then, it felt as if the heavens had opened their doors. The crowd grew quiet, as if holding their breath for the miracle that was about to occur, as he began to sing the opening lines of Frankie Avalon's, *Venus.*

Every word dripped like honey from his lips. Tim had even glanced shyly around the room, making eye contact, "drawing" the audience in as he serenaded them with his velvet voice and powerful vibrato. His eyes had claimed Jamie's for only a brief second before moving along, and that's when the attraction had hit her full force.

She'd continued to watch him, and by the time Tim Cunningham had finished his song, her heart had melted.

People stood up from their chairs in a rush. They

whistled and clapped wildly as Tim stepped down from the stage. Wearing a sheepish grin on his face, Tim had taken the time to shake hands with some of the patrons who were complimenting him on his magnificent performance. Then, he'd calmly walked to a table, taken a seat, and drunk a beer...alone.

Jamie had tried to keep up the conversation with her friend, but her mind was far away. She kept glancing at his table waiting to see if a hidden girlfriend might suddenly appear, but no one ever came.

"I know who you're looking at," her friend remarked with a Cheshire Cat grin on her face. "You should go over and talk to him."

"I can't help it," Jamie announced. "He has the most beautiful voice I've ever heard."

"Go over and talk to him, Jamie! It's not like he's going to bite your head off or anything! Besides, he looks lonely." Her friend offered sad, puppy-dog eyes, and practically pushed Jamie out of her chair.

Jamie took a deep breath, exhaled, and made her way slowly through the smoke-filled room. She barely noticed the crowds of people ordering drinks at the bar; the bystanders who were watching people out on the dance floor; and, a stranger whistling at her as she walked by. None of this was remotely important. There was only *him.*

With every step closer, Jamie's heart beat harder in her chest. Reaching her final destination, she'd stood there for a few moments attempting to build up the courage she needed to speak.

"I'm Jamie," she said, nervously.

Like a true 'gentleman'–the ones who Jamie thought didn't even exist anymore–Tim had stood up and shook her hand with *both* of his. The diamond horseshoe ring he wore on his right pinky finger glimmered in the lights.

"Tim," he'd replied in a shy, quiet tone.

Jamie looked at him and then glanced down at the table, hoping with all her heart that he would invite her to take the vacant seat beside him.

"You can sit down if you want," he said, quickly. "Uh...would you like me to get you a drink?"

"I'd like that a lot." She smiled. "Just as long as you'll be my company."

He went to the bar and ordered, returning to the table they now shared. His stunning voice, alone, had Jamie daydreaming about sharing far more than a table with him in the future. Soon, the picture of a dream house that they would one day inhabit together appeared inside Jamie's mind.

"They'll bring the drinks in a few minutes," he said, shrugging his shoulders. "Seems they're really busy tonight."

Jamie smiled wide. "They all came to hear you."

Jamie was always so happy after she'd found out what Tim had been thinking that same night–that same blessed meeting...

The fragrant bouquet of her perfume had invaded his senses. To him, he'd told her later, that night was pure heaven. He'd not only seen how remarkably beautiful she was, but he'd also been amazed that she was pure elegance and absolutely adorable at the same time in her tight blue jeans and black T-shirt with *Hard Rock Café* inscribed across the front. Her petite features, pouty pink lips, and emerald green eyes were perfectly blended into a soft look that had reminded Tim of a mix between Scarlett O'Hara and Elizabeth Taylor–and his imagination had run wild. He had been afraid that his eyes would betray him; that she would know he was thinking how drop-dead gorgeous she was.

But Jamie *had* wanted him to see her as the girl in his song. She longed to see that passion in his eyes that night, so she would've known for a fact that she'd been beautiful in his eyes. After all, for her, it had been love at first sight.

The waitress brought her drink over. It had been such an extraordinary meeting that Jamie could still remember the coaster that'd read, *Miller-Lite* on the table.

"That was the most beautiful song I've ever heard." Her words had made Tim's face turn blood red.

"Thank you," he replied, in a very humble tone. "I *love* to sing. For as long as I can remember, I've always dreamed of being a singer."

"You *are* a singer." Jamie knew then that she'd been looking at him like a love-struck teenager, but she couldn't stop herself. Lightning had struck!

Moving closer to Tim, she'd made sure to tell him the words she knew he wanted to hear. "And you're the **best** singer I've ever heard."

In that smoke-filled bar, where some unknown karaoke singer was now butchering Hank Jr.'s, *There's a Tear in my Beer*, a single, solitary tear had streamed down Tim Cunningham's face. And the world had shifted under

Jamie's feet.

Jamie loved to think about that first night. They had been married now for almost a year, and she loved him more every day. He played his guitar and sang for her whenever she asked him to, and he'd written so many beautiful songs just for *her*, that Jamie was filled with thanks every single day that the "powers that be" had brought Tim into her life.

2

She'd been born Jamie Louise Finney, in a town called Bath, New Brunswick—a lovely Canadian province.

The fourth of five siblings, Jamie had been a beautiful child—the apple of her father's eye. Her hardworking father was her idol, as well. While owning his own appliance store, Jamie's mother, Becky, rounded things out by managing a restaurant at a local truck stop.

Jamie loved ice skating and had, at just three-years-old, started learning to ice skate. She'd become quite proficient over time, and had harbored the dream of one day becoming a professional figure skater.

Her school had an ice rink in their freezing cold basement, and Jamie could always be found there after school skating with her classmates. They would all take turns warming their hands by an old wood stove that sat in a corner near the benches. She and her friends talked about which boys were cute, who they wanted to marry, and how cool the *Boston Bruins* were—fairly normal conversation for little girls with big dreams.

Effie was her playmate when she was just a little girl. Effie was a lovely little doll who Jamie used to play dress-up with, and took her for strolls in her small, dainty baby carriage. Although Effie was only made of cloth, she was truly Jamie's best friend. She loved to be smothered with angel kisses and hugs, and Jamie took her everywhere. Effie also got spankings sometimes, for talking back or not minding her manners but, for the most part, she was a good little dolly. Nowadays, poor Effie lived all alone in a small hope chest in the bottom of their bedroom closet. Her 'old' eyes now sad–the once best friend of a little girl whose big dreams had changed.

Once in a while, when Tim was at work, Jamie would take Effie out and give her a hug, remembering all of their beautiful times together.

But other times, the 'darker' memories occurred. One day in particular stuck in Jamie's mind because of how hard she had cried. Dressing Sammie, her cat, in a lovely blue doll dress, Jamie had taken him for a walk in her baby carriage. As she'd come around the corner, Sammie sprang from the carriage and darted off down the street in his girlie dress. Jamie ran as fast as she could to try and catch him, but he'd been too fast for her. And she never saw him again. After that, Effie had been the only one donning the dress and accompanying Jamie on her walks. At least Effie wouldn't disappear.

When she turned eleven, Jamie and her family moved from Canada. The economy had been so bad in the North, that her father feared they would lose everything if they stayed. Jamie's Aunt, who lived in Lubbock, had persuaded her father to sell the appliance store and move to the Lone Star State. So, selling everything they owned, Dad had loaded everyone–including their golden retriever –into his beige Ford station wagon and headed for Texas.

Soon, her father drove a bus for the Lubbock School District, before eventually moving on to truck driving for *LIGON* truck lines. A decision he would probably not have made...if he'd known. One night, after driving for far too many hours, Dad had fallen asleep behind the steering wheel just as he was passing through Amarillo...on his way home. Yet another who disappeared.

Jamie had spent the rest of her teenage years in Lubbock. Working on and off after she graduated from high school, Jamie attended Texas Tech University when she could afford the tuition for a semester. She wanted so badly to get a Bachelor's degree in English literature and teach grade school, and had just managed to get her U.S. citizenship about eight months before she'd met *the one*.

3

Tim's childhood memories of inferiority whirred inside his head like a fan in a turbine. He would rather forget them all, which was the real reason why he hadn't yet shared them with Jamie.

I'm not good-looking, Tim thought as he drove. *I don't know* ***what*** *Jamie sees in me.*

Pushing away the negative thoughts, he decided to concentrate on how proud he was to now be living in Lubbock. The people he'd met were so warm and friendly; it was like he'd been transported back in time somehow. Here, in what felt like actual 'home,' everyone still wore Stetson hats, cowboy boots, and Wrangler jeans with the big belt buckles. Everyone knew everyone–everyone helped everyone. To Tim, they were the genuine article.

Tim was a short, flat-topped Sergeant stationed at Reese Air Force Base and had been there for five years. He thrived on hard work, the wonderful people around him, and nostalgia. Lubbock was a place for Tim that not only personified a 'present' filled with kindness and honor —but also a truly mystical past. It was cool living where *Buddy Holly* was born; he just wished that he could have met him before he died. But he never lost hope that he could perhaps meet other local heroes, like *Delbert McClinton, The Flatlanders, or Mac Davis.*

The *Strip* was a blessing. The myriad of clubs offered Tim a chance to perform and do what he truly loved. Lubbock, within the city limits, was 'dry,' which meant no alcoholic beverages could be sold in stores. But the *Strip*, located on the outer rim of the wonderful city, was lit up like downtown Las Vegas and sold alcohol of any and all kinds. Not only was this an added extra, but being able to perform and have even had the opportunity to meet Jamie, were truly things that Tim was thankful for.

He was so excited pulling into the driveway that he could almost feel the light in his green eyes sparkle. He was so thrilled to be with his Jamie, the light of his life. The weekend had finally appeared and they would have some time together. What Tim was hoping for was that he could talk Jamie into getting a pet in the next couple of days. A small thing to some, but Tim wanted more than anything to add something "permanent" to their relationship, and a pet would announce to the world that they were a true item that would last forever.

The next day, Tim dragged Jamie into the pet store. The walls of the fish section were painted as if one were actually submerged in the beautiful ocean. The images of whales, sharks, and coral reefs surrounded them on all sides. Someone had obviously spent a great deal of time painting the mural, and it was really quite impressive.

The other end of the store had a small room with a variety of birds; the brilliant colors of the parakeets and finches, combined with the beauty and elegance of lovebirds, and a pair of heavenly white doves. All had their gazes locked on Tim, pleading with him to be the 'chosen one.'

"Um...you know, my birthday's coming up soon,"

he said to Jamie, the light shining in his eyes. Perhaps she'd fall in love with one of the animals and that could be his present. But she'd said not a word.

But what did happen, as far as Tim was concerned, was also fate. The "meeting" took place that day–the same meeting that a person always reads about in a book, sees in a movie, even hears in a song. Coming around the corner, waiting for Jamie to decide, Tim had stopped dead in his tracks; the black and tan Dachshund was no more than eight weeks old.

What set this one little guy apart from the rest of the litter was that he was slightly bow-legged. He sat all alone, off to one side, watching his brothers and sisters playing happily amongst themselves. A sad, lonely look was planted firmly upon his face, and the little almond eyes looked up at Tim as if he had heard the announcement of Tim's birthday and wanted more than anything to be the gift. Like Tim, this was a little boy who needed to be loved, and Tim was the savior he had longed for.

Tim stooped down to see if he would come to him. While the other pups were running around, exploring their surroundings, this one wagged his stubby tail, and trotted straight to him.

He looked at the man with his almond eyes, and tried to climb onto his knee, but he was too little to reach it. Tim picked him up and held him close to his face, as he stood back up.

The puppy was warm, soft, and velvety in his hands. His tail was wagging as fast as it could between his fingers, and he was licking his face vivaciously. Tim started to chuckle, as it tickled him a bit.

This encouraged the puppy even more as he floundered around in his hands. Tim held him out, smiling and staring at him, while he continued to lick at the air as if he were still licking his face. He held him to his chest and gently rocked him back and forth.

The pup could hear the sound of Tim's heart beating—he settled down and grew comfortable in his arms.

Jamie smiled and gently stroked his soft coat.

"Go ahead," she said, scratching behind his ears, "Happy birthday, Sweetheart." She could see the happiness in his face, as he nuzzled the velvet fur of the little pup with his nose. He raised his tiny head, and Tim could feel him trying to wag his tail between his fingers.

He picked out a thin, black, nylon leash and a black collar with rhinestones on it, and made his way to the checkout counter.

"Did you find everything alright?" the clerk asked. She was a pretty teenage girl with black hair and blue eyes.

"We sure did," Tim said. The puppy was squirming and grunting a bit.

"I'm surprised *that* one sold at all," she said, "because he's so bow-legged, but he's actually the only one we've sold."

"Well, I thought he was the cutest one out of all of them," he replied.

Jamie opened up her purse and drew out their checkbook.

"That comes to one-hundred and sixty-seven

dollars," the clerk said. She winced a bit and rang it up on the cash register. Jamie looked at Tim quickly for a moment, as she thought the price was a bit steep for a bow-legged dog. Tim sighed with a quick breath, and looked into the puppy's eyes.

"Guess it's too late to turn back now, huh little fella?" Jamie shook her head and then wrote out the check.

"He's had his first set of shots and been de-wormed, but you'll have to follow up with the rest of them," the clerk said, as if it would ease the pain of the price.

They made their way out of the store to the parking lot, and walked to their blue Toyota Corolla, which had seen its better days.

"I suppose you want me to drive now, huh?" Jamie asked, playfully sarcastic, then smiled at him.

"If you don't mind, I want to hold on to this little guy and try to think of a good name for him."

Jamie started the car, checked for oncoming traffic, and pulled into the street. Tim was gently petting his dog. When he held the puppy up and kissed him behind his soft, velvety ears, he wagged his tail. After some time had passed, she looked over at him and asked, "anything yet?"

"Well, I don't know," he replied, "what do you think about *Spanky?"*

"I'm not really crazy about that one," she said with a bit of a sneer, as she looked into the rear view mirror. "Why don't you try again?"

He held the puppy up and studied him closely.

Suddenly, it came to him, the *perfect* name: "How about Buddy?" he said aloud, for Tim absolutely *loved* Buddy Holly and his music. He was one of his favorite singers, and it was the perfect name for his new companion—it really fit.

"I like that one a lot better, Tim," Jamie said with a smile.

He looked at Buddy and repeated his name to him once more, then he looked at his wife with a sparkle in his eyes. "Thanks, Sweetheart, I know we really don't have the money for this, but thank you for letting me get him, he's a much better gift than an aquarium." He leaned over and kissed her on her cheek and she smiled softly.

When they finally reached their small apartment, Tim knew that Buddy was ready to go outside. "He's going to need some puppy chow," Jamie said.

"I know, Sweetheart, would you mind going without me? I need to walk him."

Just as she was taking in the last of the groceries, Buddy bowed up his back like a question mark to do his business.

Tim shot a quick, playful glance at Jamie, watching for her reaction. "Get that hump outta your back!" Tim yelled, his sides splitting with laughter.

Jamie started laughing, too. "Stop it, Tim! That's disgusting!"

As she was pulling out of the parking lot, Tim shouted, "You better pick up a bag of those rawhide bones, too! We don't want him chewing up any of our shoes!"

Buddy sniffed around awhile longer then toddled

back over to Tim. He picked him up and kissed him behind his ears. "Good Boy!" he said.

Jamie returned a half hour later with the rawhide bones, and Tim scattered them around the apartment. She also bought him a little squeak toy to play with.

They had *Hamburger Helper* for dinner that night, and Tim held Buddy in his lap as they ate, occasionally slipping him a noodle now and then. At one point, Tim put a noodle between his lips and lifted Buddy up to it. He tugged at it with his puppy teeth as Tim bit it in half. "Yes, sir!" he said, delighted. "Just like Lady and the Tramp!"

"Do you want me to set out another plate?" Jamie asked sarcastically, not knowing whether to be mad or laugh.

Tim grinned. "Naw, we're good," he said, slipping him another noodle.

After dinner, Tim took Buddy out for another walk then helped Jamie clean up the kitchen. Buddy sat behind Tim's legs as he dried the dishes, and whimpered a bit. The radio was on, and U2 was playing *With or Without You.*

Tim turned around, picked Buddy up, and started dancing with him, singing to him in his best *Bono* impersonation. He cradled him like an infant and rocked him from side to side. He rubbed his fat puppy tummy and Buddy wagged his tail. He was really enjoying the attention his new daddy was giving to him.

Jamie wound up the dish towel and popped Tim on the rear end with it. "You know he's not sleeping with us," she said in a most serious tone.

"I know," he said, as he lifted him up onto his

shoulder. Tim began patting his back as if he were going to burp him. Jamie reached to pet him and Buddy licked her hand.

After one last trip outdoors, it was time for bed. Tim took a shoe box from the closet, dumped out the shoes, and stuffed it with a couple of hand towels from the bathroom. He put Buddy in it, pointed at him, and said very sternly, “STAY!”

He repeated the command again as his finger pointed at him. He turned off the light and crawled into bed next to Jamie—the silence was broken after about thirty seconds.

Light whimpering started at first, which Tim had expected. He tried to ignore him, but Buddy’s bleating became louder and louder as he ran around the dark bedroom in search of Tim. He pawed at the bed, screaming as he tried to climb on top of it. The bed shook a little as Jamie snickered and tried not to let Buddy hear her.

“He sounds like a chimp!” Tim said, sitting up in the bed, amazed at how something so loud could come from something so small. Jamie burst into uncontrollable laughter at this because it was true. She could just picture a frantic chimpanzee racing around the room, screaming and bouncing off the walls. Tim had really hit the nail on the head with that one.

He sighed in the darkness, then reached down and picked him up. As he started to lie back down with Buddy, Jamie burst into one more fit of laughter as the sounds of flatulence echoed in the darkness—Tim had performed *shave and a haircut—get lost,* on Buddy’s tummy.

Tim laid his head back on his pillow and smiled,

for Buddy's whiskers were tickling his face. He was still whimpering as his tiny body lay on the pillow next to him. They lay there cheek to cheek as Tim cupped his hand over him, and finally they fell asleep.

4

After church on Sunday, Tim and Jamie took Buddy to the *Walk of Fame.* It was one of Tim's favorite places to go because it was peaceful there; there, he could *dream.* He had taken Jamie several times when they were dating and it held very precious memories for him, *of her.* They had held hands and walked together, as he first told her of his dreams to be a singer.

Now, as he stood before the statue of Buddy Holly —posed forever in his stance, holding his guitar and staring down at the neck of it—Tim could hear *Brown Eyed Handsome Man* echoing in the background of his mind. He wondered what it must've been like to have known him—to *be* him. Ah, the dreams were still so large now, as if Tim could simply reach out, grab that golden ring, and become the next great music man.

Tim walked over to Buddy's memorial plaque and read it, as he had done so many times before:

BUDDY HOLLY 1936-1959 — BUDDY HOLLY CONTRIBUTED TO THE MUSIC HERITAGE OF NOT ONLY WEST TEXAS BUT THE ENTIRE WORLD AS A MUSICIAN AND COMPOSER. IT IS SIGNIFICANT THAT THIS FIRST PLAQUE ON THE "WALK OF FAME" BEAR HIS NAME. THE CITIZENS OF LUBBOCK PAY TRIBUTE TO AND HONOR THEIR NATIVE SON.

Tim wondered if he would ever have a plaque one day with such nice things written on it about him. Yet another facet of that far away dream...

Buddy sat down beside Tim and looked between his owner and the statue; his sweet almond eyes so full of charm and intelligence that it looked like Buddy knew everything Tim was feeling without Tim needing to say it.

Picking him up in his arms, Tim pointed at Buddy's namesake. "This legend is where your name comes from, little guy!" Buddy wagged his tail, as Tim kissed his best friend and smiled at Jamie who was walking up beside them.

When payday came around once again, Tim purchased a book about Dachshunds, and sat on the couch reading it with Buddy in his lap.

As Jamie ironed and folded clothes in the bedroom, Tim drank in the historical and magnificent words that the author had to say. *Dachshunds originated in Germany in the 18th and 19th centuries. The term, "Dachshund," means* badger dog. *They were bred long and lean with short legs specifically to hunt badgers. They enter into their burrows and attack them. Fearless hunters, they will fight to the death, and have even been known to hunt foxes and wild boar.*

"Hmm," said Tim. "So you're a *veeshious leetle veener sneetzel*, huh?" Buddy gazed up at his master's suddenly odd tone and cocked his head to the side.

Laughing to himself, Tim looked back at the book. *Dachshunds bond very closely with their families. They like to curl up like a doughnut when they sleep, and they like to perch in high places, like on top of a couch. They love to play by their own rules, and can be very stubborn.*

"You sound like a regular James Dean," he mumbled to himself.

Putting the book down and retrieving a bag of Frito's from the kitchen, Buddy suddenly perked up—far more interested in the salty treat than anything about his species.

After being fed one, Buddy made it quite clear that he wanted another. After setting the dog on the floor, Tim brought his voice to "master status." Pushing Buddy's eagerly wagging rump onto the floor, he yelled, "Buddy, SIT!" Of course, rather than obeying (which was much less fun), Buddy started jumping up and down, begging for another snack. Tim wanted to make sure at this young age that his best, furry friend knew who was in charge, and repeated the action. After a few minutes, it was clear that Buddy finally realized that 'daddy' wasn't going to give him another treat, so he finally settled down.

Tim slowly lifted a Frito from the bag. "Buddy, s*prechen sie Deutsch!*" he said firmly. Buddy just sat there and stared.

Again, Tim gave the command, only now the voice was one of pleading and not commanding. "*Spurr-e-chen! Spurr-e-chen!*" he said, drawing out each syllable; slowly coaxing his best friend.

"Buddy, *sprechen sie Deutsch!!*" But Buddy showed no sign of sprechening in the least.

Tim turned as Jamie giggled, and emerged from the bedroom. "I think the correct term would be *Sprechen Deutsch.* Honey, you're asking him if he *can* speak German."

Tim looked down at Buddy; father and son seemed to sport the same exact look of pure and utter puzzlement.

"Are you sure?" he asked. "It just doesn't sound

Hitler-'esque' to me."

Jamie's smile grew wider. "You're so silly, Sweetheart. He's only a *puppy.* I doubt very much that he was born with the knowledge of his German descendants." Shaking her head, Jamie returned to the bedroom.

Tim got down on all fours and started bowing up and down, attempting to entice Buddy to jump and play. Tim laughed as Buddy's tail began to wag so fast that it looked like the furry one was a helicopter trying to take off the launching pad. Tim smiled. "Let's prove her wrong, pal. Siege Heil! Siege Heil! Siege Heil!" Buddy jumped into the air as Tim laughed and whispered to his best friend. "That means Salvation and Victory!"

Buddy barked.

"See? I knew you knew German!"

Tim woke up the next morning and took Buddy out for his morning walk before he left for work. Finishing his coffee, kissing Jamie goodbye, he headed for the 'coal mines.' But as all new fathers feel, Tim's heart broke as Buddy scraped and jumped against the storm door, seemingly crying out for Tim to return.

Sighing heavily, Tim turned his head and stared back at Jamie through the door. He could tell she felt sympathy for him. Placing her coffee down on the counter, Jamie strolled over to Buddy in her pink pajamas with teddy bears, and picked him up so he could get a bird's eye view of his father's departure.

Tearing himself away, Tim got into his car and stared back, framing the picture of his two loves in his mind. Jamie was smiling, waving one of Buddy's little paws 'bye-bye' for him. All Tim could feel was the heartbreak radiating from the small almond eyes as he forced himself to pull from the driveway and head out to the real world.

Jamie made the bed, washed the dishes, and took a shower while Buddy scampered behind her like a little baby duck. His screams and howls grew to a hideous crescendo when she wandered too far from his sight.

Tripping her way around the house, trying to avoid the obviously upset puppy, Jamie could barely deal with him anymore. Blowing the bangs from her face, she put her hands on her hips and stared down at him. She had now chosen the pose of the disciplinarian, but she simply couldn't begin 'barking' at him. After all, Jamie knew in her heart that all Buddy wanted was to be with Tim. Buddy missed him and was still, most likely, a little frightened because the apartment was such a new and different playground for him.

She sighed deeply and stared into his heartbroken eyes. "C'mon boy, we've got some work to do."

It took her a week to teach Buddy how to work around the house and wait—**patiently**—for Daddy to come home. But in the end, Buddy had finally *sprechened.*

The year that followed was filled with many things —issues that all new parents face—as Buddy found his voice and began to settle in to his new and loving family.

Being educated at all turns, Buddy had learned phrases like, "Wanna go bye-bye?" In fact, he learned this one so well, they had to start spelling it instead of saying it, just to keep him from scrambling to the door and doing somersaults that could ultimately cause brain damage. Every time the word was uttered, Buddy was ready for another great adventure into the big outside world. Of course, as any child will do, Buddy soon figured out the spelling of the command as well—so Tim ended up taking him absolutely everywhere.

Buddy had also grown in stature. He was bigger now and his nose had grown longer. His once soft puppy fur had turned into that of an adult; coarse, yet with ears that had remained velvety soft. He'd learned, "Are you hungry?" And he also learned absolute table manners by using Tim's shirt as a napkin while he ate.

Tim's book had been right. Buddy *loved* to perch on the back of the sofa, although he was nowhere near the category of *Rebel Without a Cause.* In fact, Buddy was the most gentle and loving little dog on the planet. He also was as full of humor as his loving owner. At times, when Buddy was on his lofty sofa perch, Tim would sit on the couch and gently curl the 'Bud-man's' legs around his neck, stand up, and wear him like a mink.

One night, as Jamie was in the kitchen preparing dinner, she looked up at Tim and Buddy's *fashion model* routine, and laughed so hard she'd nearly fallen over. Buddy absolutely loved to make his parents laugh; he apparently had a heart that was full of emotion for the people who truly cared about him.

There were strange things that Buddy did on

instinct alone, like pulling at their arms with his paw whenever he wanted them to pet him, or put their arms around him. Sometimes if they stopped petting him when he wasn't ready, Buddy would nudge their hand a few times with his cold, wet, nose, begging for them to continue. And the hugs were constant. Buddy spent many a moment standing in their laps, putting his paws around their necks, and burying his chin in their warm flesh. Even to a stranger, Buddy seemed to be the most charming and most heartwarming animal in the world.

Having his neck kissed was also a gesture that Buddy made sure to attempt almost every morning. Trying to wake Tim from his sleep, Buddy would put his neck on Tim's face and rub it back and forth until he either smothered to death or deigned to wake up. If Tim attempted the 'move' of groaning and rolling away, Buddy would simply climb over the top of him and continue as if he'd never moved. And Buddy ***always*** won. Tim would awaken, kiss the coarse little neck, and escort Buddy into the great, wide world.

As his feet found the floor, Buddy would jump off the bed and do—as Tim coined the phrase, *'The Dance of the Deer.'* This consisted of prancing around in circles, as if he were chasing his tail, while 'be-bopping' from his hind legs to his front legs. To Tim and Jamie it was more than just cute!

Tim even got to the point where he could read his mind. If he was out of water, Buddy would give him a certain look—with his ears raised up, and his head cocked. The psychic connection father and son had found would have Tim simply getting up and refilling his water bowl.

He had to buy Buddy a new collar, for he had outgrown the small rhinestone one that he had bought for him that first day at the pet store. And as it is with children who cross over into the adult world, Buddy received his own classy, black, mature-looking gift–a collar that was real leather that he loved to wear. Tim called it his 'necklace,' and if anyone dared take it off, Buddy made sure they knew he was more than a little upset about it. Tim also presented Buddy with his very own identification tag, etched with his brilliant namesake, *BUDDY HOLLY*, along with Buddy's address in case he ever got lost.

"Can you at least take that thing off of him before we go to bed?" Jamie asked, irritated. "It drives me *nuts!*"

Tim threw her a small smile. "I can't. He loves to hear himself jingle, Kitten. Besides, he feels naked without it." Buddy looked at Tim as he said these words, then raised his ears, cocked his head, and slowly looked over at Jamie with pitiful, watery eyes. In fact, he seemed to call forth the ghost of a battered and abused animal in order to stare at his mistress with pure sadness in his eyes. He reached his hind leg up–never taking his eyes from hers–and scratched at his collar, relishing in the music.

"See, Honey? Just plain *naked*! He needs it!"

"You," she began, pointing at the furry-covered, Oscar-winning actor. "Are a stinker, young man!" Then she tussled his head and went to the kitchen for some potato chips.

Tim thought long and hard about what to get Jamie for her 25th birthday. It was in two weeks and he wanted to plan that Saturday to be a truly precious and fun evening for her; he wanted nothing more than to treat her like a Queen. So, during the two weeks he had left, Tim worked late every other day just to make the dollars needed to give her the greatest birthday ever.

When the Saturday came, Tim wished her a happy birthday over coffee. She didn't say anything although Tim knew, as he watched her glance into various empty corners, that she was looking for the gift that she knew Tim would never forget to give. He had a hard time keeping a straight face though, wanting to keep the surprise for as long as possible. In fact, Jamie was so odd-acting that Tim practically burst with laughter, needing to leave the room in order to keep up the charade.

It was almost noon when Tim asked Jamie if she would mind doing the grocery shopping. "Buddy and I aren't feeling well today," he fibbed.

Jamie played along or, at least, Tim hoped she was playing along. After all, an argument was not what a birthday should be about. When she returned from her shopping trip, the first item that Jamie saw was her mother's pick-up truck. Tim could see through the window the soft smile that spread across her beautiful face—she was absolutely glowing.

When she opened the door and stepped into the room, Tim and Becky yelled *"SURPRISE!"* And Buddy, not to be outdone, ran up to her wearing his little aluminum birthday hat sitting squarely on his head.

She picked him up and kissed him, laughing as Buddy's whole body seemed to wag with excitement. Jamie's eyes fell on the lovely cake sitting on the table.

The pink frosting and sugar roses were truly beautiful, and the joy of her day showed brightly in Jamie's eyes. The *Happy Birthday, Jamie!* was highlighted by two pink candles announcing the fact that it was twenty-five years to the day since she had been brought into the world.

She was still holding Buddy as Tim lit the candles. Placing him on the floor, Jamie fell into her mother's arms and reveled in the kiss and hug from the best friend she'd ever known.

"Happy Birthday, Sweetheart!" Mom said, patting her on the back.

"We won't embarrass you by singing *Happy Birthday,"* Tim laughed. "But you *have* to blow out the candles!" He popped her on her bottom as she blew them out, and they all applauded–Jamie was overjoyed.

Tim excused himself and disappeared into the bedroom. When he returned, two brightly-wrapped gifts filled his arms. Handing Jamie a small gift bag first, he watched in silence as she reached in and pulled something out that was wrapped in delicate tissue paper. Carefully unwrapping it, Jamie stared down at the royal-blue feathered rose.

She gazed at Tim and smiled. The emotion in her eyes told him just how beautiful she thought the gift truly was.

"I love you, Sweetheart," Tim said, very softly, placing a kiss on her lips. Handing her the second gift, which was all laced up in white paper with bright yellow ribbons and a matching bow, Tim watched her open the gift very gently, and smiling wide at the large box filled with *Russell Stover* chocolates–her absoltute favorite.

"Thank you, Sweetheart! You sure do know the way to a woman's heart," she swooned, batting her eyelashes at him.

Becky and Buddy were both on the same wavelength. As Buddy issued a bark, begging to share in the sugary prize, Becky spoke up too, "Now, I want one of those!" She laughed, setting them on the table.

Tim trembled a bit as he handed Jamie his final gift. His look was more than a bit odd. From his face turning red to the holographic, silver paper that was wrapped around the gift, everything seemed a bit out of place.

"I hope you like this one the best, Sweetheart," he said; his voice shaking a bit as he spoke. "With *all* my heart."

Becky offered the intelligent 'Mom' smile and looked down; already knowing what the holographic paper was hiding.

Slowly, Jamie opened it, being more careful than she had been with the previous gift seeing as that her closest allies were all acting like something in the room had seriously changed. As the mystery started to reveal itself, tears began to rain from her beautiful, green eyes.

The gold Victorian picture frame was stunning all on its own—but inside that magnificent gift was a heartfelt letter that Tim had written for her. The ink was dark blue; the paper was burned around the edges and had been mounted on dark blue velvet, making it look as if it belonged in a true palace to a very real princess.

As Jamie read the words, every emotion possible appeared in her eyes.

'SHE HAD A BEAUTY THAT FAR SURPASSED ALL THE ANGELS IN HEAVEN; HER LOVELY GREEN EYES BURNED OF A GENTLE SPRING AFTERNOON, WITH A COOLNESS, AND A RADIANCE, THAT MELTED MY SOUL WITH HER VERY GLANCE IN MY DIRECTION.

HER VELVET SOFT, WAVES OF HAIR FELL LONG AND DEEP, GLEAMING LIKE SPUN GOLD, PAST HER GENTLE SHOULDERS, AND SMELLED OF THOSE SOFTLY FRAGRANT FLOWERS.

HER LIPS WERE OF A GENTLE PINK, FULL AND MOIST, RISING AND FALLING SLOWLY. THEIR PERFECT MOVEMENTS WERE LIKE WAVES OF TENDERNESS FROM A LONELY, NEVER ENDING OCEAN.

TO LOOK UPON A WOMAN SO BEAUTIFUL—MORE BEAUTIFUL THAN ANYTHING THAT COULD EVER EXIST—TOOK MY BREATH AWAY AND MADE MY HEART HURT WITH PASSION UNENDING.

SURELY THE LORD UP ABOVE PUT EVERYTHING SWEET AND PRECIOUS INTO HER, FOR SHE IS TRULY A VISION OF LOVELINESS.

HER HANDS WERE SOFTER THAN VELOUR AND EQUALLY TENDER. THEIR WARMTH ENGULFED ME WITH A FEELING OF PURPLE TWILIGHT, LIFTING ME HIGHER THAN I SHALL EVER KNOW. MY HEART BEAT EVER FASTER, SO I COULD HARDLY BREATHE, UNTIL THEY LEFT MY HOLD.

SHE HAD THE MOST BEAUTIFUL VOICE—THAT OF A SMALL KITTEN—AND WHEN SHE SPOKE, IT WAS A SOFT AND CARESSING MUSIC TO ME. I WOULD STAND HYPNOTIZED, LONGING TO HEAR MORE.

SHE IS WHAT KEEPS ME LIVING. TO SEE HER

BEAUTIFUL ANGELIC FACE ONCE MORE WOULD BE ENOUGH TO KEEP ME THROUGH ETERNITY.

MY LOVE FOR HER IS LIKE A FLICKERING CANDLE, MOVING WITH THE RHYTHM OF HER SOFT AND DISTANT SHADOWS, IN THE BACKGROUND OF MY MIND.- Love, Tim'

There was nothing more that could possibly be done or said, as Jamie entered Tim's arms and cried a river of true love's tears. Her whole body shook from the deeply felt words. Becky made sure to take the frame in order to keep the magical words in one place.

Tim looked over at Becky; even *she* had tears in her eyes. Jamie couldn't stop. She kissed him and kissed him, soaking his face in her salty tears. Soon, Tim felt his own tears arrive as Jamie whispered to him, *"You...are...the most...beautiful...man...in...in the world!"* She spoke between sobs, taking the Kleenex that Becky pulled from her purse.

Tim rocked her in his arms. "Aw, it was supposed to be a *happy* present," he said, winking at Becky. Jamie slapped him on the chest playfully with her hand, and issued a chuckle. The love she had for her 'music man'—for his lyrics...his words...that burned into her heart and soul were fierce.

Managing to regain some composure, Jamie slowly calmed her breathing and felt a wave of exhaustion take over.

Tim looked over at Becky who, quite graciously, took the hint. She smiled. "Well, kids, I'm going to take Buddy outside for a while. Between all this crying and those chocolates just sitting on the table calling out to him

—and me—he needs a little air."

Jamie's silence remained after her mother left the house. But soon, she was staring at the Victorian frame and beautiful rose and began to wonder aloud. "I don't mean to be rude, Honey. But how could you afford to do all this?"

Tim looked down at the floor and shrugged. "I sold a bunch of my old Elvis records."

Jamie gasped. "Those were collector's items...*antiques!* Why would you do that? You love Elvis so *much!"*

He cupped her face with his hands, and stared into her now upset eyes. "*We-ell,* let's just say I love you a little more than I love Elvis."

Giving her a quick peck on the lips, Tim spread his legs into a wide karate stance—waving his left hand high in the air as if he were conducting the *Joe Hershel Orchestra* via satellite. He sneered and twitched his upper lip at her, and in his best *West Memphis* accent said, "Elvis may be the Kang uh Rock, baby, but *you're* the 'Quain' uh muh... uh muh *heart."*

Then came the swift side-kick, as Tim handed an invisible guitar to an invisible Charlie Hodge. He got down on one knee, thrust both of his arms out straight, and 'cut' his invisible band. Tim would've handed her a scarf, but he didn't have one.

Jamie had always thought that Tim should have been on *Saturday Night Live.* He could do so many amazing impersonations, and he sounded *exactly* like the person he was impersonating—he could actually *contort* his face to take on every look and every movement of the

King and so many others.

Jamie smiled at the man who truly owned her heart. Sometimes this incredible man would even find a way for Michael Jackson to *moonwalk* through her kitchen; spin around while tipping his invisible hat, thrust out his pelvis, and shout, *"Sha-moan-uh!"* Then, he would grab his crotch...and take out the garbage. Jamie laughed to herself knowing that only a true man could do that many moves and **still** tend to the household chores.

"It's okay," he said, as he stood back up. "I want to get all of those albums on CD anyway."

As the tears stopped and the laughter ensued, Becky came back with Buddy, and Jamie started making a pot of coffee while Tim sliced into the birthday cake.

"Becky, I'm getting out of the Air Force in a few months," he said, serving her a piece of cake. "My time is up, and they're closing the Base down shortly after that."

Becky sighed. "I knew this day would come," she said, as she put a piece of cake in her mouth. "What are you going to do when you get home?"

Tim sat down and dove into his cake. Thankfully for Buddy, crumbs fell to the floor like a beautiful rain of sugar, and he slithered between the table legs to snatch it all up.

"My brother's been talking to the people at the place where he works—they make gift wrap there. The job is waiting for me and he said all I have to do is fill out an application."

Tim continued, "I worked there loading trucks on the dock before I joined the Service. It was hard work but the pay was good. I won't be loading trucks anymore, but

I'll still be making good money."

The coffee had finished brewing, and Jamie added the three steaming mugs decorated with one-million-dollar bills to the sugary picnic. Even she knew from the tension building in the air that her mother's silence was about to come to an end.

"Tennessee is a long way from home, Jamie. Will you be happy there?" she asked, as Jamie handed her a cup.

Jamie walked back to the refrigerator and reached inside for the creamer she knew her mother liked. Not only that, but it gave her an extra few seconds to think about the answer she was about to give. "I'll be happy *anywhere,* as long as I'm with Tim, Mom."

She handed Tim his coffee, and the three once again sat in silence. From creamer to adding spoonfuls of sugar, it seemed that any other subject had been put on hold. As the women watched, their smiles returned when Tim put four spoonfuls of sugar in his coffee and stirred it very carefully, as if mixing a chemical that would somehow save the world.

When he looked up and saw both sets of eyes staring back at him, he grinned. "I like it sweet like my women." Taking a sip, he batted his eyelashes at Jamie, drawing out a sweet set of giggles.

"We have a little money saved now," Jamie said to her Mom. "But we're going to have to stay with his folks for a while, until we can get settled financially and get a place of our own."

"What are *you* going to do there, Sweetie?" Becky asked.

Jamie shrugged. "I've got some college under my belt, so I'm sure I'll be able to find something."

Becky looked at Tim, knowing what the outcome of the conversation was going to be even though she simply could not give up that easily. "Are you sure you can't stay here?"

Tim put his coffee down and shook his head. "There aren't any decent jobs here, Becky. I've been looking at the classifieds in the *Avalanche Journal* for months now, and there's nothing here that pays any higher than minimum wage, and we're struggling. As much as I love Lubbock, we just can't stay."

Becky sighed into her coffee mug, trying to stop the tears from forming. "Well, I guess there's not much more to say about it. I love you, Tim. And I know you'll take care of my daughter. You're both grown, and I want you to be happy." She looked at Jamie as she finished her statement.

As the birthday progressed, the love and tears came in waves. But after finishing their cake and coffee, and saying their goodbyes, Becky left.

"I'm *pooped!*" Jamie exclaimed, blowing her bangs out of her eyes as she plopped down on the sofa. "Will you hang my picture up for me, Sweetheart?" She couldn't wait to see it on the wall—on *her* side of the bed, of course.

"Show me where you want it," he smiled, as he carefully picked up the expensive Victorian frame and walked into the bedroom.

"I want it here," she said. "No...wait, a little more to the left." Tim banged the nail into the wall and hung the picture, straightening it as best he could.

Jamie, the queen of consistency, backed to the other end of the room to make sure it was straight. "It's a little crooked, Honey," she said quietly. Pointing to the left, and offering her words in a soothing tone, Jamie did all she could not to annoy him. Tim sighed and smiled as he straightened it–making it look exactly the way she wanted.

"It's *bee-yoo-tiful*, Sweetheart!" she crooned, staring at it.

Tim yawned and stood beside Jamie, enjoying the sound, smell and feel of his birthday girl. "I'll clean up the kitchen if you want to get a shower."

"Deal!" Laughing, Jamie kissed him and started digging through her dresser, scrambling to find the comfortable pink teddy bear pajamas to end her birthday off just right.

"Happy Birthday, Kitten," he said.

Tim took Buddy out and cleaned up the kitchen while Jamie showered and relaxed–making sure to let her have the full 'birthday' treatment.

When Tim hit the shower, Buddy jumped up on the bed and stared at Jamie, jingling with every move.

She patted him on his head and admired the lovely gift that Tim had made for her. She put her hands over her heart as she read the beautiful words once more, reflecting on the special love they shared.

If words could be a painting," she thought. *"Then this would certainly be a DaVinci.*

She smiled to herself as Leonardo emerged from the shower. "Jamie, where's the Comet?"

"It's under the sink, I think," she laughed. She knew what was coming. Tim–her own OCD twin–was calling out to *Rainman*–the character he always played when his rooms were not as clean as they should be.

"*Have* to use the *Comet*," said Dustin Hoffman in his perfect role. Scrubbing in slow, rhythmic circles, Tim continued, "yeah...*definitely* Comet... The bestselling brand name on the market...yeah...*exactly* two hundred thirty seven strands of hair in the drain...yeah. *Definitely* two hundred thirty seven...and Charlie Babbitt farted in a phone booth...yeah..."

While Rainman counted the stains in the commode, Jamie got on her knees and prayed. "Lord Jesus, thank you so very much for a husband who loves me and has such a loving and kind heart—he's the *best* birthday gift of all, *Amen.*"

After the cleanliness was achieved, Tim got under the covers and Jamie cuddled next to him. Putting her arm around him, she kissed him on the back of the neck. And, as all good fathers do, Tim cuddled next to Buddy, put his arm around him, and kissed *him* on the back of the neck; A loving family that shared all moments of affection.

As Jamie lay in the darkness, she smiled a sweet smile. She realized that Tim had changed in the last couple of years, for he was no longer a sad and lonely wayfarer. It felt almost like a miracle. He was actually starting to live.

5

On the Monday morning after Jamie's birthday while driving to the base, Tim was taking the time to reflect on how he had met Buddy Holly's guitar player, Tinker Carlen, at a bar called *Alpha's Cantina*. Tinker was one of the original band members of *The Crickets*, and Tim remembered how amazing it was to be in his presence.

Alpha's was a place that most people would call the quintessential dive. It was a small, white building on the outskirts of town, located three miles from the Air Force Base. Right inside the door was a pay phone, and a small dance floor sat on the left side of the building. On Friday nights Maggie Tilton, the bartender, would spread sawdust on that broken down floor, and people would dance the *Texas Two Step*—a tradition carried on at all the nightclubs in Lubbock.

On the far wall of the dance floor hung a brightly-lit sign that read ***BUSCH!*** The walls had dark paneling, and the place had an aroma of stale cigarette smoke and popcorn. To the right, just inside the entrance, stood an old jukebox filled with 45 RPMs. Tim remembered the moment like it was yesterday, still hearing the song, *Rednecks, White Socks, and Blue Ribbon Beer,* by Johnny Russell, playing in the background of his memory.

The old cigarette machine stood next to the jukebox, and there were six small tables in front of the bar. Amber votives were burning and flickering in the dimly-lit room, offering a darkness that was supposed to cover up the fact that the place had seen far better days. The room was split, and on the other side a pool table sat, ready for another beating. This was the place where friends could smoke, shoot, and drink their chosen poison at the two cocktail tables in the corner.

The bar itself was old, yet some would call it rustic. The stools were worn and torn in places but, like an old couch that'd been sitting in the living room for far too long, they were more than comfortable. A large, illuminated popcorn machine was staged at the far end of the bar, and Maggie had been eating a handful which she'd doused in Louisiana Hot Sauce. Several bottles of this heart-stopping condiment were spaced out neatly across the bar; their backs looked like small, red soldiers framed in the mirror that ran the entire back wall.

Also on the mirror was a sign that stated: *'WE WANT TO BE A PALLBEARER AT YOUR FUNERAL BECAUSE WE'VE CARRIED YOUR @&! FOR SO LONG WE WANT TO FINISH THE JOB!'* The joke was known by many; it was public information that many people had unpaid tabs there.

Underneath the mirror were shelves filled with liquor bottles, and on the inside of the bar sat everyone's favorite beer cooler.

Tim had been talking with Maggie when the aforementioned song ended. Taking a sip of beer, he'd walked over to the jukebox and tossed in his quarter, choosing Buck Owens, *My Heart Skips a Beat*, to brighten up the bar.

He had just returned to his conversation with Maggie when the door opened. Through it appeared a man in his late fifties, with black-rimmed glasses and grey hair. His striped, light blue Western shirt, blue jeans, and cowboy boots had certainly been the perfect Texas dress code. Slowly he'd walked over to the bar and ordered a whiskey on the rocks, then sat down quietly and listened to the music.

Maggie served him his drink and waited with her conversation, wiping the counter off with a damp rag.

After the man had lit a cigarette and taken a few sips from his drink, Maggie spoke, "Tinker, this man over here plays guitar and sings. Why don't you tell him who you are?" Tinker and Maggie had sent a smile between them.

Tim, not knowing who he was or what the conversation was about, got up and introduced himself.

The man named Tinker had returned his handshake. "You're a singer, huh?"

"Yes, sir," replied Tim politely, still not knowing what was going on.

"Well, I remember a little ditty I wrote back in the 1950's called, *That'll be the Day,"* Tinker said, leading him on.

Tim tried to hide his disbelief and glanced up at Maggie. He wanted to keep his polite tone, but the man named Tinker simply sat there and looked at him, waiting for him to say something.

"Uh, sir. *Buddy Holly* wrote that song," he made sure to keep his respectful tone.

Tinker chuckled. "Son," he said softly. "I'm Buddy Holly's guitar player, and I can tell you quite honestly that I wrote that song."

Tim's mouth dropped to the floor. The next few hours had seemed to race by in the blink of an eye, as Tim hungrily drank up the information that his new acquaintance gave him—like a starving lion that'd suddenly been given a piece of steak.

Tinker related chapters from the life of his idol that evening. He'd even told Tim about the time that Buddy's dad had been looking for him to help with some work, but Buddy had just disappeared, not resurfacing until several hours later. His father was angry with him and demanded to know where he'd been. Tinker said that Buddy had been in the barn, carving *Peggy Sue* into his guitar.

As the memory faded, Tim brought his mind back to the present and walked into work, humming the famous song inside his head. At around ten-thirty the phone rang out in his office, and Tim slowly reached for it as he continued reading some inventory spreadsheets.

"Sergeant Cunningham. Can I help you?"

"Tim?" the voice asked on the other end. "This is Maggie, from Alpha's. Is that you?"

"Hello Maggie! Yes, it's me, how are you? I haven't seen you in a long time! You won't believe this but I was just thinking about you on the way to work this morning."

"Boy! You sure are a hard man to track down, I've been trying to reach you for over a week now," she said, in a slightly anxious tone. "Are you still singing these days?"

"A little, I suppose, I'm training my dog to howl," he said, laughing.

Maggie's tone continued to be super serious. "Listen, there's a guy who wants to meet with you. His name is Rusty Jackson. He came in last weekend and told me that they're having a benefit for a little girl with Cerebral Palsy in a couple of weeks.

"I told him all about you and how well you sing and play the guitar, and he's looking for someone who can play rhythm guitar and sing vocals with him. Are you interested?"

Tim was so overwhelmed with excitement, he could hardly contain himself. "You bet I am!"

"Okay," Maggie answered. "I'll give you his number—you need to get in touch with him right away."

Tim scribbled down the number. Taking deep breaths throughout the conversation, Tim set up the meet with Rusty and the rest of his band for six o'clock that night.

He and Jamie arrived at Rusty's enormous ranch-style home and knocked on the door. After a few moments, a man about five inches shorter than Tim answered it. He was wearing a brown Western shirt, a cowboy hat, and boots, and yet again spoke 'Texas' with every word and movement he made.

"Mr. Jackson?"

"No, I'm Acie," he said, thrusting out his hand. "Acie Penton. You the new guy?"

Tim smiled. "I think so. This is my wife, Jamie," he said. Jamie smiled and extended her hand.

"Well, ain't she the pretty one!" Acie grinned. "Come on in, we're just messing around in here a bit; we're trying to figure out what songs we're gonna play."

The King of Hearts

The living room was filled with a variety of guitars that were neatly arranged in a semi circle around the room. Each one had its own separate stand; and the instruments gleamed, as if calling out to the music men in the room, begging to be played. Rusty was talking to a man holding a fiddle, when he looked up and saw Tim.

He stood up and smiled. "I'm glad you could make it, Tim. Maggie said all kinds of good things about you! Let me introduce you to the rest of *The Sucker-Rod* band."

The fifty-six-year-old Jackson was six-foot-three and very skinny. The man owned his own plumbing business and his worn and weathered face carried the years of hard work, yet his kind smile definitely showed through. And there was a spark in his eyes, as if a mischievous young boy was dancing inside his soul ready to throw down, forget the rusted pipes, and concentrate on making the music that would have the fans cheering.

"This cantankerous little cuss here, is Acie Penton. He's our bass player." Acie grinned broadly and shook his hand once more.

"This is Marty York, our fiddle player–the best there is in Lubbock." Marty switched his fiddle to his left hand, so he could shake hands with Tim.

All three stood back, and Tim spotted the tall, thin young man sitting behind an expensive drum set, keeping quiet.

Acie pointed at him and said proudly, "This here is T.J. '*The Spider*' Cobb. We all call him *Spider* 'cause he can play them drums like he's got eight legs!"

Spider wore round, gold rimmed glasses, and had long brown hair tied up in a ponytail. He was wearing a red *Budweiser* baseball cap and T-shirt which had a cartoon picture of *Beavis* with his finger in his nose, as if telling the world exactly what he thought of them. Underneath the comical picture was the word *Metallica.* Tim guessed his age to be twenty-two or twenty-three–a young musician just starting out who still owned the talent and ego that they all began with.

Spider didn't say anything—he just lifted up a drum stick and twirled it around. Tim laughed to himself. There was that ego in spades, always making sure that everyone in the room knew he not only spoke the 'music-talk,' but he walked the walk as well.

Tim couldn't wait to see the supposed eight-legged beast play his heart out on a really cool drum solo. Tim and Jamie smiled, and waved back at the spinning stick.

"Well, I guess we need to see what you can do, Tim," Rusty said, lighting up a *Marlboro.* Jamie sat down on the couch as Tim pulled his black, Alvarez guitar from its case.

"That's a nice piece," Acie said.

"Thanks," Tim replied, as he put the strap around his neck.

As the rest of the band took their places and began to tune up, Rusty asked, "Do you know *The Green, Green Grass of Home?* That's a pretty simple one to start out with."

"Yes, sir. I do." Tim was trying not to show his nervousness, but he heard the small giggle from the drums, probably wondering why anyone would call Rusty 'sir.' They began the intro and the fear left Tim in seconds.

When he started to croon into the microphone in

his soft, velvet voice, Tim knew that he was back in the only element he ever knew and understood completely. Rusty looked over at Acie and raised his eyebrows.

When he finished, Acie was the first to comment. "Man, you're really good! I think he's a keeper, Rusty!"

Rusty just smiled and took another long drag off his cigarette. Tim liked Acie right off the bat, not because of the compliment that he had just given him, but because there was a certain comic relief in his demeanor; a calming force who knew he was good with his music but didn't take life too seriously.

Acie was a fabulous bass player. He was a professional on the electric, and was able to switch to an old-fashioned *doghouse* bass in the blink of an eye, with no worries whatsoever. Tim liked the stand-up bass the best because it would thunder off the walls as if the gods themselves were answering the music call. The house shook when Acie played it, calling out to Thor first with his mighty hammer to come down to Earth and tell the world that this was the band with the might, courage, and power to make it all the way.

Tim liked the *way* he played it too. He would dance with it while bobbing his head and rock it back and forth, slapping out the rhythm on its huge strings. It was amusing to watch such a short man playing something that was bigger than he was, like his own personal strength was somehow related to the instrument.

They played *Mama Tried* next, and Tim *really* got into that one, especially when Acie started in with his slick bass backbeat.

Spider stuck to his guns and was a man of few

words that night, leaving his drumsticks to do all the talking for him.

"Doggone it, Spider! Can't you play that danged song any faster?" Rusty hollered.

Spider did a rim shot.

They played it again, and Tim sang it even *better* the second time around. He could tell that he and Acie were starting to bond in a very musical way.

Next came *Amarillo by Morning*, where Marty really shone on his violin solo during the music break. Tim and Jamie *both* watched him like hawks as he played it, mesmerized by the beauty and intelligence he used to to bring the music to life.

Marty could see that they were watching him, so he did it again for good measure. He seemed like a simple, easy-going man, whose only care in the world was making the beautiful vibrato that echoed from his strings.

Tim and Jamie liked them all—even Spider—who reminded them of the *Darlings* from the Andy Griffith Show.

Finding that rhythm with the new guy, the band continued on, and played two more songs before calling it a night.

"Tim, you're a good singer, Son! We'd like for you to sing with us at the benefit. Can you be here and practice with us for the next two weeks?" Rusty lit another cigarette.

Tim looked around the room at everyone. They were all smiling at him, except for Spider who was still twirling his drumsticks around, pretending to bang out some *Motley Crue* song on his drums.

"Yes, sir, I'd love that!" Tim said, "Do you care, Jamie?"

She beamed with excitement. "Not at all! You guys sounded great!" she giggled, as if she were taking her place as the new 'roadie.'

Marty spoke up. "It's for a good cause, too, Miss Jamie. The little girl's name is Crystal Baker and she needs to have some surgery, only her parents don't have the money and she ain't but eight-years-old."

"Of course," Jamie said sweetly. "I hope we'll be able to raise the money she needs."

Rusty crushed out his cigarette, put his guitar down, and shook hands with them. Acie was still smiling as he shook Tim's hand. "I sure do like the way you sound, Tim. Good job!"

Shaking hands with Marty, Spider gave them a quick salute with his drumstick before they left.

When they got home, Tim let Buddy out of the bathroom and took him outside, while Jamie changed into her pajamas and brushed her hair.

Tim felt as if he were in another world, still stuck in the realm of the music, not wanting to leave...but Buddy was not to be denied. After a few moments he grabbed Buddy's squeak toy, which he had nicknamed, *The Binky.*

Tim got down on the floor and started playing tug-of-war with Buddy. After all, he had to satisfy his biggest fan. He clamped down on one end with his teeth, with Buddy on the other. Both were growling, grunting and tugging like the 'manly-men' of long ago using their strengths to win the war.

"Make sure you brush your teeth before you come to bed, Tim. I don't want to kiss you with dog spit all over your mouth!" Jamie's voice echoed from the bedroom. Tim sent her a fierce growl, eliciting a new set of giggles.

The night had been very, very good!

6

The next evening, Tim cleaned up and changed clothes to go over to Rusty's house.

Jamie looked up from her place on the couch and smiled. "Tim, I'm not going with you tonight. It's your time, hon. I want you to go and have some fun with those guys. I love you; it's time you made some decent friends."

"But I want you to go too, Sweetheart, I *like* being with you."

She sent him a smile and a kiss. "You need to bond with some males, Tim. I don't want to be in everyone's way. Besides, I want to enjoy the benefit and be surprised. I don't want to be burned out on the night you guys play.

"Buddy and I are going to watch some TV and share a bowl of popcorn." She kissed him again, as Buddy reached up and licked his face, giving his permission for Tim to go out and enjoy the night. Jamie laughed. "Now you go and have some fun, and I'll see you when you get home."

They had a really great rehearsal. Afterwards, everyone was laughing and cutting up. They were so excited, knowing that they had definitely come up with a decent list of songs to play to get the crowd excited and bring the money in for Crystal's surgery.

"What exactly is a *Sucker-Rod*, Rusty?" Tim asked.

Rusty lit another *Marlboro* and exhaled. "A sucker-rod is part of a drilling tool used to pump oil from the ground."

"I think it's pretty cool," Acie added. "No one has *ever* used *that* name for a band before."

Rusty looked at him and grinned. "And no one ever will again."

On Friday, Rusty and Marty were in the kitchen making drinks. When they returned to the living room, Acie had just finished listening to a song that Tim had written.

"Hey guys, you should come and listen to this...it's really good!"

Rusty, Spider, Marty, and Acie stood around Tim in a semi-circle. "It's called *The Vagabond*—go ahead Tim, play it again!" Acie was seriously excited.

Tim started in with the intro, finger-picking and making a bass backbeat with his thumb on the top two strings of his guitar. The song had a lonesome, yet haunting midnight-train-yard sound to it, as he began to sing the words.

♫*"I left home ten years ago and caught a northbound train to Omaha;*

"The reason why I left my wife is written in a letter to my mama.

"But this train keeps on a rollin' and I still keep knowin' I'm not goin' back;

"'Cause this broken heart she left me with still keeps me livin' here out on the tracks.

"I've found it hard to make a livin', and workin' always puts me in a bind;

"'Cause, to be a bum and a vagabond don't give nobody nowhere peace of mind." ♫

As he finger-picked the music break, Spider and Acie tapped their toes to the rhythm.

♫ *"I know I'm gettin' older, but I still ain't missed the bust from the blowin' stack,*

"and all the songs I've written still keep up with the rhythm of the tracks.

"Sometimes, I take a look back on my life and try to weigh the bad things from the good;

"I've come to the conclusion that my mama did the very best she could.

"I know these nights keep gettin' colder, and the only warmth I've found is a bottle of booze,

"and a fire inside a cardboard box, my tattered coat and torn-up worn out shoes.

"But this train keeps on a rollin', and I still keep knowin' I'm not goin' back;

"'Cause the pain from all my hopes and fears, lies painted in a tainted photograph." ♫

"Did you really write that, man?" Spider asked when the song came to an end.

Tim looked up at him in amazement, for it was probably the first real sentence he had ever heard the man say.

"Yeah, I wrote that for Merle Haggard when I was living in the barracks. I was hoping that maybe one day he would hear of it and want to record it."

Rusty looked over at Marty, and once again raised his eyebrows. "It's good—I'll give him that.

"A friend of mine knows Merle, Tim. If you want to

make a cassette tape real quick, maybe he can get him to listen to it."

"Do you really mean it?" Tim asked; his heart was practically beating out of his chest. He felt as if someone had just told him he'd won a million dollars. After all, that's how much a dream would be worth.

"Don't get your hopes up, Tim. I can't guarantee anything, okay? Rusty has some pretty good recording equipment, so let's just have you and the guitar on the demo."

Rusty set everything up and Tim made his recording.

As the night began to wind down, Tim and Acie were as thick as thieves and decided to try *Maybe Baby,* by Buddy Holly. It was so good, it was immediately added to the repertoire of music that Rusty was compiling. Rusty sang *Release Me*, by Ray Price, and one of his very own, entitled *Jack's Gonna Drive Tonight.*

The last song they rehearsed for the night was *Don't Be Cruel.* Acie did an outstanding job, bobbing, rocking, and slapping the strings—*The Jordanaires* would have been proud.

Rusty set his guitar on its stand afterwards and went back to his other comfort, lighting up a *Marlboro.* Everyone was excited about how good the song sounded, but Rusty remained quiet. Staring at his cigarette as he exhaled, he began twirling it between his thumb and fingers, as if he'd somehow taken over the body of *The Spider* behind the drums.

"Boy," he said, raising his black cowboy hat up on his forehead. "I haven't heard that song in quite a while."

He shook his head, reminiscing on past memories, and took another puff of his cigarette.

The memory entered the room for all to hear, as Rusty's thick, deep voice brought the picture to life. "I remember when Elvis performed in Lubbock. It was at the Fair Park Coliseum. I think it was April tenth of...*fifty-six*." He shook his head and smiled. "I can't remember. Anyways, my band was one of the opening acts for him. The place was packed! I remember he came out in that gold suit of his, and it lit up like the fourth of July in there with all them flash bulbs going off, and I ain't kiddin'!"

The band sent their smiles and laughter into the room, but the envy glowed in their eyes as they wished with all their hearts they could've been in the presence of the real, true 'King' of Rock-and-Roll.

Rusty continued, "If I'm not mistaken I think he did two performances that night; one was at eight and the other one was at nine forty-five. We played before he went on at eight." He paused and took another puff.

"After the show, he came backstage with the rest of us and talked for a while. I remember he sent someone to get us all a bunch of cheeseburgers."

Tim's mouth was watering; not for the cheeseburger, of course; he was like a kid in a candy store, for he had never met anyone who had actually known Elvis.

"How tall was he?" Tim asked.

"I reckon he was about as tall as me, give or take an inch."

"Did you eat the cheeseburger?" Tim asked eagerly, imagining what a cheeseburger from the *'King'* would taste like.

"'Course I did," Rusty said, grinning and living on Tim's purely innocent enthusiasm.

"Well, how was it?" Tim demanded. He wanted to know every single moment of that glorious evening.

Rusty crushed out his cigarette in an ashtray that was already overflowing, and pushed his hat up once more. Looking into Tim's eager face, he said, "I ain't never been much of an Elvis fan, Son. But I've got to say it was the best *danged* cheeseburger I ever had in my life! He was a really nice fella, too; he didn't act like he was any better than the rest of us."

Tim went on and on about Rusty's story when he got home. Except for the part when Rusty had admitted he wasn't really a fan of Elvis—which made even Buddy gasp—he told every single detail over and over again, as if stuck in the mystery and brilliance of what a night with Elvis would've felt like.

Jamie had never seen him so enthralled about anything before. She giggled as she held him in the darkness and listened to him mimic Elvis offering him one of his delicious cheeseburgers: "Hey, Fren', would yuh lak uh *chee-burgra?*"

Tim sounded *exactly* like him, and she giggled even more as she imagined—for an instant—that it was actually the *King*, himself, she was holding onto. *Yeah, right—as if*, she thought, cuddling closer to the real man she loved.

Rusty gave them a day of rest on Sunday. Everyone had worked really hard the previous week, and he knew they needed a break. So Tim took Jamie to the skating center after church.

It was a nice place, where the aroma of hot dogs drew them almost immediately to the concession stand. It had a ski-ball game and several arcade games lined up against the wall, where a teenager was working diligently to make sure that *Pac-man* survived. The D.J. booth was filled with 45 RPM records and LP's, with a few CD's stacked neatly on the counter to make sure that all who walked by knew they were representing the present as well as the past. *The Last Mile*, by *Cinderella* bellowed off the walls as they walked in and rented their skates.

Tim and Jamie skated over to the concession stand immediately, and he bought them both a hot dog and a cherry Slurpee, getting 'in' to the fun, teenage world of long ago. After they'd eaten, Jamie took his hand and led him out to the middle of the rink. Tim wasn't a very good skater, but he loved to hold her hand, and loved to watch ***her*** skate. To Tim, she looked like an angel from heaven, defying gravity as she floated around the rink.

Don't You Forget About Me played next. Jamie glided around on her skates in a figure-eight, displaying some truly elegant moves. She turned and put her arms around Tim, skating backwards with him as they zigzagged slowly between the other people so Tim wouldn't lose his balance.

Looking at her in her shorts that showed her well-toned calf muscles from her years of ice-skating in Canada, and a pink T-shirt that had kittens on the front, Tim was lost in her eyes and her movements. In fact, he barely noticed that there was anyone else in the building—

completely mesmerized by the one and only being in his world.

She had taken the bow out of her hair before they entered the skate center, and her long brown hair flowed out behind her like an angel's soft wings, spreading a hint of lavender into the air, transporting Tim to a calm English meadow in the countryside. He loved the way she smelled, moved, smiled—he loved every detail of her...passionately.

After the song was over, Tim finished his Slurpee and excused himself for a moment, not knowing that while he was gone, Jamie would skate to the D.J. booth and make a special request.

When Tim returned, he watched her as she floated gracefully around the rink. She beckoned tantalizingly with her fingers to come closer, smiling tenderly at him. Skating carefully to her, he took her soft, warm hand and barely breathed, feeling as if he'd been summoned by a princess.

The lights began to dim, and Tim and Jamie began to glow as the room lit with moonlight. The giant disco ball above them twinkled in effervescent starlight, and fog poured forth, as her favorite song in the world began to play. He looked at her and smiled shyly, as Frankie Avalon began to describe her in his beautiful song:

♫ *Venus if you will, please send a lovely girl for me to thrill,*

A girl who wants my kisses and my arms, a girl with all the charms of you,

Venus make her fair, a lovely girl with sunlight in her hair,

And take the brightest stars up in the skies, and place them in her eyes for me. ♫

For Jamie, Tim was the only one that could do justice to her song, for she had never heard it before until the night Tim sang it—to *her!* Even the mighty Frankie Avalon had no idea how to speak to her heart.

After the evening had come to a close, Jamie and Tim again took Buddy to the Walk of Fame and spent some time with him. Jamie took pictures of Tim with Buddy and laughed when she snapped one of Tim standing next to Buddy Holly's statue, wearing Buddy as a mink scarf.

Tim smiled back, as a shot of sincerity rose inside his soul. There were times he could barely breathe around his true love, and this was one of them.

"I never in a million years would have imagined myself being married to someone as beautiful as you," he said, kissing her softly.

"I saw all those guys looking at you, and you made me feel so special because you only looked at me. And I *love* the way you look at me, Jamie! I'm so deeply in love with you that it makes my heart hurt."

Jamie hugged him and put her head on his chest. "You *are* special Tim; you're the man of my dreams and I could never imagine myself being with anyone other than you. I am *very* much in love with you. You make me feel like I'm the most beautiful woman in the world."

Tim stroked her face. "That's not exactly difficult, seeing as that you *are* the most beautiful woman in the world."

They walked for a while longer, and then took

Buddy to *Taco Bell.* It was the perfect end to a perfect day, as Buddy shared his burrito with Tim and wiped his face on his shirt.

Tim was going through the *Avalanche Journal* the next day, when he found the advertisement for Crystal's benefit:

"A dance and benefit will be held for Crystal Baker, 8 years old, of Lubbock, at the VFW this Saturday at 7 p.m. Crystal has Cerebral Palsy and is in need of surgery. The dance will feature Rusty Jackson and his Sucker Rod *Band,* The '57 Chevy's, *and* The Longhorn's. *All proceeds will go to the Baker family.*

"For more information, please contact Maggie Tilton at 792-7694."

There was a picture of a smiling Crystal beside the announcement, and Tim's heart was moved with compassion for the young girl. That was the *exact* thing Tim loved about Lubbock: "We take care of our own," he thought, fighting back tears as he stared at Crystal's picture.

Tim called Rusty and asked if he could bring Buddy with him that evening to rehearsal.

"I guess so, as long as he's housebroken, Son."

"Thanks, Rusty," Tim said. "He is, and he loves everybody! He won't be any trouble—I'll even bring a blanket so he won't get any hair on your couch."

Rusty's smile seemed to jump through the phone line. "I just hope he likes Earnest Tubb."

Tim got dressed and tied a red bandana around

Buddy's neck, to make sure he could hear himself jingle.

"Now you look like a true Texan! All that's missing is the cowboy hat!"

Buddy did his *dance of the deer* and ran to the door when Tim jingled the car keys. Buddy always knew he was going *somewhere* whenever he did this, and Buddy was more than eager to see something new.

When they arrived at Rusty's, everyone laughed as Buddy barked his greetings in German.

Tim held him up and commanded him to say hello to everyone, "Buddy, sag "Hallo" zu jeden!"

He sprechened very kindly to them in his hoarse, raspy bark, and Rusty grinned.

"That's pretty cool, Dude," Spider said, "but you should train him to attack when you say, 'Corn on the cob!' or something like that." Buddy was wagging his tail and squirming in Tim's arms; for some reason he wanted to give Spider a hug.

"Well, I don't want him to hurt anyone, Spider. Besides, he likes pork chops more than corn." Marty chuckled.

"Don't you think he looks like Clint Eastwood?" Tim asked.

Acie heard Buddy's tags jingling under his bandana, and thought they sounded like spurs. "Yeah," Acie said with a smile, "he *sounds* like Clint running the hundred yard dash!" Everyone doubled over in laughter; Rusty choked on his cigarette smoke.

Tim laughed too, as he thought of Clint Eastwood running as fast as he could through the desert in his cowboy boots and spurs, wrapped in his serape that he always wore in his spaghetti westerns, with his cowboy hat and unshaven face, and puffing on a stale cigarillo that he had been gnawing on for days.

Spider joined in. “He sounds just like *Rod Stewart* when he barks!” he interjected, reaching over and taking him from Tim. “But we'll forgive him.”

Buddy started rubbing his neck on Spider's face.

“He wants you to kiss his neck, Spider,” Tim told him.

“Uh...I think I just want to be friends for now, little dude,” Spider said, playing along.

Tim squinted his eyes and clenched his teeth, then mimicked Clint, “Get four coffins ready!” Bursts of laughter roared from the room at Tim's expert impersonation.

Buddy chose his favorite right off the bat, wanting to sit on Spider's lap during rehearsal. But the drums scared him, so he decided to enjoy the rest of his visit perched on top of Rusty's couch.

Practice went really well that night. The whole band felt that Tim was a very gifted musician—frankly, Tim had astounded Rusty so much in the last week that he wanted to spotlight him and let him sing most of the songs they had compiled. Tim was going to make his *debut*, so to speak.

Rusty added *Folsom Prison Blues* to the list, along with Tim's song, *The Vagabond*. He told Tim that he wanted him to sing that one by himself, right after *Don't Be Cruel*.

By Wednesday, Tim started to grow restless. He had made a few mistakes at work that day as he tried to stay focused on the benefit. *What if I forget the words? How many people will be there?* he thought. The ideas, concerns and worries beat on his brain hard, as if Spider was inside his mind working his drumsticks. Tim took a deep breath and exhaled, taking comfort from the fact that Rusty and Acie would be right there, so there was *nothing* to be afraid of.

Jamie knew he was starting to feel tension and pressure. She watched him pace back and forth, trying to remember lyrics and chord changes. She did reassure him but, she knew Tim like the back of her hand, and left him alone to concentrate.

"You'll be perfect, Sweetheart. I just know it! I am so proud of you for doing your part in helping that sweet little girl. And no matter what, her family will love you for it. *She'll* love you!"

That was it. The light bulb came on like the door to Heaven had been opened for him to peek inside. Tim had found his answer. *"She'll love you..."*

Friday was their final rehearsal and everything sounded perfect. They took a break and Rusty went to the kitchen to make a drink. Tim concocted a prank to play on him, so while he was busy in the kitchen, he quickly told everyone what he wanted to do.

When Rusty returned, Marty said, "Hey man, do you mind if we try *Amarillo by Morning* again? I think my bottom string was out of tune on that one and I need to do a sound check."

Rusty took a sip of his drink and set it on the end table. "You wanna take it from the top, or in the middle?"

Marty glanced at Tim. "From the top, if you don't

mind."

"Hey Rusty, do you mind if I play your black, Fender Stratocaster?" Tim asked.

"Knock yourself out, Son." Rusty started singing the song, but when Marty's violin solo came up, Tim hit the distortion pedal. Rusty, not expecting it, jumped about two feet in the air, clutching his heart.

Tim started shredding the strings with pentatonic scales and doing finger-taps on the neck as he played Marty's solo in the glorious heavy metal style.

Spider played the drums with all eight of his legs when Tim started head-banging and stretching the strings with gross misuse of the whammy-bar.

Acie and Marty were rolling with laughter to the point of tears, as Rusty stood there staring at Tim with his cigarette dangling from his lower lip—still clutching his heart.

Then, Tim started writhing like Jimi Hendrix on his knees and licking the neck of the guitar with his tongue, as Spider went on with his 'Metallica' drumming.

The funny thing was, *Amarillo by Morning* actually sounded pretty good as a vamped-up rock song that David Lee Roth and his boys from *Van Halen*, could do justice to.

Acie was laughing uncontrollably! He could just picture a shirtless George Strait wearing leopard skin pants with seven inch leather-heeled cowboy boots and a cowboy hat, doing a David Lee Roth back-flip, like he did on the back cover of *Van Halen's* first album.

When he had finished, Spider was almost hyperventilating. Acie and Marty were still laughing and wiping their eyes.

Rusty could barely breathe, "Son, are you vexed with a *haint?*"

Acie walked up and put his left hand on Tim's forehead and lifted his right hand in the air. "Ho! *Demon* 'co-moucho' soul-*uh!*"

Rusty chuckled.

"Where did you learn all of them *pentagonic* scales?" Acie asked Tim, smiling wide.

"Washington," Tim replied. But no one seemed to understand the joke. He looked down and continued, "I didn't have any friends when I was in high school, so I spent a lot of time playing *Van Halen* and *Stevie Ray Vaughn* records."

"That's really cool," Acie said. "Did you take lessons?"

"No, I learned them all by ear. I *can* read music, and once I learned the chords I just practiced all the time. I almost drove my folks crazy with it."

Tim put Rusty's guitar back on its stand and bummed a cigarette from him.

Rusty, still wide-eyed, shook his head and lit it. "Got the jitters?"

"Yes, sir! I'm a little nervous," Tim replied, as he took a drag and inhaled deeply. He looked down at the cigarette and slowly exhaled the smoke.

"You're gonna do just fine, Son. We've done this a million times and, if you make a mistake, no one's gonna notice 'cause they'll be too busy dancing'," Rusty said, patting him on the shoulder.

Spider got up from his drums and started for the kitchen to get something to eat. Acie looked at him and announced, “Dang, Spider! If you get any skinnier, you’re gonna look like a skeleton! Heck, we can almost see your spine from the front, *now!*”

Spider didn’t say anything. He was wearing flip-flops and everyone started laughing when he walked because it sounded like his bones were clicking together as they smacked against his feet.

The boys in the band were one–a unit that played off each other as well as their instruments did.

Tim couldn’t sleep that night—he was excited, nervous, and had more than a bit of anxiety. Buddy followed him to the kitchen for a glass of chocolate milk. Tim took a few gulps then let Buddy lap some from his glass. The night ahead was going to be a long one, wondering whether his true debut was going to be a failure, farce…or miracle.

He and Jamie had coffee together the next morning, as she headed out for the grocery store, leaving her ‘men folk’ at home to practice on the guitar.

Tim paced continuously until it was time to get dressed.

Jamie watched him as he buttoned up his black Western shirt with the white seams. “Why do you like to wear black?”

“Johnny Cash wears black,” he announced, as if it were a truly silly question. Looking in the mirror he watched his fingers tremble as he fastened the last button.

“I know he does, Sweetheart. But why do *you* wear it? I think you look much better in blue.”

Tim examined himself in the mirror then looked down; the feelings washed over him like a river of sadness.

"I think it's because I want to feel invisible when I'm up there. I want people to see what's in my heart, and not what I'm wearing. I've seen all those singers on TV, Sweetheart–Elton John, Michael Jackson...even *Elvis.* I just don't think they understand what they're supposed to be doing when they're up there in front of all those people."

He swallowed hard, trying to make his words come out right. "Honey, all the diamonds and rhinestones in the world can't make you smell the beautiful scent of lavender or honeysuckle, but your heart can.

"If you close your eyes and hear a kitten crying a block or two away, you don't have to *see* him to know that he's lost, or lonely, or hungry...you can feel it in your heart and *hear* it in *his*, no matter how far away he is. Does that make sense?"

He looked into the eyes of the woman he loved. "If you close your eyes and smell the fragrant smell of a rose, you don't have to see it to know what it is, your heart tells you what it is, and all of your senses are governed by your heart."

Tim looked at his own reflection in the mirror, as a tear slipped from his eye.

Jamie's voice was quiet, as she truly felt the love, passion and devotion Tim held for the 'other woman' in his life–the joy of playing music to a crowd that would gain something from the experience. She smiled. "In that case, I guess blue really isn't your color, Sweetie."

Tim nodded and took his guitar into the living

room. He couldn't afford to 'lose it' at this point in the evening.

Cautiously, Jamie asked, "Are you nervous?"

Tim kissed her on the cheek. "Every time," he said, nodding. "Every single time."

7

They arrived at the VFW at 5:27 P.M. and the grand parking lot was already a quarter of the way filled up. Tim had to be there at 5:30 to help Rusty and the rest of the guys set the equipment up, and he was already sweating, knowing that the crowd would be large.

Tim parked the Toyota, opened the door for Jamie, and retrieved his guitar from the trunk. The VFW was a massive building and Tim could barely contemplate what it would be like at full capacity. When they entered, they saw Rusty and Marty at the bar, and sent them a wave.

Tim saw Crystal and her parents off to the side, and he and Jamie immediately walked over and introduced themselves. Tim bent down and talked to Crystal. She was partially paralyzed and her head was frozen to the right. She had limited movement of her hands, but she smiled at Tim as if it were a truly glorious day and she was running down a beach, glad to be a part of the magical gift called life.

Tim kissed her on the cheek. “Aren’t you pretty?”

The smile of the young girl grew wider.

“My name is Tim, Sweetheart. I’m going to sing a *very* beautiful song tonight just for you.”

She struggled to move her arms and touch him, but they wouldn’t move. Tim gently held her hand and kissed her on the cheek again. The nervousness seemed to disappear in Crystal’s presence. It was as if all that mattered was making this girl smile for the rest of her life.

Jamie sat at a table close to the stage and handed Tim his guitar, trying to stop the tears from falling as she thought about how unfair it was that such a small girl had to go through such large pain.

Rusty and Spider started bringing in the amplifiers. "I'm gonna go and help them, Sweetheart." Tim kissed her, then walked across the dance floor to the stage, watching Spider assemble his drum set like a mechanic restoring the perfect antique car.

"Will you and Acie start bringing in the microphones and stands, Tim?" Rusty asked.

Tim leaned his guitar against the back wall of the stage and smiled, wondering for a moment if Elvis ever helped *his* band haul in equipment. He laughed as he imagined Elvis arriving in Hawaii in his helicopter, going backstage after his limo driver had dropped him off, and commandeering Charlie Hodge. *"Hey, Chollie, ya wanna grab thuh uh-thuh end uh this amp? Less giv'ees fellas a han' with this stuff."*

"Sure thing," Tim said. He and Acie brought his stand-up bass in first.

Acie's face was beet red. "Good thing I love this, because this thing is a real test to haul all over town," he said, grunting as he pulled it from the truck bed. "It's a good thing Rusty's got a pick-up!" Tim grabbed the bottom half of it and aided his new friend.

Once everything had been set up, Tim looked around, taking in the full site. The stage was three-feet high, covered in navy blue carpet. He shook his head in wonder—this was *the* place—*the* carpet—that he would debut upon. It was like a dream come true. Tim grew a little nervous as people walked by, watching them set up. The tops of their heads came up to Tim's knees and he marveled at the size of the ballroom.

The dance floor was directly in front of the stage, and at least four times the size of *Alpha's* floor—or the entire building, for that matter. A couple of people were already sprinkling sawdust on it from cans that looked like *Comet* cleanser.

The tables were on the outskirts of the dance floor. Each one was draped with a dainty banquet cloth that fell to the floor; and crystal candle votives decorated every table top, emitting the rich scent of black cherry into the massive room.

Rusty turned the power on when everything was in place, and Tim plugged his black Alvarez into a *Peavey* amplifier and began his sound check.

Rusty tapped on all of the microphone heads, checking to make sure that each and every one of them could be heard at the back of the room. "CHECK-ONE, CHECK-TWO, CHECK-CHECK!"

The last one was too loud, as feed-back reverberated off the walls and ceiling. Some of the people covered their ears.

"That one was *too* hot!" he said, shaking his head and grinning at Tim.

"Let's get tuned up and take a break!" Rusty hollered.

Tim thought he sounded like one of the trail bosses from the Old West. *"Let's head 'em up and move 'em out!"* He snickered.

After everything was ready, the band members

congregated at Jamie's table, talking and laughing, trying their best to keep calm before the big performance. Rusty, Marty, and Acie gave her a big Texas hug, and Spider managed a shy handshake and a smile.

Marty gazed at her. "You sure do look beautiful tonight, Miss Jamie!"

"Thank you, Marty!" She hugged him again.

Jamie did look ravishing. She was wearing a knee-length denim skirt with a sleeveless, royal-blue silk shell that offered a small, tantalizing glimpse of her God-given gifts. A small sapphire pendant hung around her neck illuminating the outfit, and her dark hair hung past her shoulders, giving off whispered hints of *Ciara* perfume as she brushed it back with her fingertips.

People were starting to arrive. Waitresses were scurrying frantically back and forth to the bar, and the aroma of roasted chicken and beef filled the building.

Rusty whispered in Tim's ear and he followed him to the bar. The rest of the band members sat down with Jamie and continued to talk and laugh with the most beautiful woman in the room.

Rusty bought Tim a beer. "Liquid courage, Son. I know you're a little twitchy but try and calm down, we're gonna be in our own little world up there, and they're gonna be in theirs—enjoying the heck out of us!"

Tim took a couple of sips and Rusty pulled out his ever-present cigarettes.

As Tim lit up, Rusty spoke, "I just wanna tell you how glad I am that we met, Tim." He pushed his black cowboy hat up with his thumb. "We all think you're a fine musician, Son—one of the best. You've got *gold* coming outta' them vocal chords of yours, and I feel mighty lucky that our paths crossed when they did."

He patted Tim on the back as he took another sip of beer. "You're gonna be good tonight, Tim. I've got a feeling inside that says so." Rusty lit a cigarette. "And I always trust my feelings. Just sit back, relax, and enjoy the music."

"I'll do my best."

Rusty looked at his watch—it was a quarter til' seven. "It's about that time," he announced, tucking in his bright red Western shirt as he stood up. The determined look on his face spoke of a man who was ready to take on the world.

They walked back to the table where everyone was sitting. "Y'all about ready?" Rusty smiled. "I do believe it's show-time!" He clapped his hands and everyone took a final drink and stood up.

Jamie could tell Tim was nervous. She whispered in his ear, "I love you. You're going to be wonderful." She kissed him on the cheek.

"I want to get a picture of everyone with Crystal in front of the stage before you start," Jamie said to the band. "I think she would love to have something to remember you all by, since she *is* the guest of honor."

Rusty and Tim walked over to where the Bakers were sitting and asked them if it would be alright to have a snapshot taken.

"I think she would really like that," her mother replied. Pushing her wheelchair to the stage, everyone gathered around her. Tim got down on one knee by Crystal's side and put his arm around her. Everyone smiled, yet Crystal's grin was the one that lit up the VFW like a glimpse of sunlight in a darkened cave.

As they took the stage, Tim looked around; his breath seemed to catch in his chest as he saw the hall filled to capacity. He guessed there were around two hundred people inside. Putting his guitar around his neck, he felt as if he were in another world, hearing Rusty's deep voice in the distance.

"Welcome, ladies and gentlemen, I'm Rusty Jackson, and *we* are the *Sucker-Rod* band! We hope everybody has a good time tonight, because we have a *lot* of great music in store for you!"

The crowd cheered.

"This is all for a good cause, folks. We have a little girl in here with us tonight that needs our help, and as a gracious and giving community I know we'll all dig in deep and lend a helping hand!"

The cheers went up once again as the crowd completely agreed with Rusty's statement.

He continued, "We have the '57 Chevys and the Longhorn band here too, folks, so between the three of us, I hope you'll find a couple of songs to dance to! We're gonna start you off with an *Alabama* song called *If You're Gonna Play in Texas, You Gotta Have a Fiddle in the Band!"*

Rusty counted off, and everyone simply fell into their world–harmonizing perfectly. Whistles and applause came in waves when Marty started playing his fiddle, and Tim felt a rush of electricity course through his veins as people rushed to the dance floor, already engrossed in the music.

Tim looked at Rusty and the rest of the band as he performed. Acie was playing his electric bass; rocking back and forth, he was lost in his own magical musical world.

Spider was getting into it too; he loved to play the fast songs. Tim stared out over the vast crowd and all of his fear and nervousness simply vanished. He saw Jamie smiling back at him. With the lights beaming, she seemed so far away, but her gaze made it very clear that Tim was the only one she was watching.

The song ended and everyone whistled and shouted, and wailed for more.

When Rusty finally got the chance to speak, he smiled. “Well, thank you very much, folks! Uh, we had fun too!”

The crowd laughed.

Rusty pointed to Tim. “We have a new member in our band, ladies and gentlemen. His name is Tim Cunningham and he’s got a voice of gold and a heart to boot! He’s gonna sing one from our own Buddy Holly, called *Maybe Baby!”*

Acie had switched over to his doghouse bass by the time Rusty began the guitar intro. People whistled and yelled as Tim started to sing and, once again, the dance floor was filled with excited couples in seconds.

Acie was slapping the strings and dancing with his bass. He spun it around once, and the sound of it thundered through the entire building. Tim was filled with hair-raising electricity and sang the notes with power, making the song his own.

A few of the ladies made their way to the stage to

get a better look at him, and Rusty sent him over a knowing grin. After all, it was always the front man who drew the ladies to his side.

Tim stared down from the stage and smiled at them as he continued to sing. During the musical break, he looked down at the neck of his guitar and concentrated on the final notes that would lead him into the second half of the song. When he finished, he received a standing ovation along with several whoops, yells, and whistles. Tim smiled and bowed, thrilled with the excitement that seemed to infuse the room like lightning.

Rusty put his arm around him. "What did I tell you, folks! Can this man sing or what!" Everyone cheered.

Rusty sang *Silver Wings* next to slow things down a bit. Couples were dancing the *Texas Two Step* and talking as he sang.

Jamie went to the bar and ordered a margarita. She was so proud of Tim, and she was really enjoying herself. Oddly enough, *Margaritaville* was the next song that Rusty chose. The dance floor began to thin out a bit during this song and everyone politely clapped after it was over.

Tim sang *Mama Tried* after Rusty's song. A few people were dancing and those that weren't, were staring at him as he sang in his velvety-soft voice. He was totally at ease with the crowd, and made eye contact with as many as he could. He saw people whispering to one another as they listened to him, and the pride beamed from his heart; he was so thrilled that he was a part of making Crystal's night truly fantastic.

Marty started his lead into *Amarillo by Morning.*

Once again, people whistled and clapped as they made their way to the dance floor. Tim *loved* to watch him play it; no matter how many times he played the song, he never grew tired of it. It was Marty's passion on the strings and the look of total tranquility on his face that fascinated Tim the most.

Rusty grinned at Tim before he started singing, and shook his head, remembering his outlandish 'prank' performance from the previous night.

A gentleman asked Jamie to dance and she accepted, smiling and waving at Tim as they two-stepped past him on the stage. He smiled back; he was so happy she was having a good time. *She looks so beautiful tonight,* he thought, as he watched her flow gracefully across the dance floor.

People stood and applauded when Rusty finished the song, as *Folsom Prison Blues* began. Acie played that slick, bass back-beat of his and the crowd went wild. When he finished, Rusty thanked them once again and looked at Tim–giving him his cue. When *Don't Be Cruel* arrived, Tim's voice entered the hall encased in a true vintage *'fifties'* sound.

He gave no introduction for Tim this time. Rusty struck the beginning licks to start the song off and Acie followed with the stand-up bass, rocking it and bobbing his head. Everyone stopped and listened as Tim stepped up to the microphone, grinned, and started his performance.

♫ *"Uh-you-uh know 'ah can be fount!"* ♫

Acie and Marty sang the background vocals of *The Jordanaires.*

♫ *"Uh settin' home all uh-lone!" ("BOP-BOP!")*
"If you cain't come around!" ("BOP-BOP!")
"Well-at-uh-least-uh please-'uhh...telly-phone!"
"Uh-don't be cruel...to uh heart that's true!" ♫

The entire place grew quiet. Women started making their way across the dance floor to the stage, absolutely hypnotized by the fact that they were staring up at a young star. Jamie smiled up at Tim, completely understanding the female fascination. He sounded *exactly* like Elvis.

♫ *"Uh-well-uh baybee if 'uh made-uh yuh mat!" ("BOP-BOP!")*
"Uh sump'm ah mat-uh set!" ("BOP-BOP!")
"PULEEEEZ-uh! fuhget'n the past!" ("BOP-BOP!")
"Thuh 'few-chuh' looks brat a-het!"
"Uh-don't be cruel...to uh heart that's true!"
"Ah don't want no uh-thuh love! 'Uh baybee it's still yew, ahm-uh thankin' of!" "HMMMmmm!!" ♫

More women came to the stage and blended in with the others, like a crowd of teenagers walking to their 'god.' The excitement was palpable as they began whispering amongst themselves, visually swooning over the man with the ultimate voice.

Acie grinned and spun his bass around. Thunder resonated off the walls as he slapped the huge strings brutally with his hand—bringing home the rock-n'-roll sound. Rusty looked back at Marty and raised his eyebrows, while Spider was in a world of his *own.*

Jamie continued to watch the women flocking around her husband. The members of the '57 Chevys and the Longhorn band were all sitting together, chuckling at

Tim's total control over the crowd.

"That boy's pretty darn good!" One member remarked.

Another laughed and playfully hit the previous one on the shoulder. "He'll be 'pretty darn good' if they start ripping his clothes off him!" They all roared with laughter.

Jamie looked back up at Tim. He started chugging his guitar like a train wheel attached to its tie rod. It was exceptional and she knew it—*she* even wanted to be up there with them!

If any of those women even THINK about touching him, I'm going to come unglued! she thought to herself.

Whistles, applause, and shouts of congratulations were bestowed upon Tim when the song came to a close.

Acie and Spider were smiling as the crowd continued to applaud. Tim slid his guitar behind his back and thanked everyone, then bent down and shook hands with some of the girls.

Rusty chuckled, as Marty and Acie stood behind him shaking their heads and smiling at the slight coos and whispers of the group of ladies crushing on their lead singer.

"Son," Rusty laughed. "I thought you were supposed to be nervous!" He turned back to the microphone.

"Okay, folks, we're gonna back out for a few minutes and let Tim *sling* you another song. We're gonna loosen the reins on him a bit and let him sing one all by himself." Rusty winked. "Apparently he already has some new fans all ready to listen."

No one left the dance floor, as Tim stood back up

and looked for Jamie. She was standing near the table staring at him in disbelief, a wide smile planted firmly on her face.

Rusty stood his guitar on its stand, and walked to the back of the stage, lighting a cigarette; Marty and Acie met him there, while Spider stayed quietly behind his drum set.

Tim nodded at Rusty, and approached his microphone. "Mr. Baker, could you please bring Crystal up here to join me? I promised her that I would sing a song just for her." The crowd clapped for the guest of honor. Tim continued, "Jamie, would you mind coming up here too, please? I need your help with something."

Everyone made a path for Crystal, as Mr. Baker positioned her wheelchair in front of the stage, so she could look up at her new hero. Tim sat down on the edge of the stage with his guitar because he didn't want her hurting her neck to look up.

"Jamie, if you wouldn't mind, could you please hold the microphone for me so I can sing this song for Crystal?" He kissed her on the cheek and everyone whistled, as Jamie blushed and smiled.

Taking the microphone, Jamie remained silent as the lights dimmed and a spotlight was placed on Tim and Crystal. He was scheduled to sing his song, *The Vagabond*, but he didn't. Instead, Tim began to finger-pick the intro to a very beautiful, and much beloved Dolly Parton tune.

♫ *"Love is like a butterfly, as soft and gentle as a sigh; the multi-colored moods of love are like its satin wings..."* ♫

Jamie held the microphone to his lips. Tim was singing so soft, it was almost like a whisper–emulating that beautiful butterfly as it gently soared on the breeze.

Not a sound rung out in the hall. Discussions had come to a close and the laughter had ceased. *Everyone* was gathering around trying to see Tim as he sang the endearing song to Crystal, as the dance suddenly transformed into a solo concert.

Suddenly, the walls began to resonate in light thunder. Tim glanced back and saw Acie's silhouette on the dark stage, slowly bobbing his head and slapping the strings of the bass that Tim loved so much.

Acie smiled at him and nodded, as if letting his buddy know that the back-beat was there for him.

Tim slowly turned back to Crystal as the rhythm echoed through the building, and continued with the song. He stared into the lovely girl's eyes and was genuinely transfixed. Crystal's gaze was filled with emotion; emotion that they would both feel long after this day came to a close. She looked as if she were clinging to his every word, as the beautiful lyrics dripped from his mouth like honey, wishing her song would last forever.

As far as Crystal was concerned, in that spotlight she had become the most special little girl in the entire world, and she longed for another warm kiss from the 'songman' for her tear-stained cheek. She could feel the uniqueness–the rare and gentle moment that Tim was presenting just to her, captivating her heart.

♫ *"Your laughter brings me sunshine, everyday is springtime, and I am only happy when you are by my side;*

"How precious is this love we share; how very

precious, sweet and rare; together we belong like... daffodil's and butterflies..." ♫

His eyes began to water as he saw the love-filled tears rain gently down her cheek. He leaned forward and gazed deeply into Crystal's eyes, as he tenderly concluded his beautiful ballad sung just for her.

♫ *"Love... is... like... a... bu... tterfly..."* ♫

When he finished there were no whistles, no applause. It was simply one of those precious moments in time; a magic spell that no one wanted to break. Tim was so thrilled, knowing that this precious child now understood how much she was loved. There was also not a single dry eye in the entire building. Even the non-e motional Spider was guilty of lifting up his glasses and wiping his eyes on his sleeve.

Rusty walked over and took Tim's guitar from him, replacing it on the stand. He didn't utter a single word to him; the only emotion that played out on the weathered face was a small tear that slipped from Rusty's eye and landed on the carpet of the stage.

Tim kissed Jamie and thanked her. He could tell by the look on her face that she was so happy she was able to be of help. And, by doing so, Tim had let the ladies know that he was most assuredly off the market.

He hopped off the stage and cupped his hands softly around Crystal's face. "You will always be my butterfly, Crystal," he said softly. Wiping her tears away, Tim kissed her on both cheeks, solidifying his vow.

Rusty walked up to the microphone and cleared his throat. His eyes were still wet as he addressed the quiet crowd. "We're gonna take a short break, folks. When the music returns, we're handing the night over to the '57 Chevys. Please remember to reach inside your hearts so we can help Crystal with her medical expenses. Thank you, Lubbock!" Everyone clapped and whistled.

Rusty then, without another word, went to the manager and wrote out a check for five-hundred dollars.

When the '57 Chevys had taken their place on the stage and begun their presentation, everyone met up at Jamie's table. Rusty gave Tim a big hug and patted him on the back. "You're really something, Son. We're all proud of you, and I bet that little girl will remember you for the rest of her life." They all made a toast.

"We did it *together*," Tim said, taking a sip of beer. "And I'll remember her for the rest of my life, too."

He smiled at his close-knit group. "I am so thankful to all of you for being my friends and giving me a chance. None of this would have happened if it weren't for all of you. I just want you to know that you are the best musicians I have ever met, and it was an honor and a privilege to be here with you tonight. I feel like we're brothers."

After the cheers, salutes and hugs, Rusty smiled over at Jamie. "Brothers with a sister, of course. Lady, you're just as much a part of this as Tim here," Rusty said. "We all, especially *me*, want to say thank you for your patience, 'cause I know it ain't been easy being without him night after night."

They all raised their drinks to the woman glowing radiantly at the table.

"Now you get out there and dance with that pretty wife of yours!" Rusty hollered at Tim. "God knows, she's earned it!"

They all took turns dancing Jamie around the floor —even *Spider*; the eyes of his band practically popped out of their skulls as Spider danced, laughed, and actually *spoke* in public.

After church the next day, Tim met Rusty and the rest of the band at the VFW to help pack up the equipment. When he arrived, Marty looked over at Rusty and they met Tim at the front of the stage.

"Tim, I've got some good news and I've got some bad news, which do you want to hear first?"

Tim looked at both of them. "I guess I want the bad news first," he said, not knowing what to expect.

Marty looked at him. "My friend said that Merle Haggard listened to your tape." Tim's eyes lit up, but Marty quickly put his hand in the air. "He said he liked it, but he doesn't record anything that he doesn't write himself."

The conclusion of the sentence made Tim feel as if he'd been punched in the gut.

Rusty put his arm around him. "It's okay, Son. It's still a good song. Besides, you wrote it, *you* should sing it! Now, are you ready for the good news?"

Tim nodded his head, hoping beyond all hope that the good news was *really* good!

"We raised six-thousand, nine-hundred thirty-eight dollars, and seventeen cents last night!"

The smile burst across Tim's face as his heart filled with joy. Rusty patted him on the back. He felt so good to know that he was part of such a generous and caring community, and that his beloved Crystal would finally get the miracle she needed.

Jamie was excited to hear the good news. They turned their film in to be developed on Monday and visited with the Bakers the very next weekend. Tim and Jamie put Crystal's picture in a frame for her, and she smiled at the gift.

Tim finally understood that one smile could actually light up the world, and Crystal's was the one he would hold close to his heart for the rest of his life.

8

Two weeks later, Rusty called Tim at work. "We've got a spot out at the fairgrounds this next weekend playing at the *Nifty-Fifties* car show, you interested?"

"You bet!" Tim answered excitedly.

"We need to practice, but it won't be every night like before, just a couple," Rusty explained.

"That sounds really good! Thanks, Rusty."

"You're welcome, Son," Rusty replied—his deep voice bellowed through the phone lines like Obi Wan to a very young Luke.

The *Sucker-Rods* practiced on Wednesday and Thursday to, more-or-less, *fine tune* and make sure they were familiar with the material.

Rusty had compiled a whole different repertory for Saturday. "You always wanna keep em' guessing, Son," he said. "A lot of those same people that were at the VFW might be there, and we don't wanna grow *stale* on em'."

On Saturday, Tim was getting ready to go to the fairgrounds and yelled, "Jamie! Bring the camera in here quick!"

Jamie wondered what could possibly be of such interest in the bathroom that a photo was warranted. Nevertheless, she scurried from the bedroom, slamming the top dresser drawer on her way out.

She doubled over in laughter as she walked through the door; the sight that met her eyes was truly hysterical. Tim was sitting on the edge of the tub holding

Buddy up in his lap like a ventriloquist's dummy. He had shaving cream caked all over his snout and chin and his whiskers were sticking out, making him look like he had a spider web covered in cream of wheat dangling from his cute puppy face.

"Hurry up before it starts to melt!" Tim was laughing so hard that tears began to fall. Buddy wagged his tail and tried not to lick, as Tim held up a Gillette razor.

"Make sure it looks like he's holding it himself!" Tim said, chuckling so hard that his face turned red. Jamie centered the shot just right through the lens and snapped the picture.

"This would make a nice *ad* in *Good Housekeeping*, or *Better Homes and Gardens*," Tim said, trying to keep Buddy steady on his knee.

Tim contorted his face and spoke in the voice of some barbaric, ancient Spaniard, *"Gee-llette, for zat 'eerie-zee-stable' fess zat weemin love!"*

Some of the shaving cream fell from Buddy's face, and Tim reached for the bathroom glass, quickly holding it under Buddy's chin. "Wanna glass of rabies?" he asked, holding it up to Jamie.

Jamie started laughing again as she watched Tim's face change—her men were truly hilarious!

"I think he would look funny with a patch over one eye and a treasure map tattooed on his shaved chest," Tim remarked, studying Buddy.

Jamie had spasms of laughter once more, imagining what Buddy would look like as Tim described him; he sure knew how to tickle her funny bone once he got her started. “How in the world do you come up with all this stuff, Honey?” she asked, wiping a tear from her eye.

Tim shrugged. “I don’t know, it just pops in there.”

When they arrived at the fairgrounds, Buddy was the first one out of the car. Jamie had her hand inside the loop of his leash and his small strength gave her a moment of whiplash as she opened the door.

“Dang it, Buddy! You almost ripped my arm off!” she hollered.

Tim laughed as he thought about Buddy running through the gravel parking lot, panting and dragging a severed arm behind him. “He wants to ride the tilt-a-whirl, Honey!” Tim said, closing his door. He walked to the trunk to collect his guitar.

“No way, Tim!” she said sternly. “There’s no way I’m letting you take him on any of the throw-up rides! Especially since *I* am the one he always throws up on!”

Again, Tim laughed, as he imagined lying down in the seat of the tilt-a-whirl, holding Buddy above his head, wearing his Clint Eastwood bandana—looking as if the outlaw dog was riding all alone. He pictured him in slow motion, spinning around in the seat spraying burrito beans all over the place, and bent over and laughed until his face turned red.

“It’s not funny!” Jamie said, although she joined in with the laughter when Tim told her about all the images floating through his mind.

The midway was packed with people and the sun was hot in the bright blue sky—a truly picturesque day. The smell of cotton candy and roasted peanuts hung in the air, as the slew of vendors lined the fairway.

Tim stopped at a chili stand where the big poster of a skull and crossbones met his eye. He read the warning: *'ABANDON ALL HOPE, YE WHO ENTER HERE!'*

On the side of the vendor's stand was a skeleton seated at a table holding a bowl of plastic chili topped with plastic cheese and plastic jalapenos.

Tim cocked his eyebrows and sent Jamie a slightly evil grin.

"Don't even think about it," she said, and kept walking. "Buddy's not the only one who can cover me in ick."

Choosing to shy away from the food that would have him hurting for days, Tim and Jamie walked toward the safer looking pink building, that had a red-and-white-striped awning calling out to the customers. The look and scent of the delicious funnel cakes and doughnuts wafted through the air.

Children were holding helium-filled balloons and chowing down on their caramel apples, as a woman standing in line at the ticket booth held a baby who was bawling uncontrollably, apparently wishing to save the 'fair' experience for a little later on in his life.

Buddy was walking alongside Tim with wide eyes, taking in all of the sights and sounds.

In the distance, Tim saw the Ferris Wheel. He could see all the small faces of children laughing and screaming as they flew slowly up into the Texas sky. Some teenagers were shaking one of the seats back and forth as it topped the crest, and a girl was screaming and begging them to stop. Tim shook his head, there would always be one to destroy the fun.

They paused at the merry-go-round, which Tim and Jamie both thought was truly beautiful. The top cascaded down in vibrant colors of red, blue, yellow and white. The horses were hand-carved and dressed lavishly in shiny varnish and glowing jewels. Each horse was a different color, and between some of them were ornate seats of gold richly upholstered in red velvet where people could simply sit and feel like royalty as they went round and round.

Carnival music poured from the speakers as children sat, laughed and inhaled their cotton candy. Parents were holding their toddlers on some of them, and elderly citizens sat upon the golden seats, enjoying the shade.

Tim could see the excited look in Jamie's eyes. He placed his guitar case on the ground in front of him and held her hand. "I'll take you for a ride on it when we finish," he said, kissing her cheek.

She laid her head on his shoulder, as they continued to walk past the many attractions before they came to the end of the midway. In the middle of the fairgrounds, Tim spotted Rusty at the bandstand, his red pick-up backed up to it, as Spider unloaded his precious drum set.

Tim could see Acie's stand-up bass tied to the nose of the truckbed, and he laughed as Acie struggled with the great instrument. The stage was much taller than that of the VFW, and Tim could feel his excitement intensify.

Several bleachers encircled the stage, offering rows of aged wooden seats to the audience. Rusty saw Tim and lit one of his *Marlboros*, waving his hand. Dressed in his black Western shirt with bolo tie and his ever-famous black cowboy hat, Rusty seemed all set to get the party started.

Tim laughed to himself as he noticed that he and Rusty matched; Tim was also wearing his black Western shirt, making them look like a cohesive unit.

Acie was wearing a black and red Western shirt with fringe on the arms, and imitation mother-of-pearl buttons, topped off with his favorite black cowboy hat. Marty was a stand-out in his bright red Western shirt made of silk. It shone brightly in the hot August sun, but his black cowboy hat was solidly in place.

Spider, as always, remained the unique band member with his black T-shirt, and hair tied in a ponytail underneath his red *Budweiser* baseball cap. Even his white tennis shoes stuck out; but that choice, Tim knew, was not an eccentricity–the shoes were all business. In fact, the shoes enabled Spider to play the bass part of his drum set far more effectively.

Tim climbed the stairs that led to the stage and looked around, marveling at the height and how far he could see. To the left was the midway and all of the rides glistening in the sunshine, and to the right were hundreds of cars; beautiful antiques that called out to the automobile fanatics that walked the grounds.

The band members waved and shouted hello to Jamie, as she offered them a smile before taking Buddy for a walk.

"It's a hot one today!" Rusty said, as he bent over with his cigarette dangling from his lower lip. As the sweat began, Rusty began arranging and stacking the amplifiers.

Acie and Tim carefully brought the bass up the stairs, as Marty started hauling microphone stands. Tim opened his case and set his guitar down on one of Rusty's stands. Tim reached out to shake his hand.

"How do you feel?" Rusty grinned.

"Nervous...as usual," Tim replied.

Rusty shook his head and patted him on the back.

"I like it when you get nervous, Son. That's when things *really* start to happen!"

Tim moved his gaze to the ground.

"Something wrong?" Rusty asked.

Tim looked over at the other guys who were working their tails off. "*We-ll*, Rusty...I've kind of been working on a song...for you."

"For me?" Rusty asked, amazed.

"Yes, sir." Tim continued, "You have such a deep voice and I've noticed how you like to sing Johnny Cash songs, so I figured since Merle Haggard didn't want to sing the song I wrote for him, maybe you would like to sing one I wrote for you."

Rusty sat down on one of his amplifiers and lit another cigarette. "Let's hear it," he said, smiling as he exhaled.

Tim took out his wallet and unfolded a deposit receipt with the lyrics written on the back. "It's still a work in progress and I don't have any fancy intros to it yet, but I think it's pretty good. It's called, *Because of You.*"

Tim smiled at the man he still worshipped for giving him the chance of a lifetime. "I started thinking to myself, *What would Johnny Cash write about if he were me?* and everything went from there."

The King of Hearts

Tim put his guitar around his neck, as Rusty held the receipt up for him. Tim put his thumb-pick on and started the back-beat of the top two strings, strumming the rest with his forefinger–producing a slow-driving, razor sharp sound that Johnny Cash would definitely have used. Tim started the song, mimicking Johnny's voice so Rusty could better understand how it was supposed sound.

♫ *"My heart keeps breakin', because you lied;*
You went and left me, and made me cry;
You're a cold hearted woman, so mean and cruel;
My heart keeps breakin', because of you".

(Chorus)
"I was so sure you really loved me,
But you just played me for a fool...
I went and gave you all my lovin';
Now you've got me cryin' over you!

"You made me love you, right from the start;
You made a bee-line, straight for my heart;
You're a good lookin' woman, so hard and crude;
And I keep cryin', because of you."

(Chorus)

"Baby, when you love me, I take my time,
But then you tell me, I'm way behind;
You rea-lly get me, so sad and blue,
And I keep cryin', because of you...
Yeah, I keep cryin', because of you." ♫

Rusty was grinning from ear to ear when Tim came to the end of the powerful song. He flicked the cigarette from the stage and began to clap. "Well, I'll be dog-goned, Son!" He shook his head and whistled for everyone else to join them. Every band member's eye turned to Rusty.

"Ya'll come over here and listen to this! I gotta say it sounds like 'Old Johnny' himself wrote this!" Rusty was ecstatic.

Everyone stood around Tim as he enthusiastically played the song again. Jamie and Buddy stood at the front of the stage and listened, applauding right along with everyone else when he finished.

"I want you to play that one today, Tim," Rusty said. "We'll be able to follow you. I don't know the words yet and I want to see how everyone reacts to it." He shook his head and smiled over at Marty.

"When did you write that?" Acie asked.

"This week."

"And that's the way we do it!" Rusty spun around in excitement. "Way to go, Tim!"

Jamie sat on the front row of the bleachers with Buddy as the band warmed up. People were wandering back and forth from one end of the fairgrounds to the other, casting hopeful looks at the band that would soon be providing the highlight of their day.

"Let's do *Blue Days, Black Nights* by Buddy Holly first!" Rusty was very cheerful. *What an honor*, he thought to himself. *First time anybody has ever written a song especially for me.*

Rusty counted off and they began the intro. Up

until this point, Jamie and Buddy had been the only captive audience members, but as soon as Tim began to sing and Rusty double-picked the rockabilly song, it was like a preacher had summoned his flock. People stopped, turned, and made their way to the bleachers to sit down and listen.

Jamie stood Buddy up on her lap and was making him dance to the music. He reminded her of the dancing gopher from the movie *Caddyshack*. She saw Tim look down, fighting hard not to chuckle during his performance. Jamie laughed as Tim shook his head at her. He knew he wouldn't be able to continue the song if his funny bone got the better of him.

The people clapped and whistled as the song came to an end, and Tim patted himself on the back for keeping a straight face.

"Thank you, folks!" Rusty said into the microphone. "We're gonna sing a classic by Hank Williams now and I hope y'all enjoy it." He bellowed out the haunting lyrics of *Your Cheating Heart,* but received only mild applause. *Dixieland Delight* came next, as more people made their way to the grandstands to become a part of the show that was building excitement with every tune.

Rusty cupped his hand and asked Tim if he knew *That's Alright Mama*. "We've gotta try and draw a bigger crowd," he mumbled.

"I sure do!" Tim replied. Starting in with the rhythm, Rusty followed with the finger-picking that was identical to Scotty Moore's version in Elvis' original recording, as Acie joined in with his thundering back-beat.

Tim's voice echoed in vintage reverb throughout the entire fairgrounds. Even the antique car collectors were craning their necks to see where the music was coming from. While Acie and Rusty played the break, Tim felt that amazing rush of hair-raising electricity go through his body, as if his very soul was being transported back to 1955.

People were starting to gather, making their way from the car show and the midway. Acie spun his bass around and slapped the strings furiously with his hand as Rusty continued with the instrumental–the musicians calling forth the listeners with everything they had.

Tim was amazed at how precisely the song was being played. He looked back for a moment and watched them finish up the remaining notes before he stepped up to the microphone and began the second half of the song.

The whistles emanating from the crowd were music to Tim's ears, like a true acknowledgement of the band's talent. Acie was really putting on a show with his rocking and bobbing bass, but Spider seemed lost, as the particular song didn't require the beat of any drum.

When Tim finished, the congregation was quite a bit larger. The din was so great that it seemed they all came together in their whistles and applause.

Peggy Sue was next and Spider's quaking drums put Tim to the test, but he was so engulfed in euphoria that it wouldn't have mattered how fast he played it—Tim kept right up with him. He moved a little in his own style and flair, but nothing like what Elvis or Michael Jackson would have done.

The large mass of people stood and applauded

when he finished Buddy Holly's famous song. Generations had passed, and yet they all still missed him.

"Thank you, ladies and gentlemen. I hope I did Mr. Holly's song some justice," Tim said politely. The crowd clapped once more, assuring Tim that he most certainly had. A clear voice rang out: "You're doin' good, man! Sing another one!"

"Thank you," he said. "I just want to say that it's a privilege to be here in Lubbock with you. I love Buddy and his music, and I appreciate you letting me sing his songs."

"Tim, why don't you play them that song you wrote?" Rusty asked over the microphone, "Folks, you're gonna love this one; it's called *The Vagabond*."

Tim was totally at ease and completely uninhibited during his performance. And, as Rusty liked it best when he played it by himself, Tim made sure it would give the crowd the *lonesome* feeling that he was trying to portray in the lyrics. *I would rather have accompaniment to add more body to it,* Tim thought, as he ended the song. *But I respect Rusty's judgment.*

And Rusty had been more than right. The crowd had been silenced as he captured their attention, but the whistles and applause had soon erupted as the cameras began to snap in Tim's eyes.

He sang *Riding My Thumb to Mexico*, by Johnny Rodriguez next. And more and more people began to arrive as the afternoon transformed into a stunning sunset.

Rusty felt the mood and, *stale* or not, he sang *Amarillo by Morning*. Tim felt that song never got old *or* stale, as Marty captivated the audience every time he played it. They stared at him, mesmerized, listening to the beautiful vibrato of the strings as he stepped to the front of the stage—his look of total peace and tranquility covered his features.

Afterwards, Rusty sang *Cry, Cry, Cry*, by Johnny Cash, as the afternoon turned to evening and the temperature dropped a few degrees to give the crowd a little break.

Rusty told Tim to sing *Because of You*, while he kept his eyes on the audience. When Tim was halfway through the first verse, Rusty spotted the news crews from KCBD and KLBK scurrying over from the *Nifty-Fifties* car show. Setting up their equipment quickly, the newsmen and women began to videotape the stellar performance.

This is it, Tim thought; his heart pounded as he focused on the second verse of his song. Everyone in the band was in perfect sync and the song was razor-sharp! Tim looked into the cameras and smiled as he began the chorus.

Rusty moved away from the mike. "*Don't Be Cruel*, Son." Tim nodded his head once to let him know that he had heard him, and continued singing.

Rusty went directly into the next song without pause, as the television stations continued to focus on Tim as he belted out the tune. Just as it had at the benefit, the crowd grew silent, completely captivated by Tim's voice. He shook his guitar and cameras began to flash as the cacophony of women slowly made their way to the stage.

Tim looked down and sent them a smile, as Acie continued to slap and rock his bass as he spun it around for the crowd's delight.

When he had finished, Rusty stepped up to the

mic. "Tim Cunningham, ladies and gentlemen!" Everyone, including Jamie and Buddy, stood up, hollered, whistled, and applauded. Flashes were still going off when Tim blew a kiss to the two souls he truly loved, and bowed to the rest of the crowd.

The television crews taped the applause and left, as the show came to a close.

"We want to thank each and every one of you for coming out today and we hope you had a great time! We also want to thank the Lubbock Fairgrounds for letting us set up and play for you! I'm Rusty Jackson and we are *The Sucker-Rod* band!" Rusty led the band with *Cotton-Eyed-Joe* as they wrapped up the killer show with a killer song.

"That'll be on the news tonight," Rusty said, as he began to pack the equipment. "You couldn't have asked for better timing!"

Tim helped load Rusty's truck, while Jamie and Buddy waited for him. "That was a good performance, Tim," Rusty said; his cigarette smoke formed a ring above his head like a translucent halo.

"Do you know why I cut the show short tonight?"

Tim shook his head. "No, sir."

Rusty pushed his hat up. "You always want to leave the crowd wanting more. Never overdo it, or before you know it your seats will start to empty out. I've been doing this all my life, Son— so always remember that."

"Okay, Rusty." Tim listened to him carefully, taking in every word that came from the mouth of his mentor.

"You got any plans for Tuesday?" Rusty asked him, tossing his cigarette into the dust.

"Not that I know of," he replied, zipping up his

guitar case.

Rusty put his long lanky arm around his shoulder. "I wanna take you to a place called the *Conference Café*; it's a college bar for the kids at Texas Tech. On Tuesday nights they have songwriter's night, and anyone can get up and sing a song they've written. What I'm trying to do is get you some exposure, and what I mean by that is I think you need to be seen and heard as much as possible...get some recognition."

Tim studied him, remaining quiet.

"It takes a while, but before you know it people will be talking about you, talking *to* you, and they'll be *wherever* they know you're going to be singing. They'll tell their friends about you and in turn, *they'll* tell friends of their own. Word of mouth travels really quick around Lubbock."

Rusty smiled. "We lucked out tonight with the news people. We were in the right place at the right time, *plus*, they taped you singing your very own song, Son! You should be really proud of yourself."

Tim smiled at him, as Rusty offered him a very fatherly hug before he left.

"You were very good tonight, Honey!" Jamie said to him as he reached the last step, exiting the stage.

Tim kissed her. "Thanks, Kitten. It was fun!"

Rusty and Spider waved at them as they drove off, while Marty and Acie shouted, "See ya later, Tim. Good show!"

"Thanks!" Tim and Jamie waved goodbye.

As they reached the entrance to the midway, a couple of girls were waiting for Tim.

"Can we have your autograph?"

Tim was shocked. He looked at Jamie, staring at the girls who were smiling anxiously. "Sure but I...I don't have a pen or any paper," he said, blushing.

"You were great!" the first female told him.

"You're the best singer in this town!" said the second. Tim guessed they were most likely college students.

"That's a really cute dog!" The first girl said, bending down to pet Buddy.

Jamie dug around in her purse and managed to find an old black pen in the bottom, looking as if she'd like nothing better than to get as far away from the girls as possible.

"Thank you," he smiled. "I really appreciate that! I'll be at the *Conference Café* on Tuesday night if you'd like to come."

Jamie shot a fierce look at him, but refrained from saying anything. Finding a couple of napkins, she handed them to Tim so he could give his scribble to the adamant girls and they could go home.

"Here you go," he said, handing the napkins to them. "*You're Friend, Tim,*" was scrawled on each.

They both smiled and watched him as he left.

"I *saw* the way they were looking at you, Tim!" Jamie huffed, unable to keep her emotions in check any longer.

Tim remained silent.

"What is the *Conference Café?*" she demanded.

"Rusty said they have a songwriter's night on Tuesdays and he wants me to play my song there." He kept his gaze firmly on the ground.

"I don't like it when all those women do that when you're singing, Tim. You're *my* husband, and I don't want anyone looking at you like that but *me*!"

Tim walked quietly through the midway. "I want to put my guitar in the trunk so I don't have to carry it on the rides, it might get broken," he said, finally breaking the silence.

Jamie knew she had hurt his feelings, and tried her best to rein in the jealous female who'd suddenly appeared inside of her. She stepped in front of him, blocking his way. "I'm sorry, Sweetheart," she sighed. "You didn't do anything wrong, and I am completely overreacting."

He put his guitar down and held her in his arms. "It's okay," he whispered, pressing her head to his chest. "I love you." Buddy sat calmly between them, as if remaining the neutral Switzerland so he wouldn't be in trouble.

"No, it's *not* okay, Sweetheart." She began to cry. "I knew you were wonderful the first time I ever laid eyes on you, but I underestimated the way you would be perceived by all these needy females. I never expected to ever feel this jealous of anything or anyone in my entire life, and I don't know what to do about it! I feel awful!"

Tim cupped her face and kissed her tears as he gazed into her lovely eyes. "I want to tell you something. I am married to the most beautiful woman in the world—I have never understood what you see in me, or why you love me, but it certainly isn't my looks." He smiled.

"You believed in me when no one else did—or even *cared*; you wanted me when all the others threw me away like yesterday's garbage, and you loved me when no one else would have me."

He took a deep breath and continued, "Before I met you, I didn't want to live anymore. I was so lonely and I could never get a date. Women would laugh at me, or if I ever *did* manage to have a girlfriend, they would take advantage of me, then toss me to the curb once I ran out of money. You never did that to me.

"I always waited for the day when you would make up some excuse why you didn't want to be with me anymore, but that day never came. I took my time opening up to you because I didn't want to have what was left of my heart ripped out and handed to me on a silver platter."

He swallowed his tears. "I've *always* loved you, Sweetheart. It's always been you, and I promise that I will love you with all my heart until the day I draw my very last breath.

"With all this," he stopped and waved his hand toward the stage. "I'm only entertaining people, and I'm using the gift that God gave me to help people. Rusty's trying to show me how; he's become like a father to me."

He thought about the man who was guiding him toward his dream. "When I'm up there I'm singing with everything that's in me, and whatever passion you hear in the music is what I'm feeling for you." He offered a sneer and twitched his upper lip, "*'Cause baby, you 'reall-uh' know how tuh melt mah butter!*"

Jamie's eyes lit up, as she playfully slapped him on the chest.

He laughed. "Now, it seems like I promised you a ride on the merry-go-round, *Chickie-doodle!*"

Jamie smiled. "You're the best looking guy in the world to me, Tim. And God knows you're loaded with talent."

Buddy was one of the three who really enjoyed his ride on the merry-go-round. Tim stood him up on the horse's saddle and he rested his paws on the pole. Jamie laughed as Buddy went up and down, looking around. He was shaking a little, unsure of what was happening to him. But after a while, Tim and Jamie sat in one of the richly-decorated seats and held hands. A true family unit, Jamie rested her head on Tim's shoulder as Buddy curled up in her lap.

Tim stayed up that night, waiting for the news to come on to see if he was going to be a Lubbock star. Jamie took a shower and joined him in the living room, wanting nothing more than to be by his side when good news was given.

Sure enough, the segment aired on the *Nifty-Fifties* car show.

"...but the cars weren't the only thing dazzling the crowd tonight, a local band had several people star-struck with a rock-and-roll review that was very pleasing to the ears."

Tim grinned as he saw himself on the tall stage with all the girls crowding in front of him. Tons of flashes were going off as he did his routine with the guitar, then it cut to the part where he blew his kiss and bowed.

Jamie watched, but Tim could tell she was trying to curb her anger at all the girls hovering around the stage. He silently turned the TV off, took a shower, and went to bed. Apparently the bad always came with the good.

After church the next day, Tim changed his clothes and went through his record albums. He found what he was looking for and drew out an LP picture disc of Ricky Nelson—it had never been opened. Turning it over, he read the song list. "Gosh!" he whispered. "It's on here."

Tim studied Ricky's picture. *I remember I was out delivering pizzas for Domino's when his plane crashed that night,* he thought to himself. Getting a sudden urge, Tim called Rusty and asked if he could come over.

"Do you think we could learn this one?" he asked, after playing the Ricky Nelson cut. "It's pretty simple and, if you don't mind, I'd really like to sing this one for Jamie. She's getting pretty upset about the girls coming up to the stage."

Rusty put the needle back on the record and listened to it again. "We'll give it a try, Son."

At the *Conference Café* on Tuesday night, the announcer called Tim's name.

Rusty lit a cigarette and took a sip of beer. "Go get 'em, Son," he said, grinning.

Tim did a quick *Rocky Balboa* 'bob-and-weave' routine, and threw a couple of jabs as Rusty chuckled at him. As Tim was walking to the front with his guitar, he heard a girl's voice. "Hey! That's that guy I was telling you about! He's really good!" Tim grinned, as he strapped his guitar around his neck. Even though Jamie was upset, Tim thought, the publicity was definitely helping his career.

"Hello everyone, I'm Tim Cunningham. I'm going to sing you a song called *The Vagabond.* I really hope you'll like it."

The room was quiet as he sang. Rusty got cold chills as his voice reverberated softly through the speakers. Whistles and applause whirled about when he finished.

"Thank you," Tim said, smiling as he took the guitar from around his neck and calmly went back to his seat.

"You did a good job on that," Rusty told him, exhaling his smoke. A man of few words, but definitely words that were filled with respect.

A young woman came over to where they were sitting and set a beer down in front of Tim. She took a chair from the table beside them and sat down.

"I'm Bridgette," she said, shaking hands with both. She was extremely attractive and her perfume smelled enchanting.

Rusty put his cigarette out and turned to watch the singer at the front of the room, keeping his words to himself.

"You've got a pretty voice," Bridgette continued. "I loved that song. Did you really write that?"

Tim didn't know what to say. "Thank you. Yes...yes I did." He smiled at her, but he was truly growing uncomfortable as she never took her gaze off him and Rusty continued to watch the stage.

"I bought you a beer. I saw what kind you were drinking and thought you might want another one," she said, stroking his flat top. "I like your hair-cut, too. It's so soft; it feels just like squirrel fur!"

Rusty looked at Tim and pulled his hat down over his eyes. Cupping his hand over his mouth, he fought hard to keep from laughing. "Are you about ready to go?"

"Yeah. I think it's about time," Tim replied, swallowing the last sip of his beer.

"What about your other beer?" Bridgette asked. "Can I at least get your phone number?"

Tim stood and picked up his guitar. "Bridgette, I really appreciate the thought and you're very pretty, but I'm married and I love my wife very much."

Tim politely said good night and followed Rusty out to the truck. Rusty handed him a cigarette and lit one for himself as he started up the engine. He just couldn't contain himself any longer. *"You're hair feels just like squirrel fur!"* Rusty mimicked in a feminine, husky voice.

Tim burst out in laughter. "The squirrel lady!" He joked, "I've never been able to get close enough to a squirrel to be able to tell what it *does* feel like. I wonder how she did it," he said, shaking his head. "I can't tell Jamie about that, but I swear she would die of laughter if it happened to someone else!"

Rusty shook his head. "True. But with you, Son, I think them cat claws of hers would've been out, and her ears would've been pinned back, flat on her head right before the attack!" He chuckled.

"I'm gonna call my friend, Byron. He owns the I-27th Club off Avenue Q. Talk him into letting us play out there next weekend."

"That would be great!" Tim said. "Can we practice that song this week?"

Rusty nodded. "Yeah, and I've been working on the one you wrote for me, too."

Tim was excited–a new booking, a good song, and a laugh over a squirrel lady. This had definitely been a night to remember.

9

The *Sucker Rod* band members practiced all week, keeping their focus on two songs—*Because of You* and the one Tim had chosen to sing for Jamie...*Never Be Anyone Else But You.* He thought the lyrics perfectly described the wealth of emotions he felt for her, and would make her know in her heart and soul that she was the *only* woman for him.

They were all set up and ready to play at seven. The I-27th Club was larger than Tim had expected, and it was jam-packed with people by show time. Everyone in the band expressed joy at seeing Jamie again, with each one reaching out to give her a hug.

Rusty couldn't wait to sing the song Tim had written especially for him.

A few people approached Tim before they started, congratulating him on the benefit for Crystal and complimenting him on his voice—some even told him they had seen him on the news.

At mid-point of the set, a few women were standing in front of Tim, watching him as he sang *Don't Be Cruel.* Jamie was among them in the very front, deciding once and for all that she would be the one Tim was crooning to. And, as she already knew would happen, his performance brought the house down.

Rusty sang *Because of You* and the applause and whistles engulfed him like a tidal wave of appreciation. Tim was terribly proud of Rusty. Sure, he had seen him laugh and smile, but he was glowing tonight as he made the song his very own. Rusty was having the time of his life, and he looked over at Tim with mutual admiration beaming in his eyes.

Just before Rusty played the beginning notes to *Never Be Anyone Else But You,* he turned the echo on, elated that Marty and Acie were harmonizing with him so beautifully.

Tim crooned out the melody, rocking back and forth to the enchanting beat. *Tim's voice*, Rusty thought to himself, *is thicker and deeper than even Ricky's was, and he's putting way more vibrato into it.* The teacher was definitely proud of the student.

Tim was staring directly at Jamie, his eyes filled with desire. He was falling in love with her all over again. Clasping both of her hands over her heart, she began to weep as he sung the second verse—as did virtually all the other women in the club. Some of them had mascara streaming down their cheeks as they moved in closer, almost pushing Jamie into his arms.

♫ *"I ne-ver will forget the way you kissed me!*

And when were not together... I wonder 'if-uh-you-uh-miss-uh-me 'cause I hope and pray..." ♫

As soon as he finished the song, Jamie grabbed him and placed a passionate kiss on his waiting lips. The other women grew frantic. Obviously not realizing that she was his wife, they rushed him like a herd of cattle going after the lone bull.

Tim and Jamie tumbled over backwards because of the weight of the pressing crowd, breaking a tuning key on Tim's guitar.

Spider immediately stood up quickly, protecting his blessed drum set. Acie and Marty raced to help Tim and Jamie.

"I love you, Tim!" An unrecognizable feminine voice rang out from someone in the mass.

Byron rushed out of his office, observing the mayhem from the rear of the building. "Dorothy, maybe you need to call the cops," he said, addressing the stunned bartender.

"Hold on for just a second, folks!" Rusty hollered. "Everybody needs to calm down!"

"I don't think it's a fight, Byron," Dorothy said, walking out from behind the counter. "I think Rusty's got it under control."

As soon as Acie and Marty reached Tim and Jamie, Spider retrieved Tim's guitar. Rusty began pulling people off the floor. Calming them down, he stood in front and lifted his right hand to get their attention.

"Everybody, please listen, there's been a misunderstanding here! That young lady there is his wife," he said, pointing at Jamie. "He's been practicing this song all week to sing especially for her."

Even though there were moans and groans, not to mention a wave of snide remarks aimed Jamie's way, the crowd was soon under control.

"Are you alright, Jamie?" Rusty asked.

She nodded. Tim was holding her tightly; his head was swimming. "What in the world just happened?" he asked, dazed and confused. "Did somebody get into a fight?"

Rusty patted him on the back. "Naw...you just got

to 'em, Son!" He said, snickering as he tussled Tim's velvety-soft "squirrel fur." The women were still standing around; some looked down at the ground, feeling sorry about what had happened.

Tim left Jamie's side for a moment, and walked over to them. "Thank you, ladies. That's the nicest compliment I've ever had," he said softly. "And I love you too..." He smiled, shook their hands, and offered hugs to a few who sent him their apologies.

Tim looked over at his broken guitar. "I won't be able to sing anymore tonight, though. *Mr. Midnight's* got a 'boo-boo'." Everyone laughed.

When Byron was certain everything was calm, he returned to his office.

"You and Jamie probably need to get on home," Rusty said. "I'll get your guitar fixed, Son–just leave it with me."

The ride home was a silent one. Jamie's elbow had been injured in the tumble, and her mind was obviously swimming with the overload of attention that was given to her husband.

Tim finally broke the silence. "That was pretty cool!"

Jamie slowly glared at him as if he were mentally deranged. "It wasn't *'cool'*, Tim. It was dangerous!

"I'm not so sure about this anymore. Your guitar is broken, not to mention my elbow!"

Tim stopped smiling. "I'm sorry, Sweetheart. I didn't know that was going to happen; I thought someone got into a fight, or something."

Jamie kept silent most of the way home. The words

had been said and now the imaginations were running rampant, wondering if this life was actually the life Tim and Jamie could stand.

Rusty took Tim's guitar to *Whitson's* music store Monday afternoon and told Billy what had happened.

Mr. Whitson put his glasses on as Rusty handed it to him. "I heard you had a new guy in the band. I saw him on the news and he sounds pretty good!"

Rusty exhaled his cigarette smoke and leaned on the counter. "He's got *pure* gold comin' outta' them vocal chords, Billy," he remarked, pushing his cowboy hat up with his thumb in his trademark gesture.

"I've never heard anything like it, and he wrote a song for me, too. I've been thinking about recording it at Don Caldwell's studio."

Billy gazed up from examining the damage. "Really?" he asked, apparently surprised. "It's *that* good?"

Rusty nodded. "You bet."

Mr. Whitson looked back at the guitar, then opened up a drawer below the counter and pulled out a screwdriver as Rusty watched him begin his expert tinkering.

"I think I can have this fixed by Friday," he said.

"By the way," Rusty began, crushing out his cigarette in a glass ashtray. "Do you still have that old flatbed trailer?"

"Sure do."

"I'm gonna ask Steve if we can park it at *Alpha's* this Saturday and set up on it," Rusty explained, "If you'll let me borrow it."

"Yeah, I can haul it out there for ya."

"Much obliged, Billy." They shook hands and Rusty eased out the door.

That same afternoon Tim bought a copy of Ronnie McDowell's album, *American Music,* and dialed Rusty's number. "Hey, man. I bought this new album today and I was wondering if I could come over? It has a couple of songs on it that I think you'll like."

"Okay, Son," he drawled. "I put your 'twang-box' in the shop, too. It should be ready by Friday."

Tim could hear him exhaling his cigarette smoke over the phone.

The two songs were *American Music* and *Sea of Heartbreak*. Tim had an absolute 'fit' over the latter; when he first heard it, the music had sent chills up his spine.

At Rusty's, Tim explained the video of *American Music,* that the band turned into cartoon hillbilly cats. Rusty chuckled at Tim as he imitated the cartoon bass player bobbing and rocking like Acie always did.

"Plus, it has that cool fiddle part in it that Marty can play," Tim added.

He listened to it once more with him. Rusty nodded. "I think that's 'do-able', Son. I'll call the rest of 'em and see if they can come over tonight."

Tim was truly ecstatic.

When everyone had arrived, Rusty told them of his plans to play on top of the flatbed trailer on Saturday night. "I'll put an ad in the *Avalanche Journal* tomorrow. My friend, Steve, owns *Alpha's*—I don't think he'll mind too much...especially if he knows he's gonna sell a lotta' beer."

They spent every night that week practicing, and Tim was confident that he could sing *Sea of Heartbreak* better than Ronnie by the end of the week. In fact, his confidence in his own ability was at a new high. He practiced the beginning of the song over and over again with Acie and Marty to make sure it was absolutely perfect.

Acie liked the song a lot; he and Tim blended perfectly on the harmony. Marty was very gifted with the parts as well, but Tim and Acie had bonded almost *spiritually* the first night they had met, and their combined tone transformed the music into an absolute miracle.

As he continued watching them rehearse the intro time and time again, Rusty thought over and over about the good idea that Tim had given him about how they should start the show on Saturday.

Billy hauled the flatbed to *Alpha's* at around noon on Saturday, blowing the air horn as he arrived. After he had uncoupled the trailer, Billy parked his blue Kenworth and pulled the air brakes. Dust from the gravel parking lot made a huge cloud of smoke as the air shot out from underneath the truck.

Rusty made the introductions. "You look just like Jerry Reed!" Tim said, smiling at him.

"Yeah, Son! *Ha-ha!*" Billy laughed, imitating Jerry.

Rusty chuckled, "You gonna stick around with us?"

Billy sighed. "Can't. I have to get back to the shop, but I'll swing by after I close up.

"But I s'pose you'll be needing this, Tim." Billy

climbed up in the cab, brought out the guitar, and handed it to him. "She's as good as new. And I checked your pick-up on the inside to make sure it was all right."

Rusty put his arm on Billy's shoulder. "Thanks, Billy, I'll settle up with you later."

Billy rolled down the window, laughed like Jerry Reed once more for Tim's amusement, and blew the air horn as he signaled his exit.

Everyone started setting up the equipment on the trailer, and after an hour had passed, a man pulled up in an old black pick-up truck with a camper attached to the back. Getting out, the stranger closed the door behind him. The sudden movement made the door clang and squeak on its hinges, announcing to everyone the years it had been on the road.

The man walked up to the flatbed. "Is Steve around?"

"I think he's inside," Rusty replied, looking toward the entrance.

The stranger watched them work for a few moments before introducing himself. "I'm Mickey Jarvis," he said, sticking out his hand to Rusty.

He bent down and shook it, then paused to light a cigarette.

"Steve told me I could set up out here with you guys today. I read the paper and I hope there'll be a lot of people here tonight." He turned to Tim. "I saw *you* on the news," he said, smiling.

Tim smiled and shook Jarvis' hand.

"Whatcha got in there?" Rusty asked, pointing at the camper with his *Marlboro* smoking between his fingers.

Mickey lit a cigarette, took a drag and exhaled. "I sell smoked turkey legs, chili, burritos, tacos, breakfast burritos, and barbecued pork sandwiches. Folks buy more of the smoked turkey legs than anything else," he smiled. "They're five dollars each but I guarantee you, you get your money's worth or I give you a refund! I've never had a complaint," Mickey proclaimed, proudly.

Rusty smiled.

"Well, it was nice to meet you. I've gotta go and talk to Steve," he stated, walking away.

"I need your help, Tim," Rusty said, after everything was in place. "We gotta make a couple of runs out to a friend of mine's place. I have to get a couple of truck loads of hay bales for everybody to sit on."

Spider, Acie, and Marty went inside to drink a beer. As two o'clock had approached, the scalding heat beaming from the summer sun had told them that liquid refreshment was definitely needed.

They packed the first load of hay as high as they could in the bed of Rusty's truck. He and Tim strapped it down and drove back to *Alpha's*. Tim laughed to himself as he thought about Jamie and Buddy sitting in a rocking chair on top of all that hay while Rusty played a cassette tape of the *Beverly Hillbillies* theme.

Rusty told Tim how he wanted to start the show. "I'm gonna swing by and see if Billy's got a spotlight we can borrow; I want it on top of the roof of the building. There's gonna be lanterns and a few lights, but no one will really be able to see you at first. When you and Acie finish with the very beginning words of *Sea of Heartbreak*, I want the spotlight to come on at the same time the music starts—that'll *really* surprise 'em!" he said, grinning at Tim.

Tim imagined the whole fabulous scene, and his excitement kicked into overdrive.

By the time they arrived with the second load of hay, Tim and Rusty both were exhausted.

Rusty looked at his watch. "It's about four-thirty now. Can you be back up here by six?"

"Yes, sir." Tim nodded briskly.

The two went inside *Alpha's.* Rusty leaned against the pay phone, deposited a quarter, and called Billy about the spotlight. "Alrighty, then, I'll be by within the hour. Thanks, Billy." Hanging up the phone, he went in to talk to the others. "Can you guys set that hay up in front of the trailer while we're gone?"

"Sure," Acie said, as Spider and Marty nodded in agreement.

"Okay, then ya'll can go home and change clothes and we'll meet back up here at six."

Rusty went back to talk with Steve about his spotlight idea and left Tim to wash up and change his clothes.

Tim was very excited when he arrived at the apartment. He picked Buddy up and kissed him behind his velvety ears, carrying him into the bedroom.

Jamie, who was getting ready when he walked in, shot him a smile.

"I can't wait to sing my new song for you, Honey!" He kissed her on the back of the neck, still thrilled by the fact that she shivered at his touch.

"I can't wait to hear it, Sweetie," she said.

Tim looked in the closet as if he had a million shirts to choose from, going for the black one with white seams. He was beginning to itch from the hay, so he wanted to get into the shower as quickly as possible.

Jamie watched him as he dressed. When he finished buttoning his shirt, he walked over to her and cupped her face in his hands. "You are *so* beautiful, Sweetheart. I love you."

Closing her eyes, Jamie threw herself into the passionate kiss, hypnotized by his *Tommy* cologne. "Tim, be careful tonight. Something happens when you guys play; I don't know what it is, but it's *something* out of this world."

The worried look came over her features. "You have this sound—*all* of you. It's different from anything I've ever heard, but it does something to people, *I* can barely hold it in when you're singing to *me!* If there's a repeat of what happened before...I think someone could get hurt. I thought that kind of thing only happened in fairy tales or on videos, but it's real!"

She attempted to smile through her worried frown. "I want you to have a good time tonight, and I'll be right up front waiting for you. I love you too—with all my heart." Kissing him again, she held him close.

"Everything's going to be just fine," he promised, rocking her gently in his arms.

They put Buddy in the bathroom–the last place he wanted to be. In fact, from the whimpering, he missed Tim already.

They arrived at ten minutes to six and the parking lot was already packed with cars. Finding a spot on the edge of the highway, he and Jamie parked, and went looking for Rusty as soon as they were inside.

The band was standing at the rear of the building; the bright red exit sign flashed above their heads as they went over the list of songs they were about to play.

"Tim, here's what we're gonna be doing tonight," Rusty said, handing him the list.

Tim stared at it in wonder, nodding his head as if bowing to the absolute superstars that the world would never know again. From Ronnie McDowell to Merle Haggard; from Waylon Jennings to Alabama to Johnny Cash—with a bit of the Eagles thrown in—all the greats were going to be sung.

"Anything more than that, and we'll just wing it," Rusty laughed.

Tim studied the list—it was amazing to see his name in black and white next to his song, completely surrounded by the greatest musicians of all time.

"So, you're a singer, huh?" Came a voice from behind him.

Tim looked back, completely astounded to see Tinker Carlen. He didn't know what to say, but he shook hands with him. "You *remember* me?" Tim asked, grinning from ear to ear.

"I sure do! I hear you've been doing pretty well for yourself these days. I saw you on the news awhile back, and last week I read you were playing out here tonight. I had to come and see what all the fuss is about." He smiled. "Would you care if I sat in and played a few songs with you?"

Tim was speechless. Rusty and the guys started laughing.

"I told him it would mean the world to you, Son," Rusty said, patting him on the back.

Tim would have never imagined in his whole life that a living legend would actually ask *him* if he could sit in on one of *his* sets. "Yes sir, Mr. Carlen! That would be great!"

"Call me Tinker, Tim. This must be your pretty wife that I've been hearing so much about tonight," he said, smiling at Jamie.

"Oh, yes...sir...I'm sorry, this is my wife, Jamie."

She smiled and shook the star's hand. "You've just made my husband the happiest man in the world. He's told me so many times about the night he met you and how you told him so much about Buddy. It's an honor, sir."

"Please, call me Tinker, and the honor is all mine," he said, tipping his hat.

The men stepped out the back door to smoke a cigarette and Jamie laughed. She knew Tim wasn't a smoker, *per* se, so she wrote it off in her mind as being a 'band-thing'. *Boys will be boys,* she laughed to herself.

"Do you think we could play *Peggy Sue* together tonight?" Tim asked anxiously.

"You got it, Son," Tinker replied, as Tim shouted with joy.

The sun had set and night had fallen. Rusty had placed an old rickety ladder at the end of the trailer so they could climb up, and as they all walked to the center, the crowd started cheering.

Tim estimated that there were probably over two hundred people there. He smiled when he saw Mickey's camper with a long line of people waiting to buy his goods. He couldn't hold it against them; the smell of the smoked turkey legs even made Tim's stomach growl.

They strapped their instruments on and Spider took his place behind his drums. Rusty counted off, and Tim, Acie, and Marty started to harmonize the opening notes of *Sea of Heartbreak.*

♫ *"Co-ome to-oo my rescue..."* ♫

The blinding lights suddenly shot across the stage, and a sea of cheers flooded their eardrums. It certainly had come together just as Rusty predicted—a perfectly professional concert.

Tim stood there preparing to sing as the entranced audience began clapping in unison. Acie's bass was *thundering* over the crowd; slapping the strings, he brought forth a mesmerizing beat. The guitars continued to loop the beginning notes just waiting for Tim to begin.

Whistles and applause roared throughout the gravel parking lot. He looked back at Rusty, who was grinning from ear-to-ear.

As Tim stepped out from behind his microphone and slid his guitar behind his back, the whistles and applause became deafening. He made his way to the front of the stage, watching to make sure he had enough slack from the line that was plugged into his guitar. Bending down, he started shaking hands with everyone in front of him.

The chant of his name reverberated like the tide of a tsunami. "TIM-TIM-TIM-TIM!" He stood and waved at them, a grand smile unconsciously filled his face.

He was mid-way down the trailer when he spotted Jamie. Tears of joy were flowing down her lovely cheeks making dark rivers through her makeup. He towered above her on the trailer as he looked down into her shimmering, emerald eyes. Kneeling, he cupped her face in his compassionate way and planted a kiss on her lips.

More whistles echoed and cameras flashed, as Tim stood and walked confidently back to his microphone. The experience was simply unreal, as he grinned at Tinker who returned his smile with a wink.

More flashbulbs went off as he shook his head, smiled and returned to the microphone. His horseshoe ring glimmered in the light as his voice cut through the crowd.

♫ *"The lights... in the harbor... don't shine... on me;*
I'-'hime like a lost ship... adrift on the sea..." ♫

He had performed perfectly. If anyone had ever deserved to sling a one-hundred-thousand-dollar, diamond studded rhinestone cape into an audience, if there had been one to sling, it was Tim at this purely golden moment.

Tim smiled and bowed. "Thank you, ladies and gentlemen. I hope you'll like this next one, too. It's always been one of my favorites," he said, humbly.

Rusty cupped his hand while Tim was thanking everyone, whispering to Tinker, "Mama Tried."

Rusty started the song and again, Tim relished in the sound of Acie's bass. Electricity shot through his soul as he felt the thrill quaking in the very planks of the flatbed he was standing on.

Again, thunderous applause came from the crowd when he had finished. Jamie whistled louder than anyone. She was so very proud of Tim. He truly dazzled her.

Rusty addressed the crowd when the song was over. "Thank you very much, folks! We're so glad that you've come to spend your Saturday night with us, and we're happy to be here with *you!* I'm Rusty Jackson, and we *are* the *Sucker-Rod* band!"

Everyone cheered as Rusty spoke to them; his deep voice bellowed across the gravel lot. "Folks, we have a special guest with us tonight. Please welcome Mr. Tinker Carlen! Tinker is one of the original *Crickets* from the band of our beloved Buddy Holly." Everyone whistled and clapped for Tinker, as he sent them a smile and a wave.

Tim gazed at Tinker with complete and utter admiration, as Rusty announced his credentials to the crowd. He thought about what it must've felt like to cruise around Lubbock in a nice car with Buddy, signing autographs, talking to girls, or just sitting around in a garage somewhere working on another hit song—sharing dreams of fame and stardom.

Tim felt that God had truly blessed him that night by sharing with him a small fraction of the person he admired and respected so much. A tear fell from his eye as he thanked the Lord for his kindness in sharing Buddy's legacy with him through Tinker.

"Tinker, do you remember that old song, *Good Hearted Woman?"*

"Seems to me like I do, Rusty," Tinker replied. The

crowd started whistling.

"What do you say we sing that song for everybody? After all, I'm sure all these gentlemen here have one with 'em tonight!" Rusty chuckled over the microphone.

"Well, let's give it a try!" Tinker said.

Rusty counted them off. It was a wonderfully warm evening, and the air was rich with talent and memories, as if the ghosts of the greats were sitting on clouds just staring down and admiring the band from up above—completely proud of the work they were doing for the crowds. Tim wished with all of his heart that he could somehow slow down time, wishing that the evening would never have to end.

Tinker sang *Raining in My Heart.* It was one of his favorites. Tim watched him as he sang his song. He could see in his face how much he truly missed his friend. Tinker strummed slowly, staring down at the neck of his guitar deep in thought and reminiscence. It was as if he were a million miles away. Tinker's face grew pale and his voice wavered sadly, as he slowly looked back at the audience with tear-filled eyes.

Tim looked away, knowing that he would cry if he kept looking at Tinker's expression. In fact, a pall of sadness seemed to float over the entire crowd, as if everyone was coming together to pray for the return of their beloved music man who was taken from them far too soon.

When he finished, there was a brief moment of silence that seemed to last forever. As Tim began to feel confident that he wouldn't cry, he swallowed hard and gradually looked over at Tinker. Their eyes made contact and Tim saw a tear streaming softly down Tinker's face. The moment had been one of sheer friendship, brotherhood and love.

When Tim sang *Never Be Anyone Else But You*, the women flocked once again to the center of the flatbed, hypnotized with longing in their eyes. He crooned the song slowly and deliberately. His velvet voice echoed softly across the parking lot, as Tinker and Rusty traded licks on their guitars and intermingled the melody, echoing in unison with Tim's haunting vibrato.

The women drew closer and began to press against the side of the trailer like cattle, their tears flowing like summer rain as they gazed up at him. Tim could see desire in some, and loneliness in others, but still he continued on with the endearing song, focusing on Jamie's beautiful face.

No one rushed him—not that night—for he had already let everyone know that Jamie was his precious crowned jewel, and he was absolutely not on the market.

Whistles, screams and applause cascaded around him as he handed his guitar to Rusty. Taking his microphone, he kneeled down and kissed his 'jewel' passionately on the lips.

Standing back up he returned to the center of the stage and pointed her out to the crowd. "This is my wife, Jamie, ladies and gentlemen. Isn't she the most beautiful woman in the world?"

Everyone whistled and shouted in agreement, as Tim continued his speech, "I love you, my Canadian Princess."

Jamie was lost to her tears when he said that to

her, and buried her face in her hands.

"You better go see about her, Son," Rusty said over the microphone.

The crowd went wild as Tim hopped nonchalantly from the side of the trailer and held her close, rocking her in his arms.

It was late when they finished the show. Tim and Tinker signed autographs for almost an hour, while Rusty and the rest of the band packed up the equipment. Jamie took several pictures of them together before putting her camera away, then walked over to Mickey's camper to stand in line for a couple of his famous–fantastic smelling–smoked turkey legs.

"I'll be right back," Tinker said, crushing out his cigarette.

He returned a few minutes later, joining the band behind *Alpha's* where they were all gathered together with cigarettes in hand.

Tinker handed something to Tim. He lit his lighter and saw that it was a 45 RPM. Tinker had autographed the sleeve of it for him. The title was *Raining in my Heart.*

"Wow!" Tim exclaimed. "Thanks, Tinker! I'll keep it forever!"

"I know you will, Son. And I expect the same kindness in return when *you* make a record," Tinker patted him on the shoulder.

"Yes, sir," Tim replied, handling the record as if someone had just placed the Hope Diamond in the palm of his hand.

"We're *gonna* cut a record, Son!" Rusty chuckled.

Tim's mouth fell open in shock as he looked at the

faces around him. It was dark, but he could make out the knowing smiles.

"Do you mean it?" Tim asked, as he felt the hairs stand up on the back of his neck.

"Congratulations!" Acie said.

"We thought you'd be surprised about that!" Marty added.

"I really am!" Tim continued, "Except for my wedding day, this is the most fantastic day of my life!"

Spider added the final remark, "It's pretty cool, Dude."

As Rusty talked with him in the presence of the whole band, which had become the closest group of friends he had ever known, Tim felt a bond that was thicker than blood run between them. They loved him for who he was and Tim returned the favor with all his heart.

"I'm gonna finance all of this, Son. I know you and Jamie ain't got a lot of money." Rusty said. "I also know you ain't got much time left in the service either, but you've got some kind of talent with music and writing songs, there's *real* heart in all of them. I think it would be a real shame if we didn't make a record together, and if you left before we made one I would be kicking myself for the rest of my life, not knowing how far either you or all of us could have gone."

Rusty smiled. "I think *you* can go all the way to the top, Tim, if you have the right people leading you in the right direction. Anyone can have a band, but it takes the perfect blend of souls to come up with that amazing sound."

Rusty took him by the shoulders; the perfect

picture of a father who is proud of his boy. “How many times have you heard ten different people sing the same song? Some are okay, some are better than others, but then this one person comes along who can turn it all around and set a fire under you! That’s what I’m talking about! That’s what *you* do to people, Son! Real *heart!*”

Tim could barely stop the tears from forming in his eyes. He was beyond honored.

“Buddy did it, and so have a lot of others.” Rusty continued, “Everybody loves the way you make them feel, Tim. You open up something inside their souls, and I would be lying if I didn’t say that I’m surprised that this has happened so fast with you, and with *us*. You’re like the son I never had, Tim. And all of us here feel the same way—we’re like brothers.”

Rusty swallowed hard; his deep, throaty voice was quivering a bit as he spoke. “Let’s take a shot at this and see where we land. Heck, guys! Let’s all go in and drink some beer together, it’s on *me!*”

“Before we go in,” Tinker broke in. “I just want to say, Tim, Buddy would have thought the world of you. I see that same look in your eyes that he had in his, and I want to wish all of you guys the best of luck. It’s a long way to the top, and when you think you’re almost there–keep reaching. I believe you’ll make it.”

Tim was beyond elated. Being compared in any way to the great Buddy Holly was something that truly took his breath away. He took Tinker’s words into his heart, keeping them there for the rest of his days.

10

Jamie was in the bedroom folding laundry and smiling, as she listened to Tim impersonating Elvis in the kitchen.

"We'd like to say to all the people watching and all the people that are here tonight, that we 'reall-uh are thankful for all the success that you've let us have 'an ever-thang."

Glancing around the corner, Jamie grinned. Buddy was standing up in Tim's lap; his upper lip was curled and stuck to his canine. He was definitely sneering. Jamie giggled.

"This is mah biggest 'rac, 'uh, record...an, 'uh, it goes 'sumpm lak 'iss."

Jamie laughed as her two men brought Elvis to life. Gyrating his pelvis, Tim sang *Don't Be Cruel*, holding Buddy's paws as he sang the ending.

♫"Waa-ll, 'ah don't want no uh-thuh luh-huv! 'Uh, Baybee, it's jest yew ahm-thankin of!"♫

Buddy's ears flopped around as Tim finished. "That's pretty cute, but I don't think Dachshunds are supposed to bump and grind."

"But he's the *Puppy Kang*, Baby," Tim said. "Just wait, he's going to perform something much closer to home for you now." *Hound Dog* came next.

"You're so silly." She kissed Tim and gave Buddy a pat on the head.

"I can't get him to do Tom Jones yet," Tim smiled.

"When are you guys going to the recording studio?"

"I don't know, Rusty didn't say. I'm going to talk to him and see if we can't go to Clovis, New Mexico and record at the studio Buddy Holly used. Ultimately, it's up to him, though, since he's paying for all this," Tim said excitedly.

"I'm so proud of you."

"It would be so neat to hear my songs on the radio," Tim said, letting his imagination run wild.

Tim picked up a copy of the *Avalanche Journal* on his way to work Monday morning, thrilled and amazed that he was staring back from the front page. It was a picture of him kneeling down, kissing Jamie with his guitar behind his back. The caption underneath read:

Tim Cunningham pauses for a little romance during his phenomenal performance Saturday night.

Tim continued to read:

Lubbock's newest attraction, Tim Cunningham, has been mesmerizing crowds everywhere with his unique flair and voice. His humble approach to music, and the heartfelt tenderness he shows to his audience is spreading like wildfire. Could this young man be the next phenomenon in Lubbock since Buddy Holly? Only time will tell.

A few co-workers stopped by Tim's office to talk with him and get his autograph. He was polite, but very withdrawn. For as proud as Tim was to serve his country, he had never bonded closely with anyone in the Air Force. He had never quite thought that he 'fit-in,' and never really felt welcome with his fellow Airmen.

It was later in the afternoon when Tim was going over some reports that he happened to look up and see the First Sergeant standing in the doorway with a cup of coffee.

Tim stood up quickly and greeted him. Chief Master Sergeant Brackett was a very kind man, and Tim had always felt extreme respect for him.

Tim had a fondness for his First Sergeant, mostly because he had a remarkable resemblance to his father; both in looks and personality. He had always felt comfortable about talking to him, especially during the years before he met Jamie.

"So how goes it, Tim?" He grinned, taking a sip of coffee.

"Good, sir. How are you today?"

Sergeant Brackett picked up the newspaper from Tim's desk. "I can't complain. I see that you're becoming somewhat of a celebrity."

Tim looked down, feeling the heat rise in his cheeks. "Have I done something wrong, sir?"

Sergeant Brackett smiled. "Not at all, Tim. I think you're a fine person. I didn't even know you could sing. Do you have any recordings?"

"No, sir. At least, not yet. The leader of our band wants to record a song I wrote for him, and I'll be recording one on the flip-side."

"I see." Sergeant Brackett reached into his back pocket and pulled out the picture of Tim kissing Jamie. "Could I get an autograph?"

Tim smiled. "Yes, sir. I would be happy to."

The First Sergeant studied Tim as he signed his

name. "You know, I've noticed that you're different from everyone else."

Tim looked at him, completely puzzled by the odd statement.

"What I mean is, you have a kindness about you that I have yet to see in anyone else around here. You're a good worker and you get the job done, but why did you join the Air Force?"

Tim sighed. "I graduated from high school and went to Nashville Tech for a year. I studied Computer Operations and did very well, but no one would hire me because I had no experience. I was tired of working at gas stations and factories...I guess my own biological clock was ticking. I was still living with my folks and I began to ask myself what I was going to do for the rest of my life.

Thoughts raced through Tim's mind, looking back on his wealth of decisions. "Anyone I had ever met who had been in the military seemed to have a decent job and was highly respected. So...I was on my way home from work one night–I was working at an auto parts warehouse at the time–and I started thinking about the different branches of the service. I decided to stop in and talk to a recruiter. I needed to grow up and learn about responsibility and how to make it on my own."

Tim mulled over that day, wondering what exactly had set him on his path. "I wanted to serve my country, but my main goal was to get a degree and be able to make something of myself. I never got my degree for some reason. I feel as if the last few years of my life have been in 'limbo'—that is, until I married my wife."

He could feel his smile emerge. "She makes me

very happy, sir. She's the best thing that ever happened to me."

Sergeant Brackett offered Tim a smile. "Well, you look very happy on the front page, Tim. I went through a similar time in my life when I was about your age."

He crossed his legs and grew comfortable, thinking back on his youth. "I've thought about what kind of person you are, Tim. I even showed the Colonel this article and he was really impressed! Anyway...this is just an idea, but I was wondering if perhaps you've thought of performing at any of the retirement homes around here? I bet the people in those homes could really use some cheering up."

Tim agreed completely. "Hey, you're right! I never even thought about that."

Sergeant Brackett again reached into his back pocket and retrieved a piece of paper, handing it to Tim. It was a list of the names and addresses of two retirement homes in Lubbock. The first one was *Golden Age Retirement*, and the other was *Bender Terrace.*

"I'll give them a call, sir," Tim said.

"I hope that I can be of help." He studied Tim's autographed picture. "I'd really like a copy of your recording, too."

"Yes, sir. I'll be glad to give you one when I have it."

Tim didn't call the retirement homes; he was so excited about the idea that he drove there personally and talked to the managers of each. "I don't want any money for this, in case you're wondering. I want to do this because I care."

Both agreed to let him sing, and Sergeant Brackett

even let Tim off work Tuesday and Thursday in order to perform.

Singing at the *Golden Age* home for two hours was a great experience for Tim, but being able to talk with the residents there and listen to them was an even greater time. They not only needed someone to talk to, but Tim was amazed that seniors were definitely a group of people who owned the most amazing stories; like history lessons at his very fingertips.

He felt sorry for some because they were so desperately lonely. It was so depressing to see a person who had worked so hard to achieve everything they had in a lifetime, only to have it taken away from them and sold, and sent to a place where no one ever visited, called, or cared because it was more *convenient*. That truly broke his heart.

There were no autographs or pictures that day. But there were tears, as Tim excused himself several times to regain his composure. The home was nice, but to Tim it was a place where people were simply forgotten.

"Will you come see us again?" Several people asked.

One elderly woman stole his heart. She was frail and tiny, with an enormous amount of sadness glowing in her eyes. Tim could tell that she had once been very elegant and dainty, just like his Jamie. She had cried when he sang *Green, Green, Grass of Home*, and her sobbing had cut right through his heart.

"Yes, ma'am, I will come back. I've had a wonderful time visiting with all of you."

He hugged some and shook hands with others.

There was even a young man who lived there. Tim didn't know what was wrong with him, or why he was there, but the man asked him if he would teach him to play the guitar sometime.

"I think I can show you a few chords the next time I come," he said, politely. The man's face lit up.

On Thursday, Tim took Jamie with him to *Bender Terrace*. It was much like the other home, and Tim quickly fell in love with all the residents.

He asked the managers if he could bring Buddy with him the next time he came, and they agreed. His Elvis impersonation would definitely bring out their smiles.

Rusty called Tim on Friday and invited him over to discuss the recording. Even over the telephone, Tim could feel the excitement was in the air.

"Rusty, have you decided which studio to do this at?" Tim asked. "I was thinking we could record at Norman Petty's recording studio in Clovis, New Mexico."

"Isn't that where Buddy Holly recorded?" Rusty exhaled, pushing his hat up with his thumb–the usual when he was thinking. "It's a good idea, but the truth is I'm not sure how long it'll take. Don Caldwell's studio is right here in town, and if it takes us a couple of weeks to do this, we won't have so far to travel."

Tim dropped his head. He knew Rusty was right.

"It'll be just as much fun and it'll still sound good, Son." Rusty patted him on the back. "If this takes off, we'll be doing a lot of traveling and maybe we can record the next one up there."

He smiled at Tim and the rest of the band. "Oh, by the way, I forgot to give this to you." Rusty pulled out his wallet and distributed one-hundred dollar bills. "Steve sold so much beer last weekend that he decided to pay us a little bit. Congratulations, Son! You are now officially a professional musician!"

They practiced *Because Of You* and *The Vagabond* over and over that night; they wanted everything just right, seeing as that recording was to begin on Monday evening.

Tim's thoughts lingered on the people at *Golden Age* and *Bender Terrace* all day Saturday—especially the sad, old woman who had cried. He sat down at the table with his guitar and etched out a song–not just for her, but for all of them. He titled it, *As Time Goes By.*

It was a fast-paced bluegrass genre song that he could envision as being from a bygone era. Tim heard the tune in his head, loving the banjo part he'd written in.

Now that he had finished writing, he looked at the paper and began to play, releasing the words from his soul:

♫"*Rambling through the sweet and gentle memories of our lives;*

I love you, a little more and more as time goes by.

Remember when you married me? I felt so very good;

I offered you a bouquet full of roses if you would.

You fill my life with happiness, and make my dreams come true;

I find each day, a tender way, to say that I love you.

(Chorus)

I'm so glad to know you're mine;

more and more as time goes by; more and more, as time goes by.

You're as sweet as springtime flowers and your heart's so warm and true;

With tenderness, I give a kiss, to say that I love you.

The evenings catch us laughing at the things the babies do,

And if I had a million years, I'd spend each one with you.

So I'll just keep on lovin' you until the day I die; 'cause I love you a little more and more, as time goes by." ♫

Here, Tim repeated the chorus and first verse, as a feeling of complete peace filled his heart.

On Monday afternoon the band members were all anxious and more than a little intimidated being inside the recording studio. They were beginning to realize that playing live and recording are two entirely different worlds.

Spider was asked to sit behind what looked like a bullet-proof glass wall designed to muffle sound.

Every member acted fidgety as the staff set them up, plugging wires and lines into various jacks. The sound check seemed to them to take forever. As easy as *Because Of You* was to play, Rusty was so nervous that it took him twenty-seven times to get it right.

Tim watched Rusty's face as he leaned over and listened to his voice being mixed and mastered. From this moment, Tim soon saw the spark beam from Rusty's eyes.

The studio had finished the production by the end of the week and Rusty was ecstatic. Except for the weathered expression on his face, Tim thought he looked like he was eighteen-years-old all over again.

The recording was truly fabulous. Tim was certain that it was as good as–if not better than–anything Johnny Cash would have written and performed.

Rusty patted Tim on the shoulder. "You've got some kind of talent with that songwriting of yours, Son! It sounds great! Everybody did a fine job!" Rusty hollered, shaking hands with Spider, Marty, and Acie. He was grinning like a wolf-pup during suckling time. "We'll start recording *The Vagabond* this Monday, Son. It's gonna sound great!"

Everyone listened to the song once more before leaving. Tim's head once again spun; the song had a powerful sound with Acie's bass back-beat, and the echo of Rusty's electric guitar and deep voice all intertwined with a vintage 1950s reverb.

And as complicated as *The Vagabond* was to play, Tim nailed it in eight takes. The harmonizing from Marty and Acie was unbeatable. Spider gave it the sparkle it needed from the drums, mimicking a train slowly rolling down its tracks. Tim relished in the fade-out at the end of it; his voice echoed in the distance, as his guitar gave a small chime like the faint whistle of a train leaving everything far behind.

He asked them to rewind the ending several times.

Rusty was bent over laughing. "Maybe we should cut it to the end and just have that on the record."

Everyone joined in, imagining a thirty-second record.

"How long will it take to get the records back?" Rusty asked.

"About four weeks, most likely. We have to finish mastering it, then it goes to *Nashville Record Press*. They send a proof back to us and then, if you guys approve it, the records are pressed."

"Hot-dog!" Rusty hollered.

Tim was really glad that Rusty was happy, and that he believed in his songs enough to invest so much money in them. *What a great friend,* he thought.

Tim and Jamie took Buddy with them to the *Golden Age Retirement Home* that next Tuesday. The residents there had quickly fallen in love with their new furry friend.

Tim placed him gently on a few people's laps who begged to hold him. He was extremely careful, knowing Buddy's nails could have scratched them if he jumped. But Buddy was, as always, kind–giving them all hugs as he greeted one and all in his doggy German.

Jamie watched Tim with the people; he melted her heart with his tenderness and genuine love towards those who needed someone to care. She quickly wiped a tear from her eye when he kissed the little lady on the cheek.

Her name was Belle, and Tim managed to make her laugh by making Buddy sing like Elvis for her. Tim also sat with the young man who had asked him to teach him how to play the guitar. He helped him make some chords on it, and although he couldn't play them, Tim told him how good he sounded.

Jamie was thinking about how deeply in love with Tim she was. *Is he an angel?* she wondered. *He is certainly mine.*

Two weeks had passed when Rusty called everyone in the band. "It's here," he practically screamed over the phone, sounding just like a kid on Christmas morning.

Even Jamie was surprised at how dynamic the proof sounded. She asked Rusty to play it over and over. "I can't decide which one I like best," she finally said.

"Just enjoy both of them," Tim replied. "We're a band and it should *all* sound good since we're all playing together."

Rusty put his arm around her. "It's because that husband of yours knows how to write good songs."

They listened to it a few more times while Rusty made drinks for everyone.

"So it's a keeper, huh?" Marty asked, to which he received total agreement from the others.

It seemed like an eternity before the next call came, but Rusty finally told them that the records had arrived. He'd ordered five-hundred copies, which he distributed equally among them.

Tim tried to give Rusty the hundred dollars that Steve had paid him for his share of the records, but he wouldn't accept it. "You wrote the songs, Son. That's fair enough."

Tim still felt that he had not done enough to share

in the expense.

"I'm gonna make sure there's a record on every jukebox in Lubbock, and I think I can get it on the air," Rusty continued. "I've got a feeling this is really going to take off. Have you thought about staying here in case it does?"

"I've thought a *lot* about it, Rusty. I want to stay here with all of my heart. I honestly don't know what to do," Tim said, shaking his head.

"It's too bad you don't know anything about plumbing, Son. I'd pay you really well," Rusty twirled his cigarette, deep in thought.

Tim looked up at him. "I know you would, Rusty. I'm going to have to go to Tennessee in a couple of weeks and fill out an application at the place that's holding a job for me...I don't have much of a choice. I only have about two months left in the service."

Rusty crushed out his cigarette. "I'll keep thinking, Son. There has to be something we can do, or the Lord wouldn't have brought us together in the first place."

11

Tim put in for leave on the following Monday. It had been almost five years since he had been home or seen his parents. He, Jamie, and Buddy would drive to Tennessee in just two weeks

Tim began to grow anxious by Friday, one week before their trip. He and Buddy were listening to his record that afternoon in the apartment when the front door opened and Jamie practically fell with the grocery bags in her arms.

Tim turned the music off and ran to catch the door for her. "I hope you bought burritos!" he said, cocking his left eyebrow up and down several times.

"Stop it," she smiled. "You're *not* giving Buddy *any* of that stuff, it sets his guts on fire and I have to leave the room every time he floats one of his big green, gas balloons across the living room, *or* under the covers! It *has* to give him a tummy ache because he *moans* when he does it!"

"I think it smells more like the exhaust from a '57 Chevy!" he said, doubling over in fits of laughter. Jamie started laughing so hard that she dropped the pancake mix.

Like the good husband, Tim ran out and brought in the rest of the groceries for her while she put them away. Buddy helped too, nosing through the bags that were still on the floor, making sure that the food *he* liked was accounted for.

"Buddy, stop it!" Jamie hollered, as he ran behind Tim for protection.

"I think he's looking for the bologna," Tim said, picking him up.

"Tim, *please* don't give him any more of that!" Jamie said, trying not to giggle. "I about got sick the last time. The string was hanging out of him, and he scraped his rear end on the patio for half an hour trying to get it out."

Tim doubled over again with laughter and his face turned red as he fought to catch his breath. "Honey, you know I was teaching him how to moonwalk. He *loves* Michael Jackson!" Tim buried his face in Buddy's neck. He was laughing uncontrollably, as Buddy wagged his tail.

"You've got him so spoiled that he'll hardly eat dog food anymore," she scolded.

"I *know* that my mom and dad are really going to like you, Kitten...especially my dad. He's really soft-spoken and kind." Tim smiled. "Just like you."

He sighed. "I remember when Mom didn't want to cook, he would make *goulash* for supper." Tim shook his head and chuckled. "I always called it *'Hot-Surprise'* because you never knew what he was going to put in it. I never did like macaroni dishes very much, and I can't stand to even *look* at macaroni and cheese!" Tim made a gagging sound and shuddered as if he had just stepped barefoot in some of Buddy's 'recycled' food.

"Why don't you like macaroni and cheese, Sweetie?" she asked, as Tim helped her put the pancake mix on the top shelf of the cabinet.

"I was a baby when it happened, but I remember

that I climbed on top of my granny's table and ate a stick of butter. I got so sick and I haven't been able to eat it since. It's just like Kryptonite to me. I guess the yellow of mac-and-cheese reminds me of all that butter."

Jamie giggled. "So you must have been a little *Curious George*, huh?"

Tim went to the bedroom and came back with an old photo album. Jamie poured herself a glass of milk and sat down.

"I know it's here somewhere," he said, thumbing through the pages.

"What are you looking for?"

"Ah! Here it is!" He handed the photo album to Jamie and pointed to a picture.

She blurted out a laugh so hard that milk sprayed out of her nose. It was a picture of Tim as a baby; Jamie guessed he was maybe two or three at the time. His hair was sticking up all over the place and it looked patchy. The parts of his head that weren't bald had splotches of hair that, to Jamie, resembled baby bird feathers.

He was wearing a tiny, green, pinstriped T-shirt that was way too small for him. His bloated tummy was exposed and his diaper was sagging halfway off. Holding a training cup in one hand and a paintbrush in the other, Baby Tim was covered from head-to-toe in black paint, and he wore a *tongue-in-cheek* grin on his face.

She wiped the milk with her sleeve between gasps of air, and dabbed the tears from her eyes. "You look like a cross between a baby Buddha and a midget plumber! And your hair looks like you fell into a waffle iron! What in the world were you doing when that was taken?" she said, still laughing.

Tim looked at the picture with a frown on his face. "I don't remember what I was doing, but I do remember getting a good whipping for it." They laughed together as Tim thumbed slowly through a few more pages of the album.

As he started to flip a page, he suddenly stopped, took the photo album from her and stared at a picture.

"What is it?" Jamie asked, trying to get a peek at what he was hiding.

Tim shook his head. "This is the night I got my first guitar. It was Christmas Eve." Tim was sitting on an old couch holding a blonde, *Ventura* guitar.

"It's beautiful," she said. "You don't look very happy about it, though."

Tim sighed. "I was so disappointed. I wanted a train set so bad. I begged Mom and Dad all year for an H.O. scale railroad set. I thought they got it for me and when they gave me the guitar, it about broke my heart."

He chuckled for a moment. "Well, if they *hadn't* bought it for me, *you* wouldn't be standing here right now. It's funny how things turn out. I didn't have the slightest interest in learning how to play it until my Uncle Roy came to visit. He's my mother's oldest brother. We were living in Cleveland, Texas at the time."

The images flooded Tim's mind. "Mom hadn't seen him in years, and when he came down, he played it one night and I was glued to everything he did, he really set a fire under me!"

Tim got up and retrieved his guitar. "Uncle Roy sang this song when he came down." Tim chuckled as he began the intro.

♫ *"Well, the liquor was spilled on the barroom floor, and the bar was-a closin' for the night;*

"When out of the corner came a little brown mouse, and he sat in the pale moonlight.

"He-ee lapped up the liquor from the barroom floor, then on his haunches he sat,

"And you could hear him roar as he staggered out the door!

"Brang on the dad-burned cat! ♫

"He showed me how to play a little bit, but it was really my grandfather who taught me and kept me interested. When we moved back to Tennessee I showed him my guitar, and he sat up with me all night and taught me how to play *The Wildwood Flower* by Mama Maybelle Carter."

"What did you used to do for fun when you were little?" Jamie asked. Taking the album from him, she sat back down to look.

"Well, we moved from Texas to Tennessee when I was thirteen, and moved in with Uncle Roy and my cousin Jerry, who was ten. We lived with them for close to a year, I guess, until Dad could get on his feet."

Tim continued to his rapt audience of one, "I remember Dad bought this blue 1964 Cadillac while we were still in Texas. I can't remember how much he paid for it, but he and a friend of his had to dig it out of a mud hole somewhere. They worked on it for a few days and finally got it running.

"Mom made some black and white leopard-skin seat covers for it. Dad thought they were *gaudy*, but I actually thought they looked pretty neat; they were really plush and soft. The whole interior of the car was white, including the steering wheel."

A smile crossed Tim's face. "I loved that car. Dad told me I could have it when I turned sixteen, but it finally conked out and he had to sell it. Anyway, to answer your question, we used to ride our bikes all the time."

Jamie sat quietly, riveted to Tim's voice, eager to learn everything there was to know about the man she loved.

"We lived on Shauna Drive in Donelson. It wasn't very far from the Nashville airport, and I remember listening to the airplanes flying overhead at night when we all went to bed.

"It was a really big neighborhood and we could ride all over the place. Dad would give me fifty cents a week for allowance. Uncle Roy always gave Jerry five dollars a week and I used to get so jealous! Anyway, me and Jerry would sneak up to the Jim Dandy sometimes and buy comic books.

"I loved *Superman* and *Batman*, but he would always buy *Sergeant Rock* or *The Avengers*. We never did have the same taste in comics. We were also never allowed to ride our bikes to the store because it was a major highway with lots of traffic. I remember Uncle Roy caught us up there one afternoon when he came into town to buy some beer. We both got the belt when we got home. We still did it though." Tim snickered.

"We all had to share a bedroom, too. We had two sets of bunk beds; I slept on the top bunk of mine, and Jerry slept on the bottom of his. My brother, Sam, slept on the bottom bunk under me.

"I used to get so mad because Jerry had to sleep with this stupid *Chuck Wagon* nightlight on all the time. Sometimes, I would get up in the middle of the night and turn it off once I knew everyone was asleep. Boy, he was a weird one. He was really skinny and had brown hair and he wore round glasses...there he is, right there!" Tim pointed at a picture of Jerry.

"He was funny though. Dad would always wake us up at five-thirty in the morning by flipping on the light switch and hollering, 'Get up!' Man, I used to hate that! Mom always made us oatmeal for breakfast while *they* always had eggs and bacon. Jerry used to prop his head on the palm of his hand and scrape the oatmeal slowly into his mouth with his spoon. Sometimes, he would snore when he did it.

"Mom made sandwiches for our lunch everyday, and we had to bring home the brown paper sack and sandwich bags every night so she could reuse them. She bought that thin, cheap lunch meat and put *exactly* two pieces of razor thin meat on the bread; then she would drown the whole thing in ketchup. And for dessert, it was always carrot sticks or celery."

Jamie stared into the eyes of the man she truly loved.

"She made the worst hamburgers I have *ever* tasted, and we had them a *lot*. She would cut up a bunch of onions and mix them in with the ground beef, then burn them to a crisp in the frying pan; the meat in the middle would still be raw. And there were definitely no treats like buns, we had to eat them on that nasty white bread.

"And then there was her ever-famous tuna casserole. The only good thing about that was she would crumple up some potato chips on top of it before she baked it in the oven. I always did my best to get the crispy part off the top because if I got any of the noodles I would have to hold my breath, take a huge sip of water, and swallow it whole before I got sick."

Tim shook his head at the memories. "The meatloaf wasn't too bad, but I was always hungry. I weighed one hundred and thirty-two pounds when I graduated from high school.

"And as far as fun went, most days we would go over to someone's house and play kick-ball or board games. We didn't have VCRs back then, so we would watch *The Munsters, The Addams Family*, or *Flipper*.

"We had to go to bed at eight o'clock on week nights. Dad would pop popcorn almost every night after we went to bed and he, Mom, and Uncle Roy would watch *Star Trek*. My stomach *ached* from hunger when I smelled it."

He shrugged. "Riding bikes was great, though. We would have races all the time. I remember once Jerry and I were racing down Shauna Court; it was a steep road that dead-ended at the bottom, and there were three or four houses down there. We were trying to see who could make the longest skid mark in the gravel. I went down first and slammed on my brakes. Then, I looked behind me and saw Jerry pedaling as fast as he could. Just when he slammed on his brakes, his banana seat came loose and he fell off the back of his bike, sliding all the way down to the bottom.

"I was laughing so hard I almost wet my pants! It looked just like that scene at the beginning of the *The Six-Million-Dollar Man*, where his plane crashes and slides all the way down the runway. He must've slid for fifteen seconds!"

"Was he alright?" Jamie asked, very interested in Tim's ongoing commentary.

"He ripped his pants up pretty good, scraped up his arms, and his bike had a flat tire, but he was okay. In a way, I kinda thought he deserved it." Tim chuckled. "He was always so proud of that bike, and I'm the one who taught him how to ride one in the first place! I had this old, beat up one that my grandpa had given to me years before. I had been asking for a dirt bike, but my parents never had the money to buy me one, so my dad painted it red and slapped a couple of plastic number *8's* on it for my tenth birthday.

"Let's see...here it is!" Tim pointed to it after flipping through a couple of pages. "Uncle Roy bought Jerry that brand new bike after I taught him how to ride one and he wouldn't even let me touch it!

"One time, Granny and Granddaddy came over to visit. They lived out in Mt. Juliet, and my other uncle, Kalvin, was with them. He's a year younger than me. He talked Jerry into sneaking up to the Jim Dandy with him to buy a pack of cigarettes. Kalvin was twelve and I was thirteen at the time, and he wanted to borrow my bike.

"I made him promise that he wouldn't skid with it or tear it up, and he promised. Later that night, after they had left, Jerry told me that there was a dead cat in the ditch on the side of the road, and Kalvin was popping wheelies on it with my bike."

He stared at her. "I was so mad, Jamie! Jerry said that the cat would fart every time he ran over it!" Tim pursed his lips on his arm and made several slow, ripping noises to imitate what it sounded like.

Buddy sat up, cocked his ears, and stared at Tim as he made the strange sounds. Knowing how he could make them himself, Buddy jumped off the couch and ran into the kitchen–jingling all the way. Stopping in front of the refrigerator, Buddy stared up at the freezer.

"Aw, look, Honey," Tim said. "He wants a burrito."

Jamie laughed at the confused dog, and waved Tim on–wanting him to continue his story.

He nodded. "Sure enough, the next day when I went to the basement there were dried cat guts and fur all in between the treads of my tires, and Jerry kept making the farting noises and I was getting more and more upset about it. When I finally finished yelling, he followed me back up the stairs, doing it every time I took a step. He was the king of torment and aggravation.

"I made him show me where the dead cat was. When we got there it was all flat and dried up like a piece of bacon. Jerry took *his* bike and ran over it a couple of times, but all it did was crackle like someone was crunching up a bunch of crackers to put in their soup.

"When I got my driver's license a few years later, I drove over to his house one day. We had moved to Franklin by then, and he and Uncle Roy only lived about five miles away. I went inside the house. Uncle Roy wasn't there but I walked into Jerry's bedroom. He was standing on a chair with his head inside his thirty-gallon aquarium. He was wearing a diving mask and had a snorkel in his mouth, and I remember shouting, ***'JERRY!'***

"He was so startled that he jerked his head out of the aquarium and water shot all over the ceiling. I was laughing hard but he just stood there; he was clutching his heart and looking at me like I was nuts!

Tim smiled. "One of the best memories I have was Christmas that year. We drove all around the neighborhood on Christmas Eve, looking at all the lights. Everyone was laughing and having a good time, and when we got back home Santa had already come. We had Christmas that night instead of waiting until morning.

"I remember opening Uncle Roy's gift to me, and it was an AFX race track! I was so happy! Jerry and I played with that thing up in the attic for weeks." Tim went to the bedroom and opened his trunk, returning with a black case labeled *AFX*.

He smiled. "I bet these things are worth a fortune because they don't make this brand anymore, and they still work."

He stared down at the cars, taking in the blue Camaro, black Firebird, the awesome police car, and two 1955 Chevys. "The track layout was broken years ago, but the cars still hold some very good memories for me."

Tim chuckled, as a new image leapt into his mind. "Jerry used to aggravate this little girl on the bus. He would pull her pigtails and then look out the window like he didn't do anything. One day she turned around and hollered at him, "Leave me alone, you 'FO' 'EYE-DIT' 'RET-NECK'!"

Tim laughed. “He got so mad at her, but there wasn’t anything he could do, and she had yelled so loud that *everyone* on the bus started laughing at him. I was laughing the hardest! He told everybody what she had called him at the supper table that night. But when we laughed, he got mad *again!* After that he was like a parrot. For weeks he kept mimicking it over and over: *‘fo’ ‘eye-dit’, ‘fo’, ‘fo’ ‘eye-dit’, ‘fo’ ‘eye-dit’ ‘ret-neck’.”*

“We went to Donelson Christian Academy at the time, and practically the whole school was made of those cheap, portable buildings. One day I went to his homeroom to ask him something, but no one was there–just him–standing at the chalkboard writing *‘fo’ ‘eye-dit’ ‘ret-neck’* on it.

“What did you ask him?” Jamie said.

Tim chuckled. “I said, “What are you doing, you ‘fo’ ‘eye-dit’ ‘ret-neck’? But he was always doing weird stuff like that.

“I remember when Uncle Roy took him to see *Star Wars.* He bought him a T-shirt with a picture of *Chewbacca* on it, and for weeks after that Jerry would make growling, gurgling, moaning sounds like *Chewie.* If Mom told him to do the dishes, he would moan like *Chewie.* If she told him to make his bed, *Chewie* would moan. One morning, Uncle Roy slapped him for snoring and scraping his oatmeal, and he moaned like *Chewie.*

“He didn’t even seem to mind getting ‘slapped’ for the aggravating things he did. I ate my lunch with him one day at school, and when we were standing in line with our trays, the lunch lady gave Jerry his hamburger and six French fries. He looked down and counted them, and said,

"Can I please have a few more fries? I'm about to starve half to death." Tim started laughing so hard that his face turned red, he could barely continue the story.

"The lunch lady yelled at him and said, "Get on outta here, boy! You ain't about to starve *'no-half-no-deaf'!"*

Jamie was laughing hysterically, just imagining the picture in her head. She looked at her beloved husband, thanking the Lord that they could actually sit down and share his boyhood memories.

12

As soon as Jamie composed herself, Tim tried to change the subject.

"No," she said. "I want to hear more. You never told me about any of these things. I really needed to laugh—and I'm interested in knowing about your childhood."

Tim sighed. "Okay, but don't say I didn't warn you!" He winked. "One Saturday, my dad was watching football on TV when Uncle Roy came into the living room and asked him who was playing. My dad made the mistake of accidentally saying, 'The Atlanta Vulcans'.

"Jerry heard him and mimicked him for weeks, making up different names for other football teams. There were the *Dallas Convoys, The Pittsburgh Squealers, The Minnesota Vampires, The Detroit Tiggers,* and so forth.

"He was as skinny as Spider and tall, too. One day, this K-TEL commercial came on advertising an Elvis record with all of his hits. It showed Elvis crying while he was singing, *In the Ghetto.* Jerry *despised* Elvis! Every time the commercial aired, Jerry got madder and madder.

"One day, after it came on, he huffed real loud, stood up, unbuttoned his shirt all the way down to his navel, and pulled his collar up. I could see his ribs! Then, he streaked some saliva down his face to make it look like he was crying.

"He looked exactly like an anorexic Mr. Spock with brown hair, wearing an Elvis suit with John Lennon's glasses. "He rocked slowly back and forth like this, Jamie:

"Uh 'po' lil' bay-buh chalt is bone in-'nuh Ghetto..."

Jamie roared with laughter as Tim over-exaggerated Elvis' voice.

"Jerry could throw his voice like an infant baby crying, too. He tried to show me how he did it, but I could never get the hang of it."

He laughed. "I also used to *love* to go to the grocery store with him and watch him do it. He would stand there in the middle of the aisle and pretend to be reading a can of spaghetti. Then he would make the crying, bleating sound, and several people would come running over from the other aisles to look around for the abandoned baby. He would stop as soon as they started building up, but as soon as they left, he'd do it again.

"Sometimes, people would ask him if he had heard a baby crying, and he'd look up from the spaghetti can and politely say, "No, Ma'am." Then he would look at them like they were crazy or something. He could also sound like a chirping cricket. I honestly thought he was going to make Uncle Roy lose his mind over that one!

"We'd be watching TV, and Jerry would start chirping. Uncle Roy would get up and start looking for the cricket, and Jerry would just sit there with a bored look on his face.

"Uncle Roy would look under the couch, the chairs, and between the seat cushions. Sometimes he would even get a flashlight from the kitchen to look in all the dark places. When he'd finally give up and sit back down, Jerry would wait for a few minutes and start all over again.

"One time Uncle Roy got so aggravated that he jumped up and shut the TV off. Then we all had to pull the furniture out from the walls to try and find a cricket that wasn't there. Even Jerry helped him look for it! They never figured it out and it was always so hard for me to keep a straight face."

He looked at Jamie, wondering when she would get bored and head for the other room. But the sparkle in her eye was still begging for more.

"When *The Incredible Hulk* started, so did Jerry. Do you remember the series with Bill Bixby? He mimicked Lou Ferrigno so *well*, that it's a wonder he didn't end up being a bass singer for some quartet. He could rattle his throat so deep that it sounded like a slow, controlled belch." Tim attempted the impersonation, making Jamie laugh.

"He was constantly growling and grunting in that voice and it was hard to get him to say anything without talking like that. I remember he did it only *once* at the supper table. '***Pass the biscuits, please!***'

"Sometimes he would swallow a bunch of air to force himself to belch. Then, he would try and draw it out as long as possible and say as loudly as he could: '***The Incredible Hulk... will continue after these messages...***'"

Jamie was laughing so hard that Tim had to get her some tissue paper from the bathroom. "Was he like that all the time?" she asked, wiping her eyes.

"Pretty much. Once he got something in his head, he *became* whatever he was thinking about."

Tim practically jumped from his chair as the image hit him full-force. "Oh, I almost forgot! One time my dad gave me a whipping for something, and he had asked

Jerry to step out of the room. I bet he whipped me for three or four minutes! After that, I had to stay in the room for the rest of the day.

"But that night, when Jerry and Sam came to bed, I was almost asleep. I heard my tape recorder rewinding by Jerry's bed. I rolled over on my back. I thought Jerry had felt sorry for me and was going to play my *Elvis* tape, but when he turned it on it was *me*, hollering and screaming, begging Dad to stop. He had turned my tape recorder on before Dad asked him to leave, and recorded the whole thing!"

Jamie was in hysterics, "I'm sorry, Tim," she laughed. "That is awful!"

"What's worse is that he started laughing when it was playing. I reached down and turned it off. I knew if I went and told, Dad would give me another whipping.

"Jerry just lay there mocking me in a whiny little voice, saying '*No, Dad, **pwease!** Not the belt with the spikes in it!*'

"***'You're such a weak little sissy!'***" Tim belched, in the voice of *The Incredible Hulk*.

Jamie could barely catch her breath. Buddy even jumped off the couch and started barking, trying to figure out how the voice was coming from his father's mouth.

"'You're a puny human!' He kept saying it over and over, Jamie. At that point, as I was lying there in the dark, I thought he sounded more like the devil than the Hulk."

Tim cocked his head to the side. "Now that I think about it, I would be willing to bet a dollar that he set the whole thing up—so I'd get whipped just so he *could* record it! I got him back, though." Tim continued, "I waited for about a week and forced myself to stay awake until 2:00 A.M. one morning.

"I quietly got out of bed, put my school clothes on, and tip-toed to the kitchen, turning all the lights on as I went. Then I went back to the bedroom, flipped on the light switch and went into the bathroom to start brushing my teeth.

"I had my ear to the door and I could hear Jerry rustling around in the bedroom getting dressed. When I came out of the bathroom, he was dressed and had his school books tucked under his arm. He walked into the living room, half asleep, and sat down on the couch, waiting for his breakfast.

"I went back into the bedroom, got my pajamas back on, turned the light off and climbed back into bed. I was sleepy all the next day, but it was so worth it."

"Tim! *Please* stop, Honey! *I can't breathe anymore!"* Jamie begged, trying to catch her breath. She thought she had never laughed so hard in her entire life.

"Pwease stop, Timmy! I'm 'waffing' too hard!" Tim mocked in Jerry's whiny voice.

Jamie's face turned from blue to purple when he said that. For a moment, he actually thought she might have a heart attack, and Buddy was rubbing his neck back and forth across her face.

Just as she was starting to recover, Tim started tickling her. "Enough! You win!" she yelled.

Tim gave her a break and helped her up. Going into the living room, Jamie practically fell on the couch.

Buddy joined them, as he crawled into Tim's lap

and started scratching his neck with his hind leg.

Tim's mind turned in a different direction. "I really hope our record does well."

"It will." Jamie kissed him.

"I really want to stay in Lubbock, but in a way I really miss my hills in Tennessee. I don't know what to do, Jamie." He sighed. "There aren't any decent paying jobs here. Rusty said if the record takes off, then we'll be traveling a lot!"

Jamie could see the excitement in his eyes. "Well," she began. "You can work in Tennessee and Rusty can always call and let you know what's going on."

"You know, I never even thought about that! You're so smart, Sweetheart!" Tim looked into her emerald eyes. "I know that you're going to miss your mother. Maybe we could come and visit her, or vice-versa."

She nodded. "Mom will be fine. I'll miss her bunches, but my place is with you. If your music takes off, then we can always move back to Lubbock."

"Can you just imagine it? What if I really *do* get that famous?" For a fleeting moment Tim's imagination was filled with pictures of riches and grandeur. A tour of Europe...a night in Paris...a chalet in the Swiss Alps—all sounded spectacular, but a dream home in the South was even more alluring, and being able to spend his time helping those who needed someone to care.

"I'll build you the biggest mansion the world has ever seen, and I'm going to visit and help all of those people at the retirement homes, too," he vowed.

"I can just picture you cruising down the street in a pink Lamborghini with your beautiful hair blowing in the wind! I would love to get you one of those royal blue evening gowns like Scarlett O'Hara wore in *Gone with the Wind!*"

Jamie grinned, as she started to share in Tim's beautiful thoughts.

"I would *love* to get another 1964 Cadillac like the one Dad used to have, but mine would be white with ruby red metal flakes in the paint, and 24-karat rims with white-walled tires." Tim smiled wide.

"I'll get Buddy his own taco stand, and get him some real diamonds for his black collar; he can also have his own harem *filled* with twitter-pated Dachsie's with *Bambi* eyes."

Jamie chuckled, and blew her bangs out of her face. "So what does your dad do for a living?" she asked.

"He's a telephone technician; he installs the phone systems for large corporations. When we first moved back to Tennessee he worked for a while at UPS loading trucks, but he finally got a job with the company he's at now. They sent him to several technical seminars to learn different things, and he's slowly worked his way up the ladder over the years. He's soft spoken, but he's also a very intelligent man. He can fix *anything* electronic." Tim raved.

"Before that, he was a television repairman for *Holiday Inn*, which is one of the reasons we moved a lot when I was growing up. They were constantly transferring him. We lived in Minnesota for a couple of years—that's where Dad's family lives.

"We lived in a trailer park the first year and we had a really bad blizzard. The snowdrifts were taller than the trailers! It was ice-cold; I bet it got down to minus forty degrees.

"I had a sled, and after the storm was over I dug it out from underneath our trailer. I climbed that drift and rode down it all day on my sled. It was so much fun.

"Mom and Dad helped me make an igloo, too! That's one of the best times I ever had with them. We used a cooler to make the bricks with, and Dad busted up an old, wooden wire spool and used one of the round ends to make a roof for it. It took two days, but we finally finished it, and I played in it for days. What's strange is that it was actually pretty warm inside!"

Tim laughed. "We moved to Plum Grove after that and I had to walk to school. I remember my dog, Dinky, followed me one morning. I should have put her in the house, but I didn't think about it. I had to call Mom when I got there to come and get her. Boy, she was so mad at me!

"After I finished the school year, we moved to Florida. I really liked it there, especially after dealing with all that cold and ice. I went to Lakeside Elementary School for the sixth grade. My first girlfriend was Melody Vaughn. What a pretty girl she was."

"Did you ever kiss her?" Jamie asked, batting her eyelashes at him.

Tim smiled and blushed. "We would sneak off and kiss behind her father's lawnmower shed; we held hands on the bus, too."

Jamie took his hand. "Isn't it nice that you don't have to *sneak* when you kiss me or hold my hand?" she whispered, kissing him on the cheek.

Tim nodded happily, as he continued with his story, "Florida is pretty much all sand, and some of us would ride our bikes on the outskirts of the neighborhood on the sand dunes.

"The streets were paved and we used skateboards too; we would all take turns riding them while holding on to the back of somebody's bike as they rode.

"We had a lot of races doing that. As soon as we were going as fast as we possibly could we would let go of the bike and see who could go the longest without falling off. Mom and Dad bought me a skateboard of my own for my birthday. I bet I fell off that thing a thousand times before I figured it out.

"I also had a box turtle named 'Peek-a-boo'. I found her one afternoon after it'd rained. I had her for a long time until I set her free in the backyard, but she never left. She liked to burrow behind our lawnmower shed, and I could usually find her in the exact same spot every day."

"How did you know it was a female?" Jamie asked.

"I could just sense it, I suppose. She had sweet eyes with long eyelashes." Tim smiled at her.

"Dad built me a really neat clubhouse one summer in the backyard, and I spent hours out there with my school buddies. We would draw comics and write ghost stories. But we had to tear it down because Dinky found a copperhead in there one afternoon. It bit her on the nose and she almost died. We rushed her to the vet and they saved her... Well...actually she saved *me!*

"I used to hunt for chameleons outside the house, too. They were everywhere! One time I found two of them and made them bite down on my ear lobes. I went in the house and Mom started laughing because they looked like earrings. Hmm," Tim said, cocking his eyebrows at her. "Maybe that would make a good anniversary gift for you!"

"Don't you dare!" She shuddered in disgust.

"Just think, Kitten. You could be the next fashion trendsetter!" Tim laughed as he described Jamie standing in the check-out line at the *Piggly-Wiggly*, whisking her long brown hair back with her hand, and *purposely* exposing the lizards dangling from her lobes. Greeting the cashier, she would politely say:

"Oh, thank you! And they change color when you stand next to foliage, too!" Tim imitated Jamie placing Hamburger Helper and toilet paper on the rubber mat.

She laughed. "I do not sound like that!"

"I don't sound wike dat, Timmy!" he said, in Jerry's whiny voice.

Jamie slapped his hand playfully, and smiled. "Continue."

"Well...I went fishing a lot," he moved on from the lizards. "I used to ride my bike down to the river and catch bluegill by the dozen! I loved the smell of the river water, Jamie, and feeling the breeze slowly brush across my face."

Tim's voice echoed as if he were in another world, waiting for the bluegills to bite. "I kept a vigilant watch on my bobber. It's a rush when the pole finally jerks in your hand! You have to be patient and *feel* when it's the right time to tug on your line to hook him!" Tim mimicked catching a fish, without even a pause in dialogue.

"I *loved* how Mom fried them up, too. My favorite part was the tail. She'd make them so crispy they tasted like potato chips!"

Jamie laughed. "More, please."

Tim rolled his eyes. "Aren't you bored of me yet? If we keep talking like this, what will we have to talk about for the next thirty years?"

Jamie laughed. "We'll think of something. Maybe Jerry can come over and burp like *The Incredible Hulk* every night."

Tim shook his head, searching for the next memory to share. "My best friend was named Flint. He could draw really well, and when I spent the night over at his house we would stay up and draw comic strips. They were always about outer space because *Star Trek* was such a big show at that time."

Tim looked down at Buddy and scratched him behind his ears. "Life was so good back then. They were some of the best days of my life."

"I never had a chance to be bored growing up either," Jamie said. "I remember my mom taught me how to cross-stitch, knit, and embroider. She was always patient and kind when she taught me, and I felt so special when it was just me and her. I felt so grown up, and we would talk for hours. I had to take piano lessons for a while, too, but I didn't enjoy that much."

She smiled. "Mom hired this *nun* to teach us. I *never* liked her–the nun, I mean. I got slapped one time because I told her that she looked like a witch."

Tim laughed as he imagined the shock on the nun's face. "You have got to be kidding me!" Tim said. "You *actually* said that to her?"

"Uh-huh," Jamie admitted. "She looked just like

this!" Jamie turned sideways, hooked her index finger and placed it beside her nose so Tim could see what the profile of the witch looked like from the side.

Tim roared with laughter as he imagined Jamie staring wide-eyed in horror at the nun, her mouth gaping open, as she wailed *Chopsticks* on the piano like Jerry Lee Lewis before blurting out how ugly she was.

"Did she stand up and kick the stool out from under her...or set the piano on fire like Jerry Lee?" Tim asked, laughing hysterically.

"No," Jamie laughed. "My mom did that when I told the nun that she looked like a witch!"

"Did she have any warts on her nose?" Tim asked, between gasps of air.

"No, but she had a big mole on her left eyebrow; maybe that's the reason she became a nun. Tim, she was so ugly that she hurt my feelings! I was so mortified the first time I saw her. She always wore her black habit and had all these beads around her. She was so old and *wrinkly!*"

Tim cackling in an old woman's voice, stroked his long, crooked witch nose up and down with his bony, arthritic fingers. *"Will you make a frail, old witch some homemade French fries, Dearie?"*

Jamie giggled at him. "How in the world do you come up with all this stuff? I really think you missed your *forté*. You should have been a stand-up comic."

As they walked into the kitchen and began dinner, Tim cackled all the way.

13

Jamie barely made it to the bathroom before she got deathly ill. Her stomach was churning, as if a roller-coaster was spinning out of control deep inside her belly. She wet a washcloth, folded it and held it to her forehead.

Buddy jumped off the bed, 'jingled' to her side, and stood up on the rim of the commode.

As Jamie sat on the floor gasping for air and panting as if she'd been running a marathon, Buddy crawled into her lap and looked up at her with his almond eyes. Buddy could always tell when something was wrong, and his look was one of sheer worry.

Jamie sat quietly and pet her friend until the wave of nausea passed. Then, setting Buddy aside, she brushed her teeth slowly and carefully so that the movement didn't spark another bout of illness, wet the washcloth once more, and returned to the bedroom. Tim was still fast asleep.

4:00 A.M.

She glanced at the bright red beam of the clock, letting her know the ungodly hour. Carefully, she crawled into bed next to Tim, as Buddy jumped up on Tim's side of the bed, burrowed under the covers, and joined his loving family.

Jamie watched the little 'hump' under the bedspread turn around three times before deflating, and then focused on the clock until she finally, gratefully, fell asleep.

The King of Hearts

Tim woke up at 8:30 that morning to find Jamie sick in the bathroom.

"Honey, are you okay? You're so pale. Did you eat too much last night?"

Jamie shook her head as another wave kept her glued to the commode. *"I...don't...know,"* she whispered between shallow breaths. "I feel like I have the flu. I'm not going to be able to go to church this morning."

Tim wet the washcloth for her. "Let me help you to bed. I think you just had too much grease with the French Fries last night."

She got sick one last time before she felt safe enough to leave the bathroom. Tim helped her into bed, placed the cold rag on her forehead, and kissed her still-shaking hand.

"Should I stay home with you?"

"I'll be okay, Buddy will keep me warm." She offered a little smile.

Hearing his name, Buddy jumped on the bed and jingled up beside her, placing his throat over her face. She giggled...he smelled like Tim's cologne. Jamie kissed his neck and cuddled him like the miniature teddy bear he was.

Tim studied her for a few minutes; a frown of worry etched on his face. "Do you need me to get you anything?"

"Maybe a cold glass of orange juice, if you don't mind," she said faintly, turning her head to look at him.

He kissed her once more. "Coming right up!" he exclaimed, rushing to the kitchen. He was concerned about leaving her but tried to remain light-hearted.

"Honey, do you think I made you laugh too hard

yesterday? Maybe all that giggling made you sick." He placed the glass on top of a napkin on the nightstand.

She managed a small smile as she remembered the previous afternoon. "No, Sweetheart. I don't think laughter causes the flu." He stood beside the bed, nervously hopping back and forth from one foot to the other.

Jamie reached out to steady him. "You go to church and I'll be right here when you get back." Buddy's tail thumped the bedspread and he rolled over on his back. Tim stared down at the small paw waving in the air, as if he were telling Tim that the protector was here and Mommy would be okay with him by her side.

Tim couldn't concentrate on the sermon that morning. The preacher was teaching about forgiving one's enemies, but all Tim could think of was his love at home, sick as a dog.

On the way home, he stopped at the *Circle K* convenience store to fill up with gas, and bought Jamie a beautiful, yellow rose. Hoping to find her a bit better, Tim was even more worried when she was once again 'manning' the bathroom.

The circles under her eyes had grown darker. "Can we please sit in the living room? I want to lay my head in your lap."

"Of course." Tim helped her to the couch. Turning on the television, he sat down and placed Jamie's head gently into his lap. In a matter of minutes, she fell asleep.

Tim made a light supper that evening, but Jamie wasn't hungry, and she went to bed early.

Tim decided to call Becky. "I don't know what's wrong with her, but she's been sick all day. She said she woke up at four this morning," Tim explained.

"I'll come over tomorrow before you go to work and check on her. Don't worry, Tim, I'm sure it's nothing. She probably has a stomach virus," Becky said, trying to reassure him.

"Okay, I'm just a little worried. I've never seen her like this before."

"It'll be alright, get some sleep, Tim."

He took Buddy out for his last walk of the night and went to bed. He lay next to Jamie, but he didn't put his arm around her for fear she would wake up and get sick again.

Becky arrived before Tim left for work. Jamie seemed fine and she even had coffee with them before he left.

He thought of her all day, and on his break, he called her.

"I feel fine, Sweetheart, I probably just had a stomach virus like Mom said."

Jamie had no viral symptoms that evening when Tim got home, and the whole household seemed to relax just a little bit with each passing hour.

The phone rang and Tim answered. "You feel like going out to the Conference Café tomorrow night, Son?"

"I don't know, Rusty...Jamie's been sick the last couple of days."

Jamie interjected, "I'm fine, Tim. What does Rusty want?"

"He wants me to go to the Conference Café with him tomorrow night," he told her, holding his hand over the receiver.

"Go ahead, Sweetheart. I'll be fine."

"I can go, Rusty." Tim looked warily at Jamie. She was wearing her pink teddy bear pajamas, looking so cute and endearing. He kept his gaze on her as she walked into the kitchen, opened the refrigerator and poured herself a glass of fresh, cold orange juice.

"I got our record on all the jukeboxes I could find, Son," Rusty said, exhaling his cigarette smoke over the phone. "I also gave it to all of the radio stations this week. I think one of them will play it. The manager listened to it and he thought it was pretty darned good!"

Tim smiled, as his heartbeat sped up with the good news. "Really?" Tim asked, his voice radiated his overwhelming joy. "That's great news, Rusty!"

He turned to Jamie. "Rusty said he gave our record to the radio stations and they might play it!" Rusty chuckled and pulled the phone away from his ear as Tim practically yelled the news.

"That's super! Tell Rusty 'Hello' for me."

"Jamie said to tell you, Hello!" Tim repeated.

"Right back at her! I'll see you tomorrow, Son." Rusty hung up.

Tim hugged Jamie and rocked her from side-to-side. "Oh, Sweetheart, I'm so excited! I think things are *really* going to start happening, now!" he said, kissing her hard on the lips.

"I think so, too," she said, hugging back. "It really sounds promising! Are you going to buy me a heart-shaped garden tub?"

Tim spread his legs in a wide karate stance and wavered slowly back and forth. *"Not 'tuh-day, Bay-beh!"*

Elvis said, twitching his upper lip and throwing a wide side-kick.

The next evening, after Tim and Rusty left, Jamie was quietly washing the supper dishes when her nausea returned like a dormant volcano that'd come to life.

———

"I think it'll take a couple of months, Tim, but I've got a feeling that we're going to start moving fast," Rusty explained, as they sat at the club.

"Jamie and I have talked, Rusty. I've *got* to move back to Tennessee, but we can keep in constant touch and if it promises to be rewarding, then I'll be right back here with you."

"Fair enough, Son. I know you gotta take care of you and yours. You wouldn't be much of a husband if you didn't. I just wish you had more time."

"I know," Tim said, taking a sip of beer. Rusty pecked out a cigarette for him and Tim smoked nervously as he waited for his turn to sing.

He sighed. "If the Base wasn't closing, I could just re-enlist and everything would be fine. Time is just not on my side this time around."

A few women recognized Tim that evening and stopped to chat with him. Some engaged in very polite conversation, while others asked him for his autograph. Nevertheless, when he began his walk to the stage he needed no introduction. Whistles and applause burst forth the moment his name was called.

A chill ran down the back of Rusty's spine as Tim's voice created the lonely, haunting sound of the midnight train yard in *The Vagabond,* just as it had the first time he had sung there.

The crowd went silent. Eyes stared and mouths gaped as *Mr. Midnight* faded out with the reverberating, yet distant cry of a forlorn train whistle.

"Thank you, ladies and gentlemen," Tim said quietly into the microphone. "We have a few records for sale if anyone would like one; the song I just sang is on it. I would just like to say I've really enjoyed performing for you tonight and thank you, as always, for your warm welcome."

Tim exited the stage to a loud, steady echo of clapping and cheering, and briskly walked back to the table.

Rusty had brought along twenty-five records with him and sold them all as quickly as a tornado falls from the sky. Several people were still waiting in line to buy one, and were sorely disappointed.

"Whew, boy! You were good, Son!" Rusty grinned, shuddered a bit, and pushed his black Stetson up with his thumb. "I don't know what it is, but you make the hair on the back of my neck stand up whenever you sing that song! I never get tired of hearin' it."

"Thanks, Rusty," Tim said, humbly "I've got a few ideas for more songs. I just haven't had a chance to iron them all out yet."

"Well, I got an iron in my closet if you need one, Son. Iron 'em! Iron 'em!" They both laughed.

Jamie listened quietly as Tim told her about how well he and Rusty's evening had gone. She didn't tell him about hers. After all, why worry him when he was this incredibly happy; there was no reason to bring down his night.

Tim was asleep when Jamie got sick again, and she was hoping he wouldn't wake up. It was impossible to be quiet but, thankfully, he and Buddy remained silent and happy off in their own little dream worlds.

The clock read *4:09*. It was as if the 'time gods' were laughing at her, making sure she knew that, once again, she was up before dawn.

"What's wrong with me?" she wondered. Jamie wept quietly into her pillow. First, she'd thought it was simply a virus, then perhaps just exhaustion from having no sleep but now, she was frightened. Many thoughts began to enter her mind as she cried into her pillow.

Her nausea had disappeared when she awoke, hearing Tim rustling around in the bedroom getting ready for work. She got up, made him some coffee and shared a cup with him before he left–still not wanting to exaggerate her fear.

After Tim had gone, Jamie called her mother and she came over.

"It won't go away, Mom. One day I'm as sick as a dog and the next, I'm fine. I'm so scared, and I have to fight really hard not to get sick around Tim because he worries about everything *so* much. Do you think I have cancer?" She began crying, as Becky held her in her arms and smiled.

"Far from it, Sweetheart," She rocked her daughter gently as she wept in her arms. "You need to make an appointment to see a doctor either today or tomorrow, because you're leaving for Tennessee on Friday."

Jamie calmed down and Becky helped her find the phone number to the Base Hospital. "I have an appointment tomorrow at one," she said, hanging up the phone. She was shivering.

Becky went over to the couch where she had placed her purse, withdrew a small, white paper sack, and handed it to Jamie. She smiled wide.

Jamie was completely confused. "I'm sick and scared, Mom. What are you *smiling* about?"

"I stopped at the drugstore on the way over, dear. I think you'll find the answer you're looking for in the contents of that little bag you're holding."

Jamie peered inside and looked back up at her mother. Her tears of icy fear now felt as warm and soft as a summer's rain as they flowed down her cheeks. She could feel the smile return to her face.

14

Jamie spent the rest of her day finishing laundry and packing their suitcases. When Tim came home that afternoon, she didn't say a word. She held him close and kissed him more passionately than he had ever known.

"Wow," he whispered. "Have you been drinking wine or something?"

Jamie laughed. "No, Sweetheart. No wine for me!"

She gazed deeply into his eyes. "I just want you to know that I love you with all my heart."

Tim smiled into her beautiful face. The dark circles had disappeared and the glint in her eyes was absolutely stunning, as if an angel were sitting inside Jamie's soul. "I love you too. I *always* have and I *always* will, even until I draw my very last breath."

She kissed him again and held him tightly in her arms.

Tim and Buddy didn't have Hamburger Helper that night for supper. Jamie made them pork chops with mashed potatoes and homemade gravy.

"You're the best cook in the world, Sweetheart. That was one fine supper!" Tim rubbed his tummy after he had finished eating, and handed Buddy one last piece of meat and a spoonful of potatoes and gravy, then he rubbed *his* tummy—two well-fed manly men.

Thursday

Tim read the note that Jamie had left for him on the kitchen table:

Tim, I had to go somewhere with Mom. I'll be back shortly in case you come home and I'm not here.

Love, Jamie

XOXOXO

She had kissed the paper with light pink lipstick. He smiled to himself as he stared down at the beautiful, elegant handwriting.

Tim was playing his guitar when Jamie came in that afternoon; Buddy was curled up on the couch beside him. She stood quietly in the doorway and waited for him to finish. Looking up at her, Tim offered a huge smile.

"Hey, there."

"I have something to tell you," she said.

Becky was standing behind her. "I'll wait out here for a few minutes," she whispered. Jamie looked at her and nodded her head.

Coming inside, Jamie closed the storm door behind her.

"What's up, Kitten?" he asked, still smiling.

She lowered her head, she looked as if she were the President behind the podium, choosing the perfect words to use for her speech. She looked back up at him. "I don't know how to tell you this…all I can say is that we're going to be hearing the 'pitter-patter' of little feet." She smiled.

Tim hoped that she had bought him a spider monkey. He leaned his guitar against the middle cushion of the sofa. "What?"

"I'm pregnant."

Tim's mouth dropped open. He was in shock. "Tim?"

He remained silent, as the list of questions ran through his head.

Jamie walked over to him and stood beside him as he sat in silence. "Tim?"

Slowly, he stood up and pulled her into his arms. "I love you, Sweetheart. Are you sure?"

"I'm *positive,*" she whispered in his ear.

Becky peeked through the storm door and saw them hugging, so she knocked. "All's well?"

"You can come in, Mom," Jamie said.

"Is everything okay?" Becky asked, cautiously, studying them both.

"We're fine," Jamie assured her. Tim smiled; his face was flushed.

"Are you alright, Tim?" Becky asked.

Tim nodded. "I...I don't know what to say," he replied, softly.

"Well, I'm going to leave you two alone to talk. Congratulations, and I love both of you. Call me if you need anything."

Jamie hugged her. "Thank you, Mom. I love you."

"How do you feel?" Tim asked, gently caressing her hair.

"I feel a lot better now that I know why I've been so sick. It was all just morning sickness!" A heavy sigh of relief came from her as she thanked the Lord that cancer was not the issue. "I was so scared, Tim. I honestly thought I was dying of something. But Mom bought me a home pregnancy test yesterday." She sighed once more, blowing the bangs from her face.

"How, do *you* feel?" she asked.

Tim shook his head. "I honestly don't know. I'm happy...excited, I guess. But I'm still a little awestruck, I suppose. I certainly wasn't expecting it," he chuckled. "Oh...I'm happy, Sweetheart. Are you still feeling sick?"

"I'm okay right now, it comes and goes. Mom took me to the doctor's office and I have to start taking prenatal vitamins now. You should see these things, they're so big a dinosaur could choke on them." She grinned.

Tim was in and out of sleep that night as reality began to set in. He held Jamie close as he stared at the clock. They had to be on the road in a few short hours.

He decided to get up before the alarm clock buzzed. Making a pot of coffee, he let Jamie sleep while he took Buddy out for his morning walk. It was still dark outside...and peaceful, as if the Lord was granting him a few minutes of silence.

Tim lit the *Marlboro* that Rusty had given to him, and smoked, as Buddy sniffed around and darted from bush to bush.

He twirled it between his thumb and fingers as he pondered over what it was going to be like to be a *daddy*. He tried to be happy; he wanted to be. But dark, hurtful reflections of his own childhood started to creep into his thoughts, and Tim felt tears run down his cheeks. Taking a deep breath, he returned to the house, telling himself that he would be a far better father than the one who'd been in his life, and strive to be the greatest support for his child.

He sluggishly loaded the bags into the trunk as Jamie finished showering, dressing, and applying her makeup. She was so happy. It was as if she was stuck in some kind of fairytale where ONLY good things happened.

Tim made her a cup of coffee, then he took his guitar and carefully wedged it between the luggage and the trunk wall to keep it from shifting during their trip.

Heading into the kitchen, he made himself a bowl of *Honeycomb* cereal and ate it in silence.

Jamie came in and kissed him on the cheek. "Good morning, Sweetheart. You look sleepy. Are you excited?" She sat down and drank her coffee while he ate.

He nodded, listening to the loud crunch of the cereal race through his head. "Yeah," he replied. "It's been a long time since I've seen my folks."

She took another sip of coffee and watched Buddy beg Tim for a piece of cereal. He picked out a big honeycomb and gave it to him.

Jamie knew when something was wrong. After all, Tim always made Buddy speak in German for his rewards. "What's the matter, Tim?"

He swallowed his cereal and tried to think of something polite to say. "I didn't get much sleep last night. Big day, you know. Big trip. I'm just tired is all."

"Well, I slept like bay–uh, I mean, like a rock," she said, switching her expression. "I'll take first shift behind the wheel so you can get some more sleep."

Tim looked up at her. "That'd be great, Kitten." He was not his usual enthusiastic self, and try as he might, he knew Jamie could see right through him.

But Jamie held her tongue, deciding to be patient

and give him more time with his thoughts. After all...the move, the baby–new things were certainly cropping up.

Tim poured himself a big travel mug full of coffee, putting eight heaping spoonfuls of sugar into it. Jamie watched him stir in a half cup of creamer for about three minutes, and fought hard to keep from laughing.

Making one last sweep through the apartment to make sure everything was turned off and unplugged before locking the front door, Tim then bent down to pick up Buddy. Coffee spilled from his mug onto the carpet. Jamie cupped her mouth so she wouldn't burst out laughing.

Tim remained silent, looking a bit like a serial killer who was about to let loose. Locking the door and the deadbolt, he walked with Jamie to the car–his coffee in one hand, Buddy in the other.

Tim walked to the passenger side, placed his coffee on the roof of the car to open the door, and then sat down in the seat, placing Buddy in his lap. Without thinking of the coffee, he closed the door behind him.

Jamie started the car and backed out of the drive, while Tim stared forward–a sullen expression on his face. The dark coffee rained down on the windshield, and Tim sat motionless as Buddy stood up in his lap and placed his paws on the dashboard to get a closer look at nature's miracle.

Jamie slammed on the brakes and Tim watched his coffee mug roll down and bounce off the hood, landing in the parking lot.

Buddy lost his balance from the sudden jerk of the car; his hind legs flew out from under him and he landed on the floorboard. Tim still didn't say a word.

Jamie looked over at him, and cupped both hands over her mouth, quietly staring at the somber profile.

Tim inhaled deeply and slowly, then let out a long, whispered sigh that sounded like a leaking *'Free Air'* line at the local gas station.

"Not even one sip," he murmured. Buddy craned his neck and bumped his head on the glove box as he struggled to take his place in Tim's lap. He continued to stare out the windshield, as Buddy turned around three times and made himself comfortable. Tim watched as Buddy completed his third revolution.

"Yeah," said Rainman. "*Exactly* three turns...yeah...*definitely* three turns...and Mommy spilled all the coffee...yeah."

Tim continued to stare at Buddy. "And you don't even *care*, do you?"

"I'm sorry, Tim. I *do* care, I didn't..."

"I was talking to Buddy," Tim interrupted her.

He handed Buddy to Jamie, then got out of the car and retrieved his EMPTY coffee mug, shaking the remaining liquid across the dirt.

Getting back inside, he took Buddy from Jamie, reclined his seat back as far as it would go, leaned his head against the shoulder strap, and closed his eyes—dreaming of the coffee that was no longer available.

Jamie released the brake, and silently drove into the darkness. Tim was slightly snoring soon afterward, so she turned on the radio. Mary Chapin Carpenter sang *Passionate Kisses*, followed by *Streets of Bakersfield* by Dwight Yoakam.

As Jamie approached the city limits heading north on I-27 towards Amarillo, Tim slept on as the DJ introduced the next song.

"Folks, next up is a song from a local band here in Lubbock that seems to be doing very well. It's a new single from Don Caldwell Studios *featuring a fella by the name of Tim Cunningham. He really seems to be making his way into the hearts of Lubbock. And I have to say the lyrics are powerfully poetic. So without further adieu I introduce you to,* The Vagabond.*"*

Jamie turned the volume up slightly and looked over at Tim. She just couldn't wake him, he was fast asleep and looking extremely happy about it. Chills ran down her spine as she lost herself in the haunting, yet beautiful sound of her husband's song. She loved him so much, and even though he was asleep his velvet voice was with her, captivating her heart. A man...a voice...the father of her precious baby growing inside of her.

Jamie watched the heavens transform from black into a picturesque vanilla sky, with orange and yellow hues that mixed brilliantly with small openings of brilliant blue. It took her breath away as she marveled in the stark beauty of it all.

She rolled the window down slightly to smell the breath of early morn. It was warm and fresh. A tear fell from her eye and she patted her stomach softly, as if to wake the miracle growing inside her.

I wish you could see this, my sweetness. It's beautiful—just like you! she thought.

Two hours had passed; Amarillo was now just five miles ahead. Jamie looked over at the two sleeping passengers and smiled. *Father and son,* she thought, shaking her head.

She pulled into the next gas station and parked the car on the side of the building. The gas gauge read three-quarters of a tank. Quietly, she opened the door, hoping Buddy wouldn't wake up but, like the man he was, he remained fast asleep curled up in father's lap.

Once inside, she used the restroom and washed her hands. Heading straight to the coffee counter, Jamie stared at all the different brands to choose from, deciding to go with the Columbian breakfast blend.

She found the largest cup available and filled it halfway. She estimated what she thought to be eight spoonfuls of sugar as she poured it from the can, thinking only of how she could give Tim back his perfect cup of coffee. She stirred and sipped it. *A little more,* she thought. She grinned, remembering how funny Tim looked earlier and still marveling at how he could drink such sweet coffee. *It's a wonder he isn't a diabetic.*

As she completed her mission of mercy, Jamie walked back out to the car and quietly opened the door. As Buddy raised his head, she could see that one of his eyes was glued shut with sleep.

"Rise and shine, Porcupine!" she said, cheerfully.

Tim opened his eyes and looked around.

"I got you some more coffee, Sweetheart." She held the large cup out to him.

"Where are we?" he mumbled, taking the cup from her, and almost dropping it because of its sheer weight.

Jamie gasped, but he caught it in the nick of time. "Just inside Amarillo," she said, still smiling.

"Thanks for the coffee, Kitten. I'm sorry I'm not with it, I just woke up." Buddy was frantically trying to get out of the car. Tim reached down and picked his leash up from the floorboard, handing it to Jamie, who attached it to Buddy's collar.

Tim opened the door, stepped out and stretched.

"I can walk him if you need to go inside," Jamie offered, politely.

"It's okay," he said. "I need to walk around and wake up."

She studied his expression. Since he seemed to be his normal self, she let out a small sigh of relief.

After Buddy finished marking every bush he could lay his eyes on, it was Tim's turn. He opted to go inside, however, rather than follow Buddy's example of targeting nature.

Jamie walked around a bit more with Buddy while Tim was inside. When he came out, he was pecking an unopened pack of *Marlboros* against his hand.

Jamie kept quiet as he peeled the cellophane wrap from the top and tore the gold foil from the corner. She watched him inhale deeply and hold the smoke in for a moment. Then, he exhaled slowly, letting the smoke exit through his nostrils.

Tim gazed at the cigarette, and twirled it between his fingers—mimicking Rusty with every move. He seemed to enjoy the sudden bout of light-headedness, as the nicotine coursed through his body, alternately back and forth between coffee and smoke.

Jamie walked toward him. "Tim?"

He looked up from his cigarette, again exhaling the

smoke slowly through his nostrils, making him look like a dragon who had just woken up and was still stoking the fire deep inside.

She contemplated asking him a question, as he stared at her blankly, waiting for her to say whatever was on her mind. Jamie looked away. "Never mind, I can drive for a while longer if you want."

He nodded, as she put Buddy back into the car. *Okay, so that's it.*

Tim crushed out his cigarette and returned to his seat on the passenger side. He held his coffee up as Buddy did his instinctive, yet autistic, triple-spin-lap-turning-dance.

Tim fiddled with the radio dial as Jamie continued to drive. "So, what's up? You're not saying much today," she said, trying to sound cheerful.

"Nothin'. Just tired," he replied.

"You're grumpy, Tim," she said. Looking in the rearview mirror, she checked the traffic all around. "You're not being *you. Please* tell me what's wrong. Have I done something?" She looked at him briefly.

The quick flash of lightning shot from her usually docile eyes. Tim turned his head away, glaring out his window. "Nothing's wrong, Jamie. I just don't feel well," he mumbled.

"You feel well enough to smoke a pack of cigarettes," she said in a slightly harsh tone.

Tim could tell she was getting angry, and he was beginning to feel like he was stuck between a rock and a hard place. He looked at her and pulled the cigarettes from his shirt pocket, holding them up between them.

"Does it *look* like I smoked a pack of cigarettes? No! There's *exactly* nineteen left in the pack. He fought arduously not to laugh, as he realized that his comment almost sounded like he was imitating *Rainman* yet again. He placed the cigarettes back into his pocket.

Looking down at the most understanding 'creature' in the car, Tim began to pet Buddy. He raised his head up to accept the warmth, as Tim scratched him behind his ears. Buddy's hind leg started pedaling with delight.

"I know something's bothering you. You need to talk to me."

"What do you want to talk about?" He was starting to push her buttons.

"If I've *done* anything, or *said* anything wrong, I would like to know. Tim, *we* don't act like this!" As she looked into his eyes, Tim lowered his head in shame.

He turned his gaze to her profile and thought about how truly beautiful she was. "I love you, Jamie," he said, softly. "But I just...can't talk about it."

Sighing, she glanced over at him, trying simultaneously to converse and focus on the increasing traffic. "You *can't*, or you won't?"

He dropped his gaze. "I... can't."

"Tim Cunningham, you tell me *right now* what's going on or I'm going to stop this car, go back to Lubbock, and you can go to Tennessee by yourself!"

There was no getting out of it—she had him cornered. Tim stared down at the floorboard, then out his window, trying to find the best words to express the fears in his heart.

She waited. Her eyes darted to him constantly,

watching him wring his hands like a sinner who was about to confess.

"Do you think? I mean...I don't know," he stopped.

She glared at him. "*What?*"

"I don't know if I can be a good father."

There. It was out! Jamie hit the brakes and swerved the car, coming to an abrupt halt on the shoulder of the interstate. A cloud of Texas dust engulfed the Toyota as she turned the key off and stared fiercely into his face.

"What are you trying to say, Tim? You don't want me to be pregnant? Is it going to 'interrupt' your plans? Complicate your life? *What?*"

Tim peered at her, tears began to form in his troubled eyes. He shook his head. "No, it's not that at all. It's just..." he looked down, cocking his eyebrows in frustration. "It's just that I'm so..."

Jamie interrupted him. "Ugly? Is that what you're trying to say? You say it enough already! Do you think I'm going to lay on a gurney somewhere and pump out a bunch of two-headed chick-a-rabbits'? You are not *The Fly!*"

Her anger was at a savage level. Tim lowered his head farther and closed his eyes, tears streaming down his cheeks.

She touched him lightly on his shoulder. "I'm sorry, Tim," she sighed. "But I'm your wife, I'm your soul-mate, and I'd like to think that we're best friends. If you love me then please trust in me. I will never, *ever* hurt you, or make fun of you, or laugh at you.

"I don't know why you have these negative feelings

about yourself. I would *love* to get my claws into the person, or *persons* who told you that you were ugly," she said, making a clawing motion with her hand. "It's simply *not* true! I know that you've never had a woman treat you decently before, but I have.

"Did you ever stop to think that God was saving us for each other? I *never* had any luck with men, Tim. I know I'm attractive, but that's all *any* of them *ever* saw in me...and they only wanted one thing. But I wasn't brought up that way. I wanted someone special. I wanted someone to make me happy and make me laugh; someone to show me that life is worth living. It was so hard, but I waited patiently. Sure, I made a couple of mistakes along the way. Who hasn't? And I regret them."

She took a deep breath. "I prayed so hard for someone good and decent that I could give my heart to, and for them to love me back, but not because I was beautiful on the outside, but because I was beautiful on the *inside.*" She smiled at him, as warm, love-filled tears joined the mascara streaming down her face. "And God gave me... *you."*

Jamie tenderly pulled his head into her arms and held him. "When we first met, you didn't look at me with lust and desire in your eyes. I could tell you thought I was pretty, but that's entirely different. You saw past my looks and went straight for my heart! I *needed* that, and I had been waiting my whole life for someone to have the instinct to do it; it was *always* you–right from the start.

"I fell in love with you at first sight, Tim, and that is a *very rare* thing indeed. It just doesn't happen that way. I knew you were special when I heard you sing *my* song. You didn't realize it at the time, but you were singing it to me. *I claimed it!*

"You're an angel, and every day that I'm with you, I believe it more and more because you see the world as it's meant to be seen." She wiped the tears from her eyes.

"I've watched you with everyone you've come into contact with. Crystal, the poor elderly woman at the retirement home.... Belle? What singled her out to you from all the rest, Tim? All the people with differences and imperfections are perfect to you, and the ones that are normal," she said, making quotations with her fingers in the air, "are the ones with *imperfections.* How are you able to do that?"

Jamie went on, making sure that each and every gift he had was known to him. "You touch *everyone* with that beautiful voice that God gave to you. They can't help themselves! I even remember the way you looked at Buddy that day in the pet store. You fell in love with him because he was bow-legged. You *knew* how lonely he was!

"I'm willing to bet if that cashier had told you that he cost a million dollars, you would have found *some* way to pay it!

"Tim, a part of your soul flowed over into mine that first night because that's exactly the same way I fell in love with you. Sweetheart, Jesus *is* the King of Kings, and Elvis is the King of Rock, Michael Jackson's the King of Pop, but you, my love, are the *King of Hearts,* because you can look through flesh-and-bone and see the heart in its true form."

Jamie was so excited as she saw the future in her mind's eye. "Our children are going to *love* you, and you're going love them! Tim Cunningham, you're going to be the best daddy in the world, and I want them to be *just like you!*

"You are the most beautiful man I have ever seen, and *my* opinion is the *only* one that matters! Do you understand me?"

Tim nodded. He could feel her heart beating as she held him close.

"Did you say, *children?*" he asked, pulling himself from her.

Jamie's beautiful green eyes were full of emotion; they cut through him like a steel blade. "They saw *two* in the ultrasound."

She let go of him and sighed, as Tim tenderly caressed her hair, and stretched towards her for a kiss.

Buddy yelped as Tim accidentally squeezed him between his knees and the emergency brake.

"I love everything about you, Jamie. And *of course* I will love our babies."

He gently rubbed her tummy. "I could never be disappointed with you or anything that comes from you. You *are* my life, Kitten–not a complication in it. And as far as my 'plans' go, they're not interrupted, they're going exactly the way God has commanded them to go—right on schedule.

"What I'm going through and feeling right now has absolutely nothing at all to do with you. It has to do with *me.* And you're right, you do treat me decently. You're the only person in my life that's ever made me feel like I'm part of the human race."

He looked away from her and stared out the

windshield. Taking a deep breath, Tim closed his eyes tight. "I think I'm ready for you to know *my* story..."

15

Jamie started the car and turned on the blinker. She was finally able to pull out after the one-hundred twenty-eighth car had passed by. Tim assembled his thoughts on where to begin, as she drove onward and searched for the I-40 East interchange.

"My last name used to be Anderson," he started.

Jamie gave him a startled look, but didn't speak.

"My mother got pregnant with me when she was seventeen. The father I have now adopted me when I was seven years old. I think of him as my *real* dad because he's the one who raised me. My biological father, James, *ironically* was a disc jockey at WKDA in Nashville when he met my mother."

Tim laid his head back on the seat, trying to focus on the images swirling in his brain. "Back then it was an AM station. Now it's known as WKDF on the FM dial there, and it's the main rock-and-roll station that everyone listens to.

"My mom's job was to get records from the shelves for the DJs. They needed her to help them line up their program lists for the evening, and play requests for the people who called in. Once the records were played, she filed them back on the shelves. Basically, she was the station librarian.

"I'm not clear on how they came to start dating, Mom hates to talk about all this, but she told me that he led her to believe he really cared for her."

Tim took a deep breath. "My mom was very young and lonely. My grandparents aren't the most loving people in the world and they treated her pretty bad when she was growing up. Granddaddy drank a lot and Granny never wanted to have any kids. As it turned out, she ended up having five. For some reason she disliked Mom the most.

"When my mother found out that she was pregnant with me, James got very angry about it. He told her that she'd ruined his life and destroyed any chance he ever had of having a career!"

Jamie winced in the driver's seat, wondering how any man could be that soulless.

Tim nodded, as if agreeing with her silent statement. "He tried every way possible to get rid of her. She was so scared, Jamie. She didn't know what she was going to do, but she was *mostly* afraid of what her parents would do to her, not to mention *me*, when they found out.

"*His* parents, my other set of grandparents, are very decent and kind people and I love them very much. They never knew what happened."

The images grew darker inside Tim's mind. His stomach churned, as if by just speaking these words he was somehow covered in sin. "One evening, my grandfather walked in as James was yelling at her. He threatened her life if she ever tried to contact him again. My grandfather is a big man, Jamie...and Mom said that he slammed James up against the wall."

Tim sighed. "Apparently, at that point, Grandpa had figured it all out. My grandfather said, 'That's the *mother* of my unborn grandchild you're talking to! If you *ever* threaten her again, I'll break your sorry neck.' And he meant it.

"One thing lead to another I guess, and they were forced to get married. Mom moved to Minnesota with Granny and Grandpa, while James stayed in Nashville. Mom said that her mother told her not to *ever* come back with her *little bastard*."

Jamie once again was jolted in her seat, just imagining the horrific people who would treat their children like that.

Tim continued, his voice full of sadness. "Apparently her mother called her every four lettered word in the book before my Mom left.

"James had driven to Minnesota at some point because the night I was born, Mom said that he wouldn't even come into the delivery room. The doctor said, 'Mr. Anderson, your wife is having the baby now.' And James replied, 'Tell her she can have it by herself! I'm gonna sit here and watch TV!'

"He went back to Nashville after I was born. Granny and Grandpa helped my mom finish high school; she had to go to school during the day and take care of me at night after she finished her homework.

"Granny taught her how to cook and clean, and how to take care of me. Mom said she was exhausted all the time because Granny kept her so busy." Tim issued a small smile as he thought back to how much love his mother had shown for him during that horrific period in her life.

He sighed. "At some point, James got fired and moved in with us. I can barely remember that." He shrugged. "I probably blocked it out."

"Granny and Grandpa loved me very much, and I remember Grandpa holding me and playing with me. He would hold me in his lap and make talk like a teddy bear. Their house has this soothing smell to it too, and every time I've been back to visit them over the years, I'm instantly transported to a time when I felt safe and secure from all harm. It's the only security I've ever known, Jamie."

She reached out and laid her hand over his.

"Grandpa had all these old toys. Heck! He *still* has them!" Tim chuckled. "My favorite one to play with was this metal wind-up tractor. Sparks would come out of the smokestack when it was running.

I barely remember my great-grandmother. She was nice, though. She made this huge humpty-dumpty doll for me and I dragged that thing everywhere! She made the best oatmeal and raisin cookies I've ever had, but she died a long, long time ago." Tim shook his head, remembering the sweet taste of those unforgettable cookies.

Jamie continued to listen to him as she merged into traffic on I-40.

"James and Mom moved to Wisconsin when I was three, I *think*. We rented a small apartment, and James got another job as a disc jockey. I remember Mom used to sit me on the kitchen sink to listen to him when he was on the radio.

"I had my own room with a few toys in it. James bought me a racetrack and set it up in there, but I was only allowed to play with it when he was with me. He didn't want me to break the cars. And he only played with me *twice*." The childhood anger still filled Tim to his breaking point.

"There was a 55-gallon aquarium in the living room that had a rock in it; it looked like one of Mom's burnt hamburger patties. We had a television set in there, too. If I'm remembering right, I believe I watched the very first episode of *Sesame Street* on it!

"James had a reel-to-reel tape recorder in the corner. Mom said he would put his headphones on and listen to himself all night when he got home. She hated that thing. She said it was all he ever wanted to do—'sit there and be in love with himself.'

"I never felt like I belonged there, even when I was that small. Maybe it was because Granny and Grandpa's house was all I had ever known."

Tim shuddered at the next thought that came to his mind. "James never wanted me to touch him. I tried several times to hug him, but he would push me away. I tried and tried to make him love me, but he wouldn't. Sometimes when he came home, I would run up to him and hug his leg. He would say something to Mom then pull me off of him like I was a dirty piece of filth."

Jamie choked on her tears, as Tim continued.

"Whenever I said, 'I love you, Daddy,' he would look at me with really mean eyes, or just ignore me. He would *never* tell me that he loved me." Tim looked down and sighed. "It broke my heart."

"One night, I was asleep in my bed and he came in. He flipped on the light and jerked me up by the arm, and started beating me all over my room with his belt. I screamed and screamed, but he wouldn't stop."

Tim's voice was cold. "Mom ran in there and

started screaming at him to quit. 'What are you doing to him!' I remember her shouting.

"He told her I was cussing and said I had a filthy mouth. He finally put me down. He was breathing hard and shaking. I was still crying, and Mom just looked at me.

"I was terrified that she might believe him so I said, 'No, Mama, I was asleep. I didn't say any bad words!' He slapped me across the face for that and called me a liar, then stormed out of my room. I was crying so hard! Mom held me and rocked me in her arms and put me back in the bed. I was horrified. I was so sore the next day I could barely move. I had purple belt marks all over my back, my legs and my stomach."

He turned to his love behind the wheel. "Jamie, I didn't say any curse words...I swear," Tim said, fighting back the tears.

Jamie looked over at him sadly. "I know you didn't, Baby. I believe you."

Tim nodded. "It was a while before it happened again. One night he was siphoning water out of the aquarium, doing a filter change. Once he'd refilled the aquarium with fresh water, he accidentally made the mistake of leaving the siphoning hose out.

"I guess, in my little mind, I wanted to help him. While he was listening to himself on his tape-recorder, I reached up and slipped the hose back in the aquarium and sucked on it. The water started flowing into the bucket, but once it reached the half way point, I couldn't get it to stop!

"I watched as it filled to the top, and I started

crying when it overflowed onto the floor. I ran into my room and crawled under my bed. I closed my eyes so tightly, hoping it would all go away. But, of course, it didn't.

"I could hear him screaming in the living room. I felt the floor quaking as he stomped into my room; he was cussing so loud that my ears hurt. He reached under the bed to grab me, but I scooted myself up against the wall. He kept reaching in until he managed to grab my leg, then he pulled me out.

"He held me up by my arm and hauled me into the living room to show me what I had done. I was shaking and begging him not to spank me. My arm was numb from hanging limp in his hand, and he beat me again."

Jamie sucked in her breath.

Tim sighed heavily, feeling the pain course through his body as if the beating happened just yesterday. "I remember opening my eyes only once. I was afraid that his belt would hit me in the face, and I saw Mom just standing there with her head down. I don't know if she thought I deserved it, or if she was scared of him, but I wanted to die because it hurt so bad. The next day I was covered with purple bruises."

He swallowed hard. "I shied away from him quite a bit after that. Then, one evening—I guess he was in a good mood—he sat down in the chair in front of his tape recorder. I was standing in the kitchen, watching him. He smiled at me and motioned for me to come over, so I went to him. He picked me up and sat me in his lap.

"'This is what Daddy does at work,' he explained. 'I talk to people over the air.'

"He put his earphones on my head and turned the tape recorder on. I listened to it for as long as he let it play. I was thinking that he *finally* loved me, and I was so happy to be sitting in his lap."

Tim shook his head at the ridiculous hope of a child. "The next day I made the mistake of wanting to be like *him.* He was at the radio station, and I went into the living room and picked out one of the reels he had stacked on the shelf next to his recorder. I sat in his chair and put his headphones on and opened the box, pulling the reel out. I didn't know what I was doing, or how to thread it to the other reel, but I accidentally dropped it and it rolled across the living room floor. The tape unraveled and went everywhere.

"I should have told Mom what I'd done, but I didn't trust her *not* to tell him. I panicked and jumped out of the chair. I wrapped the tape up as quickly as I could, but it was obvious that someone had touched it. I put it back inside the box and placed it on the shelf where I found it, then I went into my room and closed the door. I *prayed* that he wouldn't notice it that night when he got home, but he did."

Tim shook his head. "Already, the tears were starting as I heard him cussing and throwing things around in the living room. I jumped once when something hit the other side of my bedroom wall."

His voice turned into a whisper. "I was sitting on my bed when he came for me. There was no sense in begging him for forgiveness, or for mercy, or telling him how sorry I was...it was over.

"He jerked me up by my arm again and hauled me

into the living room. Only this time, he threw me across the room after he had beaten me and I hit my head on the wall."

"My God," Jamie whispered.

"I was in a daze but I remember Mom was yelling at him. He shouted at her to keep me out of his way! I remember Mom picked me up off the floor and carried me into my bedroom. She changed me into my pajamas and put me in my bed, and then woke me up a couple of times during the night to make sure I was alright. I started to jump like a scared rabbit every time the door opened.

"The next day, after he had left for work, Mom came into my bedroom and told me that I had to stay in my room when Daddy was in the house.

"'Why doesn't Daddy love me?' I asked her.

"I know now that there was nothing she could have said that I would have understood. She just held me and said that it didn't matter...because Mommy loved me."

A wealth of emotions swept through Jamie's mind. She didn't know what to say, because at that point she was just as mad at Tim's mother as she was at the disgusting creature who he had called Daddy. A mother should certainly walk out and save her child! But Jamie remained quiet, shaking her head in disgust.

"I stayed in my room after that, and never made a sound when he was home. I don't remember how much time had passed, but there were times when he wouldn't come home at night; then it got to where he would only show up once or twice a week. Eventually...he didn't show up at all.

"Mom was scared. I don't know why she didn't go

back to Minnesota. I wish she would have. The next thing I remember, Granddaddy, my mom's father, came to where we lived in Wisconsin and drove us back to Tennessee. We had to live in a room he built in the basement, but it wasn't too bad.

"As irony would have it, their house was four houses down from the one we lived at later with Uncle Roy, on Shauna Drive. Kalvin and Aunt Lizzie lived there because they were still kids. Uncle Roy and Aunt Sheila were grown and they had moved away.

"I had to walk on egg shells with Granny and Granddaddy. They didn't like me any more than James did. Granddaddy used a switch from one of the trees in the front yard to whip us with."

"Jesus," Jamie whispered. "Nobody should go through a childhood like that."

Tim sighed, as if accepting the fact that beatings were everywhere. "I got whipped the first day I was there because Kalvin told Granny that I wouldn't let him play with any of my toys. He never even asked me if he *could* play with them.

"Those two were basically left to their own devices. They were spoiled rotten to the core. Granny never wanted them anyway, so instead of raising them properly, she let them do whatever they wanted as opposed to listening to them whine and cry all the time.

"The only time *they* ever got the switch, or 'a lickin' —as they liked to call it, was if they talked back or got smart with them.

"She wasn't anything like my other granny who loved me, and gave me ice cream cones and homemade chocolate chip cookies. I can't remember a single time that she didn't look at me with hatred in her eyes.

"From the first day that Mom and I got there, anytime *anything* bad happened, or got broken, or if there was an argument, it was always my fault. There were no questions or explanations, just an automatic whipping."

Tim continued on, as Jamie sat silent, confused and infuriated that anyone had ever dared to lay hands on her love.

"Granddaddy owned a frame shop and Mom worked there with him. I don't know how much he paid her, but I remember on my fourth birthday she got me this little plastic board set with a magnetic bulldozer inside it. There was a magnetic pen that you held on the bottom of the board to drag the bulldozer around in the sand. I thought it was pretty neat.

"We were down in the basement when I opened it up and she said, 'Son, this is all I could afford to get you for your birthday; keep it down here and play with it all you want. But keep it hidden, because if Kalvin gets hold of it he'll tear it up and you won't have it anymore. Do you understand?'

"I hid it under the mattress. We went back upstairs that day and everyone was in the kitchen. Granny was making lunch, and she looked at me with those hateful eyes of hers, and asked, 'Did you get anything for your birthday, Tim?'

"She *knew* Mom had bought that toy for me because Granddaddy had to take her to the store to get it. I looked at my mom before I answered her, and she lowered her head. I wanted to lie but she nodded at me to tell the truth."

Granny told me—ordered me, more like it—to bring it up so everyone could see what I got." He turned to Jamie. "She had this evil smirk on her face that I will never forget. Even at *four,* I knew what she was doing!"

Jamie was speechless. So far everything that Tim had told her about his life was worse than any horror movie she could ever imagine.

Tim studied her reaction before he continued. He noticed that her knuckles were bone white from the death grip she had on the steering wheel. He stroked Buddy's soft coat as he slept on oblivious, thankfully, to a life of pain.

"I did as I was told. I went back down to the basement and pulled my birthday present out from between the mattress and box springs. I was determined not to cry at the inevitable. I hugged my plastic board and took it back upstairs.

"I walked over and handed it to Granny. Kalvin ran up and snatched it out of her hands and started banging it on the table. I watched him as he ripped the plastic from the board so he could get the bulldozer out, and my heart sank.

"The sand from my gift was all over the kitchen. I looked at Granny and she was glaring at me, as if she was daring me to do something about it.

"My mom was standing by the basement door with her head hung down, crying. I think I felt more pity for her than I did for myself."

"Why didn't she *do* anything?" Jamie asked, trying to maintain her emotions. "She was your *mother*, for gods sake!"

Tim looked at her. "What *could* she do? We were living in their house, and Mom had nowhere else to go."

Jamie shook her head. "She *should* have done something!"

Tim shrugged. "Kalvin ran off into the living room with my bulldozer and Granny smiled at me. She put her hands on her cheeks faking a surprised look, and said, '*Uh oh! It's all gone!*'

"I guess it made her mad that I didn't cry because she stomped over to the basement door, grabbed the broom and dustpan, and handed it to me telling me to sweep up all the sand."

Tim paused for a moment. "Have you ever read, *Flowers in the Attic*, by V.C. Andrews?"

Jamie shook her head.

"I have," he said. "That tale of terror wasn't *fiction* to me."

He sighed. "Granny made us leftovers for lunch one day. I ate everything on my plate except for my cornbread. I kept choking on it. I don't know if it had too much cornmeal in it, or what; but to me, it tasted like she had poured a cup of sand on top of it. I really didn't think I would get into trouble, but if I would've known what would happen, I would've eaten it."

"What happened next, Sweetheart?" Jamie asked, softly. "I'm listening to every word you're saying, so you take your time...okay?"

Tim nodded, trying to get his words out between the sobs. "I took my plate over to the trashcan and I buried the cornbread as deeply as I could. Then I covered it up with some of the trash that was in the can.

"Aunt Lizzie watched me do it. After I sat back down, she just looked at me and grinned, then went and told Granny what I had done."

"How old was Lizzie?" Jamie asked.

"She was eight at the time," Tim replied. "Granny stomped into the kitchen and dug through the trash until she found it. Lizzie just stood there with her arms crossed, smiling that evil smile.

'Do you think my food tastes like garbage?' Granny asked.

'No Ma'am,' I said. 'I just couldn't eat it, Granny. It made me choke.'

"She went and got the switch and spanked me hard. When Mom got home that night Granny told her what I had done, and then she told her that she was going to lock me in the attic until I was hungry enough to eat her 'garbage'.

"Mom started crying as Granny dragged me up the stairs. Granddaddy was drinking a beer and laughing; I guess he thought it was cute or something. When we reached the top of the stairs, I saw a wasp nest in the ceiling with a bunch of dead wasps scattered all over the floor.

'Here's your light!' Granny said to me.

"It was a single bulb in a ceramic socket on the ceiling. A long, cotton string was tied to a small chain that I could just reach to turn it off and on. There were piles of old clothes all over the floor. Some were on hangers, and hung on a bar that was nailed between the rafters. Man it was hot up there.

"On the other end of the attic was a twin bed with a stained mattress and box springs that sat under a big, rusty fan in the window. There were no sheets, I had to use the musty clothes on the floor.

'You can knock on the door whenever you have to use the bathroom,' Granny told me and then she showed me a skeleton key. 'You can have water, and I'll *give* you one peanut butter sandwich a day and that's *it!* By the time you get out of here, you're going to think my 'garbage' is the best food you've ever had!'

Tim sighed. "I was *so sorry* that she hated me. I would have gladly thrown my arms around her and told her that I loved her, if I would have seen just one tiny spark of compassion in her eyes, but she only stared at me with that normal face of hatred and disgust.

"So...I watched her turn around and walk down the stairs. I could see her through the railing. She *slammed* the door at the bottom and I heard the key turn in the lock."

Jamie was *choking* back her tears now, trying hard not to cry. "How...*long*...?"

She felt her heart breaking, as if some invisible giant hand were squeezing it with all its might. "How *long* did she keep you locked up?" Jamie glanced at the road, then back at Tim.

He could feel his bottom lip quiver, as if he were sitting in that attic once again, detesting his life. He bit down hard to make it stop.

The light green eyes were as translucent as glass. Jamie felt as if she could see for miles in them—deep and bottomless—storing all of these hideous memories in his mind. She had never seen such desolation, fear, and loneliness written so blatantly on someone's face.

"I was so little...I had no comprehension of time. I could see day turning to night through the window fan, but they all ran together. If I had to guess, I would say a little over a month."

Jamie gasped in horror. She was truly amazed that *The King of Hearts* still had one of his own, considering the monsters that had tried to crush him along the way.

16

"Where the *he*..." Jamie tried to compose herself. "*Where* was your mother?"

"Mom brought my sandwich to me every night when she came home, along with a clean change of clothes. And she was allowed to bathe me every other day, but I wasn't allowed to say anything to anyone. I had to go straight to the bathroom with her and not say a word as she ran my bath water and bathed me.

"Granny would stand at the bathroom door with a switch in her hand to make sure we didn't talk. *Once,* Mom managed to sneak a candy bar up to me in her pants. She opened it and whispered, 'Eat it as fast as you can. Don't let Granny catch us.'

"I gobbled it down as fast as I could, and she crumpled the empty wrapper up and shoved it back down her pants."

"What on earth did you do up there when you were all alone?" Jamie asked.

He sat in a long silence, staring out the window. Jamie didn't ask him again. She checked the mirrors occasionally, trying to keep her attention focused on him.

Finally, after about fifteen minutes, he politely asked, "Would you mind if I had a cigarette?"

She smiled at him when he finally spoke. At least he wasn't shutting her out. Tears streamed down her cheeks and she wiped her nose with her arm, struggling to keep from breaking down completely. "Baby, you can smoke all the cigarettes you want."

He rolled his window down slightly, and pulled one from the pack in his shirt pocket. He exhaled slowly and deliberately, watching the smoke escape through the window. "Sometimes, I would unplug the giant fan in the mornings when I woke up so I could hear the birds singing. The fan didn't blow any fresh air *in*; it drew the heat from the attic *out*. There were no toys up there, no board games, no radio, and no books...*nothing*.

"Most of the time I sat Indian-style in the middle of the mattress and stared through the metal blades of the fan while it was running. The roaring noise soothed and comforted me thankfully, because if it had been only silence, it would've killed me.

"I depended on it for security like I depend on you...and Buddy when I cuddle with you at night, if *that* makes any sense. That's why I have one blowing in our bedroom at night. I can't sleep without it.

"I spent many a sleepless night in boot camp because there were no fans in our dormitory. Most nights, I did double...sometimes triple shifts at fire watch. The guys really admired me for it because they could rest. The drill instructor *never* found out; we had a list posted with every man's name and time that they had to stand at post.

"I watched over them as they slept. I never said a word and I never made a sound. I walked past each one of them and stood in front of their bunks and listened to them breathing. It soothed me. Sometimes I would wonder what they were dreaming about.

"The fan was my only friend. I would plug it back in whenever it got too hot for me. I mean, it was *always* hot up there, but when the sweat would literally rain from my face, I would plug it back in and lay down.

"I used Granny's dresses that hung on the bar to dry my sweat off with. I *especially* liked to use this fancy black one with white lace because I sweated so profusely that it would be white with salt when it dried." Tim chuckled at his mischievousness.

"I watched the wasps fly around the light in the late part of the morning. I was scared of them at first but they never bothered me. The light was quite a distance away from my bed, and I don't think they liked the fan. I would lie very still so I wouldn't attract their attention or provoke them.

"I guess I became part of the woodwork to them, and they didn't see me as a threat. They would roost on their nest in the evening, and I knew it wouldn't be long before Mom would bring my sandwich to me.

"In the afternoons I would watch the other kids riding their bicycles up and down the street. The next-door neighbors had two little girls who liked to jump rope and play hopscotch. Sometimes their mama would sit on the porch with a glass of tea and watch them play. A couple of times, their daddy played with them when he got home from work. He tickled them until they were screaming and laughing, and begging him to stop."

Tim had longed to be one of those happy children, a member of a family that only showed laughter and love. "He put one of his little girls on his shoulders and ran as fast as he could around the yard with her. She bounced up and down, laughing hysterically, and pulled his hair as if she were holding the reins of a horse. He didn't yell at her or spank her because it hurt, he just laughed, and I laughed, too!

"When Mom brought me my sandwich, I would save it until the afternoon turned to dusk. Then, when everything outside was quiet, I would unplug the fan and sit in the middle of my bed and listen to the crickets as I ate my sandwich.

"It was then, every night, that a breeze would blow in and cool my face. I closed my eyes and relished in it; I *knew* it was Jesus because he always smelled like fresh rain.

"When my eyes were closed, I tried to think of all the things that I could smell. Mostly it was the aged wood of the attic along with the musty clothing, but if the breeze was just right, I could smell the faint hint of roses and honeysuckle once in awhile. It was beautiful.

"When dusk turned to darkness, Jesus sent lightning bugs for me to watch. I sat for hours and watched them through the fan cage. And when I grew sleepy, I would lie down, close my eyes and listen to all the different sounds outside.

"One night I heard a kitten crying somewhere in the distance. It was so sad and heartbreaking to listen to. It was like me, like we were two lonely souls crying out for a friend.

"He moaned for so long, Jamie, it was pitiful. I could feel his loneliness and his broken heart. I knew he was hungry, scared and lost. I cried so hard for him because there was nothing I could do."

Tim stared down at Buddy, grateful that he was now a savior to a beloved animal. "There was one day in particular when I was feeling really lonely. I watched through the fan cage and was so happy that the sky was finally overcast. The temperature dropped and the wind began to blow.

"I put my face against the fan cage and enjoyed the coolness that blew in. When I opened my eyes, there was a small whirlwind made of leaves dancing back and forth on the ground below me. I couldn't tell you if it was a miracle or not, but in my heart I *felt* like it was God. He was spending time with me, and stayed there for an hour or so before He went away.

"I smiled as I watched the leaves dance. I felt so peaceful and calm. Something inside me told me that I was going to be happy one day. I just had to get through this part of my life."

He swallowed the memories. "I prayed a lot, Jamie —every morning and every night. I always asked God if He would send someone that would love me."

He looked at Jamie. Tears were softly raining down her face. He raised Buddy up and kissed him behind his velvet ears.

"Sweetheart, what happened when she finally let you out?"

Tim pondered for a moment, and sighed deeply. "That was the last *horrible* day I had, but it was also one that I will never forget.

"She waited until Mom got home. I heard the door being unlocked and I thought she was bringing me my sandwich as usual but, instead, she told me that I could come down, get a bath and eat supper. I was happy, but I was also very scared because I was so used to being up there.

"By that time I almost *didn't* want to leave, because when I was up there no one beat me, or yelled at me, or called me bad names.

"It almost hurt to speak because I hadn't spoken for so long. Mama gave me a bath, and I was so happy that I was going to have something to eat besides peanut butter..." He stopped for a moment.

Jamie looked over at him and he wiped his tears on Buddy's coat.

Buddy opened one eye as Tim held him tightly. "Mom walked with me to the kitchen and I sat at the table. Kalvin and Aunt Lizzie were told to stay in the living room with Granddaddy. I was so hungry, Jamie.

"She set my plate on the table in front of me..." Tim began crying. "It was the cornbread that I had thrown in the trash that day and there were cigarette ashes all over it. Beside my cornbread were some butter beans with white mold on them, and beside the beans was some moldy, dried-up macaroni and cheese.

"She stood there with that switch in her hand. I looked at Mom and she had that 'hang-dog' expression on her face, and didn't say *anything.*

"Granny said, 'You're *going* to eat my 'garbage', Tim, or you're *going* to starve. And if you throw up at my table, you're *going* to eat that, too.'"

Jamie cried uncontrollably and gripped the steering wheel fiercely with both hands.

Tim continued, "I looked up at her; she was glaring at me with unbelievable hatred. She smirked when she saw the tears form in my eyes. I asked her for a glass of water. That was probably the nicest thing she ever did for me, because she let me have one.

"I got through the cornbread pretty easily. I took huge bites and drowned it with water, then gulped it down. The beans smelled horrible; I stirred them up so I wouldn't have to look at the fuzzy mold…"

Jamie interrupted him, "Baby, that's *enough*!" She wiped her burning eyes. "You don't have to talk about this anymore. I…I *have* to pull over, okay? I can't drive anymore." She was shaking horribly.

Tim could see the monumental rage shining in her eyes. "I'm sorry, Jamie. I didn't mean to upset you, but you wanted to know."

Her look was a mixture of anger and trauma. "***You*** don't have *anything* to be sorry about, Tim! I'm…enraged and in…*shock* at how your grandmother–how *any* grandmother could… And how your *own* ***mother*** could just *stand* there and *let* someone do these things to her *own child!* You were just a *baby* for God's sake!

"If anyone even *dares* to lay a hand on one of my babies *I'll tear them to pieces!"*

Tim and Buddy decided to be quiet, as Jamie restarted the car and pushed the accelerator through the floorboard. Seeing a billboard that advertised a gas station at the next exit, Jamie took the ramp like a racecar driver out of control.

Tim and Buddy were jolted back and forth as Jamie displayed her rage by whipping the steering wheel, and screeching to a halt beside pump number three, switching the engine off.

"I'll fill the tank," Tim said, quietly. Jamie sat

there speechless and nodded her head.

Buddy sneezed on Tim and wagged his tail. He could tell that Buddy was anxious to take a bathroom break. Opening the door, Tim exited the car, making his way toward the gas pump.

Jamie looked in the rearview mirror. She felt as if she had aged ten years in the last few hours. "I need to get my make-up bag out of the trunk," she said, taking the keys from the ignition.

"Okay," Tim replied as he opened the gas tank and unscrewed the cap.

She sighed. "I might be a while...I've got to put myself back together."

Tim nodded at her and fumbled with the gas nozzle.

Jamie dug through the trunk and found her bag. Walking towards Tim, she cupped his face and kissed him as a tear slipped from his eye. "You don't have to cry anymore, hon. You've been through enough hell today," she said softly. "I can't imagine in my most frightening nightmares what all that must have been like for you, but ***I*** love you...*until I draw my last breath.*" Jamie smiled, as she quoted his beautiful words.

"I'm not an angel, Jamie. I'm just a victim of unplanned parenthood," he said, looking into her beautiful mascara-smudged face.

Jamie shook her head. "No, Tim. You are the *victim* of abuse and neglect, and your mother did absolutely *nothing* to protect you. I'm so sorry that you had to relive that, but I honestly think you *needed* to let your feelings out. It's the only way to let go and move on." The gas nozzle clicked off and Tim topped off the tank.

"I'll pay it while I'm in there, Sweetie. Are you going to walk Buddy?" Jamie asked.

Buddy was standing up against the door wagging his tail so hard he could barely stay on his feet. Tim smiled. "Yeah, I think he's about to wet his pants."

Jamie giggled. "It's nice to have you back. *I've really missed you...*," she whispered, handing him the car keys.

As Buddy earned his freedom and began running from bush to bush, Tim thought about everything he had told Jamie. She was right. He felt as if he had been living under the ocean, held down by thirty-foot waves. He had been drowning in his past. He had been kicking furiously in the icy depths to reach the surface for each small gasp of air, but the ocean of pain and anger continued to pull him in deeper.

His unrelenting love for Jamie, and his *trust* in her, had forced him to keep kicking and talking. With her support and love, he had finally broken through to the surface, and taken that much-needed breath.

It was over. God *had* heard the prayers of a sad little boy from long ago. That very whirlwind....*had* answered those prayers...by sending him Jamie. There was no doubt in Tim's mind—she was his savior.

17

Tim and Buddy were sharing a stick of *Slim Jim* beef jerky when Jamie came out of the store. She had been in the restroom for so long that he'd gone in and bought a couple of the extra long ones while he was waiting. Tim loved how the spicy grease of the meat sticks *oozed* out as he chewed them.

He had since moved the car to the side of the building, and saw her looking around. Tim honked the horn, as he and Buddy tugged on the last bit of meat together. Buddy's furry lips tickled Tim's and he chuckled, as he bit the beef stick in half.

As they readied themselves to continue the journey, Jamie took her place in the passenger seat and held onto Buddy so tightly, that it looked as if she was already practicing the *protective mother* phase.

Buddy struggled to reach Tim but finally gave up, knowing that he was safe in his mother's arms. Doing his triple-step turn-around routine, he made a nest in her lap.

"How are you?" Jamie asked.

He glanced over at her and smiled. "I'm feeling better, how are you?"

Jamie sighed and blew her bangs out of her face. "Tired," she replied. "*Very* tired."

"How's the morning sickness?" he asked.

She pulled on the latch and reclined her seat back as far as it would go. "It comes and goes. I had a spell when I was in the bathroom, but I think it was my nerves more than anything else." She stroked Buddy's fur and he sighed deeply.

"Umm...Jamie? Please don't say anything to Mom about what I told you, okay? It happened a long time ago and it's a sore subject."

"It should be!" she said, angrily. "Don't worry, I won't make this any harder on you than it already was. I won't say anything, Tim. But I can tell you right now that I don't like her. I'm not going up there to fight with someone I've never met before, but there's no excuse for what she did... *Excuse me*, I mean, what she *didn't* do," she said, sarcastically.

Tim looked over at her. He could see that she was tired. Deciding to let the conversation go, he turned the radio on and ran the dial up and down until he found a good radio station to listen to.

Jamie closed her eyes, and she was soon fast asleep. ...Wasps were everywhere. She was walking through a rolling meadow of Black-Eyed-Susan's with Effie. She swatted at them but they wouldn't leave her alone. Holding Effie close, Jamie tried to cloak her from their stingers but they swarmed around her.

Jamie screamed for help but no one came to her rescue. She ran as fast as she could through the meadow, but the heat was stifling—almost unbearable. Tripping over something, she fell down hard, knocking the breath from her lungs. She gasped desperately for air as she lay on top of Effie, doing her best to protect her from the violent predators.

She felt the wind from their wings as they flew about her face and crawled through her hair—they wanted *Effie!* She closed her eyes tightly and hoped they would go away.

The time seemed to become an eternity. The fragrance of the meadow had disappeared and was superseded by a strange new odor—it was old and musty. Slowly, she opened her eyes and looked around—the wasps had vanished. Her knee was bleeding badly. Effie was okay but she was scared. Jamie looked around; she had tripped over a loose board on an old wooden floor and ripped her knee open on a nail.

The room she was in was very dark, but she could see a light at the other end of it. Standing up slowly, she tried to stop her head from spinning, but the dizziness and nauseous feeling was taking her over.

Wearily, she walked through the darkness, clutching Effie safely to her bosom. Onward, toward the light... But with each step she took, Jamie knew that something was different—something was *wrong.*

She was caught in a vacuum and couldn't stop the suction. It pulled her slowly and deliberately through the darkness. Panic engulfed her and sweat rained from her forehead as she gasped at the horror that lay ahead. It was a massive, rusty fan that stretched from one end of the wall to the other.

The roaring blades were too much for her to bear. She could feel her soul diminishing as she realized that she and Effie would soon be pulled into the evil device and torn to bits. She cried and screamed, but suddenly...it *stopped.* The roaring vacuum ceased. She looked around and saw a young boy staring at her—he was holding the plug in his hand. He had saved them...

She recognized the child; it was Tim when he was four years old. He stood there, shirtless and wet, quietly looking at her. She could see his ribs, and his pale and lifeless eyes were framed by the deep, dark circles underneath.

"Tim!" she cried out. Shaking her head, she wept as she reached out to him. But he simply stood there, not even trying to come to her.

"Come here, Baby. I'll take you far away from this place." She held out both of her arms to him, but he didn't move an inch.

"I love you, Tim. Please take my hand," she pleaded with him and cupped her hands over her mouth—he was so close to death. He lowered his head; it was clear that he had given up on his hopeless little life.

He looked toward the fan blades and a small bed materialized out of nowhere. The mattress was filthy and stained. He waited until the apparition was clear and then slowly climbed on top of it. Sitting Indian-style in the middle, he remained silent and stared out the window.

Jamie limped over and sat down beside him—her knee was in excruciating pain and blood dripped onto the floor. She watched as a river of sweat poured from his forehead, listening to his shallow breathing.

"Tim," she whispered, tears streaming down her face. He turned his head and looked at her, seeing *Effie.* He stared at her for a long time; desolation lit his face.

Jamie looked down at Effie, then back up at Tim. She smiled and held her out to him. *"Here. She wants to be with you. Her name is Effie,"* she whispered.

Tim smiled and looked around cautiously to see if

his grandmother was watching, then he reached up to take her. The second he touched the doll, Jamie was jolted from sleep. Tim had slammed on the brakes in the middle of the interstate.

"What's going on?" she asked in bewilderment. She wiped the tear away, raised her seat back up, and looked out the window.

"I don't know," Tim said. "The traffic just came to a sudden stop. Sorry...my mind was somewhere else."

He rolled the window down and craned his neck out to see how far the traffic was backed up.

"What are you doing?" she asked. Buddy tried to appear invisible and slinked over into Tim's lap.

"I'm trying to see what it is," he grunted. The cars inched forward.

"Someone probably has a flat tire up there, and everyone has to slow down to look at it. *Roadside Entertainment*," Jamie remarked.

"If that ever happens to us, I'll set a coffee can out and sing while you're changing the tire. People can give us their spare change as they pass by." Tim chuckled.

"I think we should stop and get a room once we get on the other side of Memphis," he said. "It's about another six hours from there and I don't want to take a chance on falling asleep behind the wheel."

"Okay," she approved. "How long was I out?"

Tim checked his watch. "About three hours."

Inch by inch, the Toyota crept forward and Tim started laughing.

"What's so funny?"

He looked down at Buddy. "We're going so slow, I

think you could actually take Buddy out and walk beside the car while I'm driving."

Soon, there was no movement at all; traffic was at a complete standstill. They had been stationary for fifteen minutes when Tim decided to turn the engine off.

"I don't think it's a flat," he said. "Not unless they've set up a concession stand next to it."

He reached over and put his hand on her. "I've been trying to think of some names for the babies," he said, thoughtfully. "Have you been able to think of any?"

Jamie smiled. She was so happy that Tim had come around. She *knew* that he would be such a wonderful father. "*We-ll,* as a matter of fact, I was thinking of naming one of them Sarah, if they're girls, of course.

"When I was little my grandfather always called me Sarah. I don't know *why* he did, but he always said it to me so sweetly, that I was thinking it would be a nice name to give to one of my own," she grinned.

"That's a pretty name," Tim remarked. "I like it."

"What names were you thinking about?"

"I was thinking of naming one of them Moriah," he said.

"That's beautiful, Tim! Where did you come up with that one?"

"I read it in the Bible a long time ago and I always thought it would make a pretty name for someone."

"It really is, Sweetheart! What if they're boys?" Jamie asked.

"I can't make up my mind. I was thinking about either Vincent or Quentin," he said. "I love Vincent Van Gogh, because he's my favorite painter, but I like Quentin because the name sounds so dignified."

Traffic finally began to move.

"I was thinking about Colden," she said. "It's a family name." She took Buddy out of Tim's lap and he grunted.

"I like *that* one a lot. I've never known *anyone* with that name before. Is it Canadian?"

"I don't know, but I've always thought it had a certain flair to it."

"It *does* have a ring to it. So...it's Sarah and Moriah, or Quentin and Colden?"

"Sounds *perfect* to me," she answered.

Traffic started to speed up, and Tim and Jamie soon discovered the cause of the delay. A tractor trailer had taken an exit ramp too quickly and turned over—freight and debris were strewn across the highway.

"It's definitely *not* a flat tire," Jamie remarked, as if Tim couldn't see the wreckage for himself.

The driver was talking with police as they passed by; he took off his hat and scratched his head. An ambulance and a fire truck were blocking the entrance to the ramp, and there was an officer redirecting traffic around the two emergency vehicles.

"I guess that guy's having a bad day," Tim said, shaking his head.

Tim drove for another six hours and passed through Memphis. His mouth watered as he read the billboards advertising tours through Graceland, and he pointed them out to Jamie. "Maybe we should stop in and say *Howdy* to lil' Lisa?"

"Yeah," Jamie said. "Maybe we can ask her to fire

up the ole' jumbo jet so we can get there a little faster."

"Ad lak tuh have a couple uh heapin' helpin's uh poke-chops an grave-uh," Tim said. Jamie giggled.

"Could you just imagine living there?" Tim asked. "We could have Rusty and everybody over *all* the time! I would get Rusty a punch-bowl-sized ashtray with a ceramic elephant holding it up with his trunk. Buddy could chew his rawhide bones on the eighteen-foot sofa in the living room."

"I would *love* to swim in his pool," Jamie added.

"We could set the equipment up in the jungle room and play music all night long. I heard that's where he recorded *Moody Blue* before he died. I would get his waterfall fixed for him, though, and sing *Blue Hawaii* to you up there."

"What's wrong with his waterfall?" Jamie asked in curiosity.

"It floods. He tried to fix it several times over the years, but it never worked."

"Maybe he should have gotten a professional to fix it for him."

Tim burst with laughter. "No, I don't think I can envision the *King* with a monkey wrench in his hands, down on his knees, asking Charlie Hodge to hand him a couple of washers." He grinned, and gave her an impish look. "Do you want me to hire that nun to play a recital for you on his gold-leafed piano in the living room?"

"No way!" Jamie exclaimed. "I'd rather have Billy Joel come over and play. I heard him on the radio one night—just him and his piano—no band. He was so funny! I think he's one of the best musicians I've ever heard."

"I'll give you that," Tim agreed. "He sure knows how to write 'em.

"I'm going to fill up and find a motel room. I'm getting pretty tired and hungry." Tim took the next exit and pulled into a *Texaco* station. Jamie walked Buddy as Tim filled the gas tank.

He went in to pay and walked back out to the car. "Guy in there said that there's a motel a couple of miles up the road," he said, starting the car.

"Hey! There's a *Kentucky Fried Chicken*!" Jamie exclaimed; her mouth suddenly began watering. Buddy stood up and placed his paws on the dashboard and Tim's stomach growled as they passed by.

"Let's get the room first then go back," he proposed.

They came to a small motel a couple of blocks away from the restaurant. It was old and run down; the sign looked like an ancient marquis from some primeval drive-in movie theater. Several of the bulbs were burnt out; the lights blinked and flickered as they attempted to orbit the name.

Tim parked the car and went inside to register.

"The room's around back," he said, handing her the key.

"I'm exhausted," Jamie sighed. "I just want to eat, take a nice hot shower, and go to bed."

"It's been a long drive, alright," he added.

Tim unloaded a couple of suitcases from the trunk and put them beside the bed.

The room itself was very quaint. The establishment looked far worse from the outside, but the room was clean and air fresheners were plugged in. Jamie decided it was quite comfortable.

"I didn't tell them about Buddy," he confessed. "They would have charged me a pet deposit in addition to the room."

"Good thinking."

Tim waited for Jamie to unpack some of her toiletries then they took Buddy with them and drove to *Kentucky Fried Chicken.*

When they arrived back at the room, Tim poured some dog food into Buddy's dish, but ended up having to share his two-piece chicken dinner with mashed potatoes and gravy with him. "You're not going to be able to do this at Papa's house," he told Buddy, as he handed him a crispy piece of skin.

"Papa doesn't allow German puppies to beg at the supper table."

Jamie laughed. "You've got him spoiled rotten, Tim, he's liable to starve."

"That's one of Dad's pet-peeves," he said with a smile. "That and empty ice trays in the freezer."

He took a deep breath. "Jamie, I don't want to start a fight, but what do you think Rusty's going to say when I tell him you're expecting? He's spent so much time and money on this record. I just don't want to lose his friendship, that's all."

Jamie looked kindly at him. It was a valid question. "Tim, if he's any kind of friend at all, I think he'll understand. I think Rusty is a very kind man. I think *all* of those guys are decent people, but unexpected things happen in life. I would certainly never tell you what you 'can and can't' do, and I'll be right beside you whatever you decide about you're music, but keep in mind you're going to have two other people who will be depending on you to take care of them."

Tim nodded his head and gnawed the remaining meat from his chicken wing.

The next morning, Tim and Jamie ate from the continental breakfast bar after they had checked out of the room. Jamie snickered as she watched Tim's discontent over the small coffee cups on the counter. He made his slow 'air-leak' sigh as he picked it up and stared at it.

"It's not much bigger than one of those paper ketchup holders at *McDonald's*," he said, sarcastically. "I think I'll wait and stop off at that gas station to get a big cup. I have to call Mom and Dad anyway and let them know where we are."

Tim stopped at the station and called. "Hi Mom, we're just outside of Memphis. We should be there by one."

He paused. "Sure! She's fine, and she can't wait to meet you."

Jamie rolled her eyes, and he put his finger over his lips to quiet her. She crossed her arms and frowned.

"Okay, I love you too. We'll see you in a little while." He hung up the phone.

"Turn sideways for a minute," she said.

"What for?"

"I just want to see how long your nose grew for saying that to her."

"It's not going to be that bad, Jamie. We're going to

have to live there with them until I can get settled with this job."

Tim purchased a tall cup of coffee and Jamie drove while he drank it.

After a while, Tim broke the silence. "There's a river where we live and I was thinking about taking you and Buddy fishing this week."

"I'd like that!" Jamie said.

He took another sip of coffee and looked over at her. "You know, life got a lot better for me when Dad married Mom and he adopted me. Sure, he disciplined me—most of the time I deserved it. I believe that a child needs to be punished for doing wrong, but there's a big difference between spanking and beating.

"Dad always used his belt, Jamie, but he was always careful not to whip me with it anywhere except for my rear end, and that's okay by me.

"I love my dad because it takes a special kind of man not only to have the heart to raise someone else's child, but also to love that child enough to give him his last name. I know I painted a pretty irresponsible picture of my mom but deep down, I know that she loves me. She could have given me up for adoption, but she didn't.

"Just like the lyrics in my song, I think my mama did the very best she could, Jamie. She was just a child herself when she had me, and so was James. It was a reckless thing for them to do, but I came to terms with all of this years ago, and I forgave all of them.

"Jesus said, 'If the world hates you, remember that it hated me first.' Please...just give my mom a chance and you'll see that she's not a bad person," he pleaded.

Jamie pursed her lips and remained silent.

"And I'm going to tell you why I have such a problem about my looks," Tim continued. "When I was in high school I had severe acne. I would get boils on my face and it was very painful. That's why my face is so pitted now.

"I begged Mom and Dad to take me to the doctor but, frankly, they didn't have the money. Mom told me that it was a natural thing that I was going through, but I was the only kid in school that had it, and no one would have anything to do with me.

"Kids can be very cruel. Anyway, there was a girl in my Biology class that I had a crush on. Her name was Brooke Jenkins, and I thought she was so beautiful. She would talk to me once in a while and I could make her laugh. It was my senior year, and it took all the courage I could muster, but I finally managed to ask her to go to the prom with me. She told me *no.*"

"I should have just left it at that but I didn't. 'Why not?' I asked. She looked at me and bellowed, *'Because you are ugly as hell!'*

"I was so humiliated, Jamie. Everyone started laughing at me, calling me names and making fun of me. I never spoke to her again."

"Did you *go* to the prom?" she asked.

Tim shook his head and took another sip of coffee. "I stayed home and watched *Dallas* with Mom and Dad that night. Did you go to yours?" he asked.

"No, I didn't," Jamie replied. She smiled at him. "There wasn't anyone I wanted to go with and, believe it or not, I just wasn't interested in going so, I stayed home."

"You better let me take over the driving, Sweetheart, the traffic is getting heavy and it's always hectic in the city. I know my way around here fairly well," he said.

Jamie pulled off the interstate on the outskirts of Nashville and Tim took over. She occupied herself with the radio dial as Tim continued their journey.

With each passing mile, Tim grew more excited and eager. He drove slowly down the gravel road as they approached the house.

Around every tree in the front yard, his mother had tied a yellow ribbon. Ed and Vickie were sitting on the front porch of their enormous brick, ranch-style house just waiting for them. They waved as Tim pulled up and parked the car.

Tim could feel the tears forming, knowing he was home.

18

Tim's parents stepped off the porch and walked toward them; huge smiles were pasted on their faces. Tim quickly got out and gave them a hug, as Jamie hooked Buddy's leash on his collar and joined them.

"Mom, Dad...this is Jamie, isn't she beautiful?"

Jamie blushed at Tim's compliment, as Vickie gave her a hug and kissed her on the cheek.

"I'm so glad you're here, Jamie. I hope you'll make yourself at home." Vickie smiled at her and Jamie smiled back, trying to force the images of evil from her mind.

"This is my dad, Ed," Tim said. He was holding a glass of tea which he handed to Vickie, giving Jamie a warm hug.

Jamie noticed that Ed had very striking features. Even though his once-brown hair was now grey, and a few wrinkles were upon his face and brow, he was still a very handsome man.

"We were just relaxing," he said. "I was hoping to have the yard mowed before you got here, and I finally finished it about a half hour ago."

The yard was picturesque and peaceful. Sunlight shone through the tops of the tall trees; the landscape was well-shaded and cool, with the ambience of a state park.

Jamie marveled over the mountains that were the backdrop behind the house. The entire landscape took her breath away. She felt almost as if she had been placed in some forgotten *Monet* oil painting that the master had overlooked. "It's beautiful," she said, breathing in the wonderful aroma of freshly-mowed grass.

"There are six acres in the front, but we have a total of forty-six acres all together," Ed said. He looked down at Buddy as Vickie handed back his glass of tea.

"And who might this be?" he asked, bending down to pet the anxious Dachshund.

"This is Buddy," Tim explained proudly.

"Buddy, Sprechen Sie Deutsch!" Buddy barked his greetings to them, and Ed and Vickie both chortled gleefully.

"He can do all kinds of neat things," Tim said excitedly. "But he mostly likes to eat Mexican food." Everyone laughed.

"It's true," Jamie confessed. "Tim has him so spoiled! But don't worry, we'll put him somewhere at mealtimes. Tim already told him that he wasn't allowed to eat at the dinner table," she added, playfully.

Ed chuckled. "I was thinking about grilling some chicken for supper."

Vickie bent down and picked Buddy up to hold him. He gave her a hug and buried his chin in the cleft of her neck. She loved his almond eyes.

"That sounds delicious," Jamie said politely, not mentioning that they had chicken the night before.

"If he starts rubbing his face all over you that means he wants you to kiss his neck, Mom. I didn't teach him that by the way, he just *does* it," Tim said.

"He seems to have a very sweet personality," Vickie laughed, rocking him back and forth.

"Yeah, he loves *everybody*." Tim watched his

mother with Buddy. "He's my best friend. I'm going to bring the luggage in," he said, looking at Jamie.

Ed walked through the yard and went around the back of the house to get the grill.

"Thanks for putting the ribbons out, Mom. That was really nice."

Vickie hugged him tightly. "We've missed you so much, Son. We wanted it to be a *special* welcome home for you. You and Jamie can sleep in our room while you're here," she said.

"Thanks, Mom." Tim kissed her on the cheek.

He hauled in two of the suitcases and Jamie followed him in with his guitar.

Jamie looked around as they entered the living room. It was spacious and warm. Two black leather sofas faced each other with a beautiful coffee table set in between. A large, white ceramic dove sat on a crocheted doily in the middle of the glass top.

Oak end tables had been placed at either side of the sofas with lamps on each one. And a big television sat in an oak cabinet right next to the fireplace—and there were stacks of videos galore.

The kitchen was behind the living area at the rear of the room. The floor was covered with honey-colored linoleum, and sunlight gleamed through the large windows. The cabinets were crafted of solid oak, the same light shade as the living room paneling, and Jamie thought it was very pleasing to the eye—comfortable and inviting.

There was a small stereo system by the back door of the kitchen with several neatly stacked LPs. A turntable was on top, a cassette deck was underneath, and a radio rounded out the system.

Jamie could smell the tantalizing aroma wafting through the house. "That coffee smells good, Vickie. Could I have a cup when we get our luggage in?"

"Sure! I figured you'd be worn out from the trip and I didn't want Tim going to sleep as soon as he got here," Vickie laughed.

"I hope you have lots of sugar," Jamie commented.

She and Vickie offered each other a knowing smile, as Jamie told her about Tim's episode with his spilled coffee as they were leaving the apartment.

"He's always been so animated," Vickie remarked, as she led them to their room.

"Is it okay if I take the leash off Buddy?" she asked.

"Sure, he'll be fine."

Jamie unhooked his leash. Buddy ran in front of the women–as if policing the area–and jumped on top of the bed.

"You can put your bags in here," she said, smiling at Jamie.

The bedroom was very snug and pleasant. Jamie looked around as she placed the guitar case down.

There was a picture of Ed and Vickie on the dresser that had been taken many years ago when they were much younger. Ed had his arm around her and they both had a twinkle in their eyes. *They looked happy together,* Jamie thought to herself.

There was a picture hanging over the bed of a white swan in the middle of a lake. It was set against snow-capped mountains and a crystal clear blue sky. To

Jamie, the scene was breathtaking.

On the opposite wall, there was a portrait of Vickie when she was very young—perhaps seventeen or eighteen years old. Her hair was so blonde that it almost looked as if it were yellow, and she had a sweet smile on her face. *She was once very pretty*, Jamie thought.

The carpet was beige and plush, and there was a white oscillating room fan in the corner. Just looking at that fan brought Tim's story to the forefront of her mind.

After Tim had neatly placed the luggage on the opposite side of the bed, Vickie proceeded to show Jamie the rest of the house. "Dad's going to put a divider along the hallway, *here*," she said, pointing at the wall midway down the hall.

"Basically, we're going to turn the other half of the house into an efficiency apartment so you can have your own privacy."

"That's really nice of you," Jamie said, smiling at her.

"It's going to be so nice to have you here with us. I told Ed that we needed to get ready to laugh a lot because Tim has such a good sense of humor.

"We've had a little bit of the 'empty nest' syndrome since Sam's moved away. He lives in an apartment in Columbia now."

They walked down the hallway and went into a bedroom on the left. "Tim, Dad's changed out the plug outlet here on the wall. We were thinking that you could use this room as a kitchen, and your stove can go here. There's another outlet over there for a small refrigerator."

Vickie walked to the opposite side of the bedroom

and stood beside a window. "We're going to tear out this window, too, and put a door in. We'll put a small porch outside, and that way you can come and go as you please.

"I've been thinking of doing this for some time now, because if there's ever a fire we'll have another exit."

Jamie hugged her. "Thank you so much for all of this, Vickie. Tim and I will try not to be a burden to you. I know it's difficult for two families to live together."

Vickie waved her hand in the air. "You won't be a burden at all."

"This will give us a chance to save some money and buy a place of our own."

"And once I start working, I'll pay half of the utilities," Tim added.

They went into the kitchen and poured themselves some coffee. Vickie lit a cigarette.

"I was thinking that Sam could take me on Tuesday to fill out my application," Tim said, starting the conversation.

"I think he's coming out here tonight to have supper with us and meet Jamie," Vickie said. "We hardly see him anymore since he's moved away. He works a lot of long hours and I think he has a girlfriend now."

Tim sipped his coffee and added another spoonful of sugar.

Ed came in and refilled his glass of tea. "So, what's it like living in Texas?" he asked.

"I love it," Tim said. "I really hate to leave, but I don't have much of a choice since they're closing down the Base."

Ed opened the refrigerator and withdrew two packs

of chicken, and began washing the meat.

"Tim's in a band down there and he's been doing really well!" Jamie raved.

"Really?" Ed asked, enthusiastically. "What kind of music do you play?"

"A little bit of everything, but mostly old country. The guys in the band are some of the best friends anyone could ever have, and they're fantastic musicians," Tim said.

"They just made a record, too," Jamie stated. "By the way, Tim, I heard it on the radio when we were leaving Lubbock."

Tim gasped. "You did!? Why didn't you tell me? You know I would have wanted to hear it!"

"You were sleeping and I wanted to enjoy it by myself," she said, matter-of-factly.

"I brought you one of my records, Mom. Maybe we can listen to it when Dad puts the chicken on the grill? I wrote both songs on it," Tim said, proudly.

"I would love to hear it, Son."

Jamie told them about all that had happened in Lubbock—Crystal's benefit, the retirement homes, and about playing music with Tinker.

Ed listened intently as he stacked the raw chicken on a large, metal pizza tray. Tim got up from the table to help him, as Jamie continued to boast about her true love's talent.

He took the barbecue sauce from the refrigerator, found the grilling fork and basting brush in the kitchen drawers, and went outside with Ed to help him load the meat on the grill.

Jamie was still talking when they came back in.

"So let's hear this record of yours!" Ed said. Tim brought it from the bedroom and placed it into Vickie's hands.

She looked at it and turned it over. She was overwhelmed to see her son's name underneath the song titles.

Tim walked over to the record player and turned it on. Everyone made their way over as he placed the needle to begin.

Everyone was silent as the haunting lyrics of *The Vagabond* echoed through the kitchen. Vickie shivered as she listened to her son's voice coming through the speakers. Ed was speechless. He put his arm around Tim's shoulder the way Rusty always did, and wore a look of sheer pride.

Vickie looked positively awestruck. After the song was over and the needle arm had picked itself up, she stared at the record. A tear slipped from her eye as she hugged her son. "It's so beautiful, Tim," she said.

Ed was choked up as well. "It's very good. I like it," he said, "I like it a *lot*."

Tim played *Because of You* for them and explained how he came to write it for Rusty.

"I'm really impressed, Tim," Vickie commented. "It sounds like you've been keeping yourself really busy down there. You're a very talented songwriter." She hugged him.

Tim looked down. "I've had a lot of fun. I've really *found* myself there, and I wish it didn't have to end." Turning around, Tim slipped the record back into its sleeve, and gave it to his mother.

"What do you say we all sit on the porch and enjoy the rest of the day?" Ed proposed.

Everyone went outside. Jamie and Tim sat on the porch swing, as Vickie settled herself in the rocking chair.

Ed lifted the lid of the grill and stood back as smoke and steam poured out. The meat sizzled as he turned each piece over and placed it on the hot aluminum foil. He took a sip of tea, closed the lid, and took a seat in a rocker beside Vickie.

The cool summer breeze whistled gently across the porch. The leaves of the trees rustled softly, as the smell of fresh-cut grass mixed with mouthwatering barbeque filled the air.

Jamie was fighting to stay awake. The peacefulness of the surrounding nature was starting to act as a tranquilizer. She looked down at the marigolds in the flower beds by the porch as she rocked in the swing. Orange and yellow blossoms with hints of black, swayed gently in the breeze. Hummingbirds darted to and fro as they drank from the feeders hanging above them. Her eyelids grew heavy. Tim nudged her with his elbow.

"I'm so sorry," Jamie said, drowsily. "It's so peaceful and calm out here that I feel like I've taken a sleeping pill."

"That's why *we* love it here," Ed chuckled. "The world just seems to stand still."

Buddy scratched at the storm door, wanting to be a part of the family reunion. Tim picked him up and set him in his lap as he sat back down next to Jamie.

"I forgot about you!" he said, scratching behind Buddy's ears.

"I think he can smell the chicken cooking," Vickie commented.

Tim looked over at Jamie. She was starting to doze off again. He took a deep breath and dove right in. "Mom, Jamie's pregnant."

Vickie and Ed looked at each other and then back at Tim.

Jamie's eyes snapped open—sleep was now the furthest thing from her mind.

"With *twins* I might add."

Ed smiled and looked at Vickie. She continued to rock in her chair. Her face was a myriad of emotions, as if she was reliving the unfortunate circumstances that had happened to her, and Tim after he was born. *Thank goodness it's not going to be like that with his children*, she thought, feeling the ultimate relief.

"Well, Tim...I'm happy for you both," she said, softly. She looked at Ed.

"It looks like we're going to be grandparents," Ed said kindly, smiling at Jamie.

"I know this is a lot to drop on you all at once," Tim said, "but *we* just found out a couple of days ago ourselves. I'm happy about it, Mom. I wish the timing could have been better, but it *is* what it is."

"I know," she said. "You're a grown man and you're married. It's part of life.

"Dad and I will do what we can, but you know that you're going to have to start working as soon as you get home permanently, right?"

Tim listened to her. "Yes, ma'am, I do."

"Your whole world is about to change," she said.

She included Jamie as she spoke. It's not the worst thing that could ever happen–the *timing,* I mean. But it's going to be a big responsibility for the both of you, especially with *two*."

"It'll all work out," Ed intervened. "Honey, they're grown and married. Once Tim gets through this transition, everything will be alright."

"Thank you," Jamie said, looking at them both.

"For what?" Vickie asked.

"For not being angry with us about this, or making us feel like we did something wrong," she said.

Vickie sat up in her rocker and smiled. "There's nothing wrong about having children, Sweetheart. Unfortunately, we live in a world where the almighty dollar makes starting a family seem like a burden, but you have a man that loves you very much, and I know he's going to be a good father and provider to those children."

She sat back and waited, as if she were choosing just the right words. "I've made a lot of bad choices and decisions in my life, Jamie. Some I can never make up for...but I'm *not* sorry for having Tim. He's the best thing that ever happened to me. Besides," she grinned, "when *is* the timing *ever* right?

Jamie looked at her for a long time. For the first time since Tim had told her about his childhood, she began to feel a small amount of respect for her.

A red 1986 mustang came out of nowhere and pulled into the driveway—it was Sam. He revved the engine a couple of times and gunned it, gravel and dust shot everywhere as he accelerated to sixty miles per hour and then slammed on the brakes.

The car fishtailed as it skidded to a stop about four inches from Tim's bumper. Everyone on the porch jumped up and gasped.

Sam killed the engine and got out of his car. He started laughing when he saw all the gaping mouths and wide, panic-filled eyes staring at him after the dust had settled.

"Sam!" Vickie shouted. "What in the *hell* do you think you're doing!"

Sam bent over with laughter. "I brought some fireworks!" he said, still laughing.

Jamie noticed how truly alike Sam and Ed looked. Sam had Ed's features; he was over six-feet tall, well-built, and had a thick head of dark, brown hair. It was so thick that Jamie thought there must have been four strands to every follicle in his head. Sam was handsome–and he knew it.

Tim was still standing speechless, with his hand over his heart and his mouth wide open. Sam walked up and gave him a hug.

"I...I thought I was going to have a heart attack just now," Tim whispered. His throat had gone dry and his skin had turned pale. "That's the only car we *have*, Sam."

Sam looked at Jamie. She, too, was staring wide-eyed at him. "I'm Sam," he said, arms extended. His laugh sounded as if it were full of a pit-viper's venom.

Ed walked over to the grill, smiling at the stunt his son had just pulled, and opened the lid. "You've got good timing, Sam, the meat's almost done."

"Good! I'm starving!" he said. "I've been washing and waxing my car all day..."

"Jamie, do you want to help me make some potato salad?" Vickie asked.

She broke her concentration from Sam. She just didn't know what to think of him. "Sure," she said, indecisively. She and Vickie went inside the house.

"So when are you gonna be home for good?" Sam asked.

"In about six weeks," Tim answered.

"It's good to see you again! I've grown a lot since you last saw me," Sam pointed out. "It's gonna be harder for you to beat me up now."

Tim smiled. It was true. Sam had grown almost a foot taller than Tim in the last few years and had put on quite a bit of muscle.

"You're gonna like working at CPS," Sam said. "It can be a little stressful, but the money is good and you get incentive pay, too. For every ten percent over production, you get an extra hour of pay!

"Petie's really looking forward to meeting you, too. I told him that you used to work in the warehouse before you went into the Air Force. I guess he talked to some of the people who worked with you and they said you were a really good worker. When do you want to go and fill out your application?"

"I was thinking Tuesday," Tim replied. "This is really the first vacation I've had since I've been in the Air Force, and I wanted to spend some time with Mom and Dad tomorrow, and take Jamie and Buddy fishing on Monday."

"Who's Buddy?" Sam asked.

Tim turned around and pointed at Buddy who was

sitting on the porch swing with his ears cocked, staring at him in confusion.

"He's a Dachshund," Tim said.

Sam reached down to pet him. "Okay, I'll pick you up Tuesday morning around eight and take you up there."

Ed loaded the cooked chicken onto the metal pizza tray and took it into the house. Buddy jumped off the porch swing and followed him in—ever hopeful that a piece might topple off and fall to its demise.

"Come and check out my stereo system, Tim. I've got this huge bass subwoofer in it!"

Tim went with Sam out to the Mustang. Once they were in the car, Sam put in a cassette tape of a group called *P.M. Dawn* and turned the volume up.

Tim quickly covered his ears as the loud music began to beat his brain like a hammer. The windows began to shake from the thundering bass subwoofer. He looked up and saw two hot wheels cars dangling from the rearview mirror—they were bouncing frantically as the music and bass raged on. Sam had tied them together at the bumpers with a shoelace. He looked again and noticed that the rearview mirror was vibrating as well.

"PRETTY COOL! HUH?" Sam screamed.

"WHAT?" Tim shouted, still covering his ears. Sam turned the music down and started laughing at Tim.

"Watch this," he said, snickering. Sam started up the Mustang and backed it into the yard next to the front porch and storm door. Then he got out and opened up the trunk. Tim sat in the seat and watched him, wondering what he was going to do.

He got back into the car, opened up his cassette

case and picked out a *rap* tape. He put it into the player and cranked the volume up. Tim had to cover his ears again. Sam sang along with the song, bobbing his head and making 'gangland' signs with his hands as the music played.

Inside the house, Vickie and Jamie were talking as they prepared the potato salad. Suddenly, every piece of glass imaginable in the house was either vibrating or shaking.

"Hold on just a minute, Jamie...***Ed!*** Go out there and tell him to turn that mess off! We're trying to talk!"

Ed just sat on the couch with Buddy curled up in his lap and grinned. He was watching the John Wayne movie that Jamie had spotted earlier.

Jamie watched Vickie storm out the front door. ***"SAM! TURN THAT MUSIC DOWN!"***

Sam leaned his head out the window. ***"WHAT?"*** Tim was snickering because, when they were young, Vickie would slap them in the mouth for saying *what* instead of *Ma'am* when she addressed them.

"I SAID, TURN THAT MUSIC DOWN! WE CAN'T HEAR!" she screamed.

"I CAN'T HEAR YOU!" Sam shouted. ***"THE MUSIC'S TOO LOUD!"*** Tim started belly-laughing.

Vickie slammed the front door, stomped into the kitchen, opened a drawer, and took out an egg turner. She stormed outside and down the steps.

Sam turned the music down as she reached the bottom step. "I turned it down! I turned it down!" he said, chuckling.

Vickie didn't think it was funny. Sam got out of the

car and towered over her, yet she proceeded to whip the tar out of him with the egg turner all over the front yard.

Tim bent over laughing as Sam flopped and jerked every time she hit him with it. Jamie couldn't help but giggle as she watched the spectacle through the storm door. Even Buddy enjoyed watching it. He stood up next to Jamie, placed his paws against the door and peered out the glass.

Vickie was worn out. Her chest was heaving violently as she stood there glaring at him. "I am *trying* to have a conversation in there! Get that car out of my yard...*right now!*" she said, gritting her teeth.

Tim was gurgling with laughter, trying to hold it in. Sam fought hard not to crack a smile, knowing that Vickie would lay into him again.

She turned towards the house and proceeded to walk back up the porch steps.

Tim burst into laughter. "Sam, you looked like this." He jerked, flopped, and flailed his arms, imitating his brother.

Sam waited until she went back inside—he grinned viciously and said, "It didn't hurt, I had everything flexed."

It was dark by the time dinner was ready. Everyone ate, laughed, and reminisced about funny childhood memories. It was a wonderful evening. Tim let Sam listen to his record and told him about Rusty, Marty, Acie and Spider.

Everyone laughed at all of the funny pictures that Tim had taken of Buddy. Vickie liked the one of Buddy with the shaving cream on his face holding the razor in his paw.

Sam was feeling very jovial and mischievous, even deciding to act like he was going to hit Tim, but Buddy started growling. Everyone sat in silence and watched.

Sam glared at him fiendishly—teasing and taunting him. He playfully hit Tim, and Buddy lurched off the porch swing and bit him in the crotch.

Everyone doubled over with laughter. Jamie was laughing so hard, tears streamed from her eyes.

Buddy jumped back on the porch swing and nested in Tim's lap.

Sam wasn't laughing anymore. "Dang, he's got some sharp teeth!" he exclaimed. He slowly walked over to Tim's dog, let him smell his hand, and then pet him on the head. Buddy decided to forgive him.

"I brought some fireworks over to welcome you home," Sam said. "You wanna help me get them out of the car?"

"Sure," Tim replied.

It was a truly beautiful display, as midnight rainbows pulsated in the evening sky. Sam had spent a lot of money on his exhibition for Tim, and even though he was a bit reckless, Jamie couldn't help but like him because he was such a big kid at heart.

When all of the fireworks were spent, and the evening started to wind down, the crickets began chirping again and bullfrogs croaked endlessly in the darkness. Jamie yawned, her drowsiness returning.

"Are you staying here tonight?" Tim asked.

"No, I've got to get back home. My girlfriend, Maria, is coming over tonight. She rented a couple of movies and wants to spend some time together."

"It's kind of late, isn't it?" Tim asked.

"I work second shift so, I'm a night owl. I usually don't go to bed before 5:00 A.M.," he said.

Jamie stretched her arms. "I'm about ready to go to bed," she yawned, fighting to stay awake.

"Me too," Tim added. "It's been a long trip."

Everyone stood and gave Sam a hug before he left. Jamie changed into her pajamas and brushed her teeth as Tim walked Buddy one last time. He put him on the bed with Jamie and Buddy snuggled up beside her. She was already sound asleep.

After Tim had brushed his teeth, he went into the bedroom and turned the fan on, then crawled into bed. Buddy changed places and curled up in his arms; soon, they were all together in their dreams.

19

Buddy was the first one awake the next morning, rubbing his neck all over Tim's face until he finally stirred.

He looked at his watch through hazy eyes. It was 6:40 A.M. Buddy did the *Dance of the Deer* as Tim sat on the edge of the bed, trying to collect his thoughts. He looked over at Jamie who was still out like a light.

Buddy started barking—jolting Tim from semi-consciousness, and he *shushed* him as he stumbled around the room searching for his pants.

"Hush! You're gonna wake up Nana and Papa!" he hissed. He attached the leash and quietly went outside.

Tim breathed the fresh morning air. It was warm and clean, and the smell of fresh-cut grass filled his nostrils once more as Buddy led him around.

He made a pot of coffee when he returned to the house. Buddy ran back in the bedroom, jumped on the bed and woke Jamie up.

She stroked his fur with her eyes closed, but he wanted more attention. Nudging her arm with his cold, wet nose, he tugged at it with his paw.

She sat up in the bed and tickled him as Tim entered.

"Good morning," he whispered. "How did you sleep?"

"Like a rock!" she whispered back. "I really love it here!"

He kissed her. "I'm so glad, Sweetheart."

"I kept thinking that your dad looks like someone I've seen before, but I couldn't put my finger on it," she said. "It came to me last night before I fell asleep. He looks like Chuck Connors!"

Tim chuckled. "I know, I used to think he was *The Rifleman* when he and Mom first started dating. He actually had to have surgery on his face when he was a kid because he was sledding in the snow one day and ran through a barbed-wire fence."

Jamie grimaced. "I like that picture of your mom, too," she said, raising her voice up slightly from a whisper.

Tim sighed and took it from the wall. He rubbed the frame with his thumb as he stared at it. "This was always my favorite picture of her," he said. "I always thought she looked like Marilyn Monroe in this picture—she was so beautiful."

Jamie peered over his shoulder and her gaze joined her husband's on the striking portrait. She kissed him on the cheek; her mind racing away from the picture and back through the stories that Tim had told her of his troubled youth. Despite all that had happened in the past, Tim truly had unconditional love for his mother.

The coffee pot gurgled in the kitchen as the rich aroma wafted through the house.

"Do you want to have a cup of coffee with me?" Tim asked.

"Sure!" she whispered loudly. "Let's sit out on the porch and drink it; I love it out there!"

Tim made them both a cup of coffee and joined her on the swing.

"I think I'm really going to enjoy living here," Jamie

said. She took a sip of coffee and gazed amorously at Tim.

Not ever wanting to be left out, Buddy scratched at the door. Tim reached over and opened it as Buddy darted out, jumped on the porch swing, and sat in between his loving parents.

"I forgot about you...*again!*" Tim said, tussling his head.

Jamie breathed the air in deeply, as far as her lungs would allow. It was refreshing. She exhaled slowly, closed her eyes, and listened to the birds singing in the park-like yard around them.

She watched as a squirrel scurried up a tree. He stopped, shook his tail, and scampered up a little farther, finally disappearing into a hole.

"I truly didn't know what to expect when we were driving up here, but this place fills me with so much peace and tranquility, Tim. I honestly feel that I belong here...I feel like I *need* to be here.

"I love Lubbock, it's always been my home, but there's just something about the hills and the mountains. I fell in love with them *instantly* and I can't explain why."

Tim hung on her every word. He rocked slowly as they glided on the homey swing and relished their morning together. "I figured you'd like it here," he said. "Maybe we could go fishing today instead of tomorrow?"

"I'd like that," she said, laying her head gently on his shoulder.

Buddy raised his head up and cocked his ears. Tim could hear his parents talking in the kitchen.

"Let's go in," Jamie suggested.

"Did y'all sleep well?" Vickie asked, as they

appeared through the door.

Jamie nodded. "I slept *very* well, it's very comfortable here," she added.

Ed and Vickie poured themselves a cup of coffee and sat at the table. Vickie lit a cigarette; Tim pulled one out of his shirt pocket and smoked with her.

"When did you start smoking?" Vickie asked.

"I don't really smoke very often," he said. "Rusty smokes a *lot* and sometimes I smoke a couple with him to take the edge off before I sing."

Vickie laughed. "Be careful, they're addictive. Before you know it you'll be making up more and more excuses why you *have* to have one."

"Jamie loves it here," Tim said, changing the subject. "I was thinking about taking her fishing today."

Vickie smiled. "I'm so glad you came, Jamie. It's going to be so nice to have someone to talk to."

"This place has really stolen my heart. I've never seen anything quite like it," Jamie said, almost mesmerized.

"Well," Ed began, "We've got all this land, we were thinking you and Tim could build your home on some of the property in the back, once you have the babies, and save a little. It might take a couple of years, but it would be nice to have you and the grandchildren close to us.

"Sam can build out here if he wants, but he's young and I think he's more interested in having fun right now."

Jamie looked at Tim and smiled. He knew that look and he loved it. Her eyes twinkled and her face glowed whenever she was excited about something. She clasped her hands together, almost as if she were praying. *She is so elegant and lovely,* he thought.

Tim smiled at her. “I think that would be fantastic, Dad, thank you.”

They talked for a while longer, then Vickie made scrambled eggs and biscuits for one and all.

Jamie wrinkled up her nose as she watched Ed drown his eggs in ketchup and stir it all together. “Ick! How can you eat them like that?”

“Watch out or I’ll throw some syrup in there, too.” He threw her a quick glance, and a huge smile.

Jamie said no more. She was afraid that her morning sickness would return, and she would offend Vickie by having to leave the table.

Buddy begged Tim in his kindest German accent for some of his eggs. Ed stopped eating and looked at Tim.

“I’m sorry, Dad.” He quietly picked Buddy up and put him in the bathroom.

“He can have any of the leftovers, but I don’t like him begging at the table,” Ed said sternly.

“Yes, sir,” Tim answered, letting embarrassment show through. Jamie didn’t say anything. She just looked down at her plate and kept eating.

Screams and tortured howls erupted from what seemed to be the deepest, darkest dungeon in all of Transylvania, as breakfast continued. Buddy’s heart was broken, because this was the very first time that he and Tim had not shared a meal together.

“Goodness gracious!” Vickie exclaimed.

Ed snickered and shook his head as the tormented soul continued to wail. “If his voice starts getting deeper, I might have to break out the silver bullets," he remarked, with a laugh.

Coffee almost sprayed from Jamie's nose as she pictured the thought of Buddy turning into a vicious, snarling, bloodthirsty werewolf, with saliva dripping from his razor-sharp fangs as he growled in German, and scraping his nine-inch talons into the oak paneling as he stomped down the hallway in search of Transylvania's best scrambled eggs.

Tim laughed too, although his heart felt like it had been ripped in half.

Ed looked over at Tim. "You know, we can build him a pen out back. That way he doesn't have to stay cooped up somewhere while we're eating, and you won't have to constantly walk him.

"I mean, you can keep him inside all you want, he's a good little fella, but it will be good for him to be outdoors on his own sometimes. It'll give you a break—so to speak."

"That's a really good idea." Jamie added. "There's so much space out there; he would love it, Tim."

Tim sighed. "You're right, Dad. I never thought about that. It does get kind of miserable when it's raining; I could make him a dog house, too."

"Sure you could! He'll be just fine, and you won't have any accidents to clean up when you get back from the store, or if you have to go places for long periods of time," Ed added.

After breakfast they all had more coffee and talked a while longer. Vickie and Tim smoked while Ed scraped the remaining leftovers into Buddy's dish.

Tim released Buddy from his temporary

incarceration, but as his best friend looked up at him with eyes that belonged behind the fences of Auschwitz, Tim's heart broke. He gently picked him up and Buddy placed his chin in the cleft of Tim's neck. He was trembling as if he had been left out in the harsh, bitter winter winds that were yet to come.

"I'm so sorry, boy," he whispered to him, rocking him from side to side. Buddy whimpered softly in his arms. Again, he found himself in a strange new world in which Tim's arms seemed to be his only refuge. He kissed him behind his ears and carried him back down the hallway.

All was forgiven when Tim walked him over to his food dish. Buddy's eyes lit up when he saw the bounty of eggs and crumbled biscuits in his bowl.

"You'd think he hadn't eaten in a week!" Vickie remarked, as Buddy scarfed his food down as fast as he could, then drank from his water bowl to wash it all down.

Ed laughed as he jumped up in Tim's lap and wiped his mouth back and forth on his shirt. Drops of ketchup stuck to his whiskers, making it look as if he'd just hunted a huge deer and had dinner in the wild forest. He nested afterwards and proceeded to lick his front paws.

"He certainly has a very unique personality," Ed commented.

Buddy raised his head and cocked his ears as if he understood that he was being addressed. He studied the stranger momentarily then went back to licking his paws, keeping his focus on the job at hand.

"Like I said, Tim has him so spoiled—it's as if they were Siamese twins, or something," Jamie added.

Ed shook his head in unbelief and smiled. "So, you're going fishing, huh?"

Tim looked up. "Yes, sir, it's a nice day and I figured we could go today instead of waiting. Maybe we'll catch a bunch of *shell crackers.*"

Vickie crushed out her cigarette and got up from the table to do the dishes.

"All the poles are out back in the shed. I believe your tackle box is on one of the shelves, too," Ed told him.

"I can help you with the dishes, Vickie." Jamie offered, heading for the sink.

"That's okay, hon, there's not that many. Why don't you go and change? Spend some time with your husband," Vickie said, smiling sweetly at her.

"Honey, I'll go put all the stuff in the car while you're doing that," Tim said, following close at her heels.

"Well, if you're sure," she said politely, not quite knowing what the correct etiquette should be.

"Go ahead, Sweetie, there'll be plenty of dishes to do when Tim comes home for *good,*" Vickie laughed.

The remark his mother had just made hit him like a ton of bricks. Tim played it over and over in his mind, as if she had yelled it into the Grand Canyon.

"Comes home for good... for good... for good..." His heart shrank—he suddenly felt like he was somehow being tugged in two separate directions. On one hand, he felt like he was betraying Rusty—he was like a father *and* a brother to him all in one. And on the other hand, he was soon going to be the father of two children. 'For good' meant forever. The chances of being in two places at one time, or very *often*, were getting slim. Was Jamie right?

Would Rusty be the kind of friend who would understand that unexpected things happen in life? Or, would he be angry and devastated because he felt that he had wasted his time and money on him?

Tim supposed that deep down, Rusty knew that this was his final chance of achieving greatness—making his mark, and leaving behind his *own* legacy for generations to come.

Rusty had played music his whole life waiting for Tim to arrive it seemed, and Tim felt as if he were about to jerk the rug right out from under him, and make him feel as if his life and friendship meant nothing to him. He felt like he was about to abandon him, and ruin his final shot to receive triumph and achievement in the music realm.

He genuinely felt in his heart that, if given the chance, he, Rusty, Acie, Marty and Spider could be at the top of the charts one day. But time was against them all. If they had only met a few years earlier, everyone's aspirations and dreams would have come true. He was confident of *that.* Tim was wearily dreading the day that was soon to come, and he sighed deeply.

in the far corner of the shed. He cringed and ducked once as his imagination ran amuck—he thought a wasp had flown over his head, but it was only the hot summer breeze blowing through the front door.

Ed's worn, brown leather recliner was sitting in front of his work bench. Over the years it had become his *Man-cave,* a place to get away from it all and tinker with things that could never be fixed. In reality, it was a place to drink a few beers and listen to the Grand Ole' Opry on Saturday nights.

Tim squirmed his way around the chair and found a small path through the junk that was stacked everywhere. He picked out two good rods and reels and made his way to the metal shelves to search for his tackle box.

He shook his head at all the mayonnaise jars that were filled with various screws, nails, hinges and tacks. He had come to the conclusion that it was part of a man's existence to hoard tons of useless hardware that would never be used—even Rusty had a vast collection.

Tim could never understand it. After all, it took far less time to go to *Lowe's* than it did to search through fifteen jars full of worthless scraps to find a certain type of self-drilling screw.

The tackle box was on the third shelf, just out of reach. He stepped forward and tripped over an old mini-bike frame. Ed was supposed to 'fix-it-up' and give it to Tim and Sam to ride years ago, but it had been placed on an imaginary *to-do* list.

Tim stepped up onto the frame and reached for his tackle box. Once he had removed it, he looked around cautiously for the killer wasps. He wished at this very moment that he was wearing a bee-keeper's suit and carrying a smoke can.

He made his way back through the labyrinth of junk, and ran out of the shed. Slamming the door behind him, Tim shuddered. He wiped the sweat from his face with his ketchup-stained T-shirt that Buddy had painted for him earlier, and opened the car door. A wave of heat burst forth as if he were standing in front of someone testing out a flamethrower. Rolling the window down, Tim loaded the rods and reels into the car and headed back to the house.

Jamie tied her hair back with a white bow and changed into a pair of denim shorts. Pulling on her flip-flops, she sprayed a hint of *Ciara* on her neck, and then turned from side to side to make sure her hair was even. She examined herself once more in the mirror, and puffed her lips out.

Buddy sat on the bed and watched her. When she saw him looking at her through the mirror, she spun around quickly and sprayed a dash of perfume on him. He wagged his tail and started scratching his collar so he could hear it jingle.

Tim was waiting for her in the kitchen. "If we catch some, will you fry 'em up like you used to?"

"I will if you clean 'em," Vickie said, and she turned to Jamie. "One time Tim caught about ten fish when we lived in Florida. He cleaned them and brought them into the kitchen, and I cooked them up for supper that night. The next day I went out on the back patio and millions of flies were swarming around this bucket full of fish guts! It smelled so horrible that I thought I was going to pass out!"

Tim blushed, and looked at Jamie. "I was so excited about eating the fish that I forgot to take the bucket out and dump it." He snickered. "Hey, Dad, when are you gonna fix that old mini-bike out there?"

"I'll get to it one of these days," he answered, shyly lowering his head.

"I'm ready to go whenever you are," Jamie said, excitedly.

"I'm ready. Will you please get the camera, Jamie? I want to take pictures of Buddy fishing," Tim said, as if Buddy were a world renowned fisherman headed out to win his just reward.

Ed and Vickie started laughing. "How in the world is he going to fish, Son? His arms are too short!" Ed snorted.

"I'm going to teach him," Tim said, with a mischievous snicker.

"That should be interesting to see," Vickie chuckled. "Absolutely, take the camera. This I've got to see!"

Tim rattled his keys as Jamie went into the bedroom and dug the camera out of one of the suitcases. Buddy did the *Dance of the Deer* and started *sprechening*, as Tim bent down and picked him up.

"Ouch!" Jamie yelped, jumping up and down as her bare thighs came into contact with the overheated passenger seat. It looked to Tim like she was pedaling a bicycle. Even Buddy was scampering around, trying to avoid the hot leather underneath his feet.

"I smell meat cooking!" Tim said. "Maybe I should

rub some barbecue sauce on your legs with the basting brush!"

"Hush, Tim! It really burns," she winced.

"I know, I can hear the skin sizzling from here!" Once again, he burst with laughter as he backed down the driveway.

"Buddy's legs are going to start flopping around like frog legs in a frying pan if it doesn't cool off soon," Jamie said, setting him in her lap.

It was a picture-perfect day for fishing. Tim stopped at the gas station/bait store and bought a cup of Canadian night crawlers.

The sun was beaming radiantly, and Buddy stuck his head out the window as Tim drove. His ears flopped about aimlessly and smacked him in the face repeatedly—it reminded Tim of the sound of a playing card shuffling against the spokes of a bicycle tire.

His jowls ruffled and beat against his gums as the wind blew into his face. Tim chuckled because he looked as if he were pantomiming the song *You Shook Me,* by *AC DC* which was currently playing on the radio.

Tim swerved to miss a dead possum on the road. "There's two dollars!" He shouted, pointing at the spot of grey fur as they zoomed ahead. It took the rank odor only a few brief seconds to penetrate their nostrils.

"What in the world are you *talking* about?" Jamie asked him, holding her nose and glaring at him as if he were crazy.

"The neighbors used to pay me and Sam two dollars apiece for them when we were younger."

"Yuck! *Tim! That* is so disgusting!" she exclaimed.

She was truly repulsed by the information.

Jamie envisioned Tim and Sam standing on the side of the highway with a shovel and a burlap sack. *"All clear!"* Tim hollered, as they both scrambled to the yellow center stripe.

"Paydirt!" Sam shouted with glee, clasping his hands together in greed.

"We struck it rich this time, Bro! Just look at how bloated and greasy it is! Don't pop it, whatever you do, we're gonna make a fortune on this one!" Tim cried.

"Let's get this hot, stinking carcass into the bag quickly before another car comes. You hold the bag open, Tim, and I'll scrape it in."

"That's not fair! You always get to do the scraping!" Tim whined in her thoughts, as Jamie felt the bile rise in her throat at the image.

"No, Sweetie, we would either trap them or shoot them, and they would pay us," Tim explained. "I guess some people *like* to eat 'possum—after all, it *is* 'the ***other***, other white meat'!" he roared in hysterical fits of laughter.

The Duck River is unusually low, Tim thought. He picked out a shady spot near the bank.

Jamie relished in the smell of the gently flowing river water as a breeze caressed her face. Something splashed in the water as she looked around—*a turtle perhaps*? Already, Buddy was slithering around in the plants marking his territory. Jamie held his leash as Tim brought the fishing poles, tackle box, and night crawlers from the car.

He rigged both poles and baited Jamie's hook for her. He knew that she couldn't stand the thought of pinching the poor things in half and impaling them. Then they both sat down together on the bank watching their bobbers float along the slow-moving current of the river.

"You have to be careful not to cross lines, Sweetheart, otherwise, it's one tangled mess," he explained.

Just then, Jamie's felt a tug on her line. Letting out a small, surprised shriek, she bit her lower lip.

"Just let him play with it for a second, Honey, and I'll tell you when to pull on it," he whispered, eager for the first catch of the day.

"Oh, Tim!" she exclaimed, gleefully. Jamie stood up and held the rod in both her shaking hands.

Once Tim saw that the line was taken, he shouted, "Now!"

Jamie firmly yanked it upwards. Her fish was caught.

Tim stood beside her. "All you have to do is gently reel him in, Kitten, and I'll take it from there, okay?" Tim's excitement for her was evident.

She nodded her head nervously as she watched her line dart back and forth in the water. Tim tied Buddy's leash to a low-hanging limb so that he could help her bring it in.

Jamie's fish finally broke the surface; it was a large shell cracker.

"Nice job, Baby! It's beautiful!" he said, in a tone of encouragement.

"Did I do it right, Tim?" she asked. Running over to him, she watched her fish flop and twirl on the line. Tim was waiting for it to exhaust itself before he handled it.

"Just like a pro!" he said, with a grin. "You have to be careful when you handle them, okay? Do you see how he has his top fins up? It's very painful if he sticks you with them. You have to wait until he stops jumping around then, gently fold your hand over his head like this, and slowly cup your hand and push them down."

Tim gripped the fish by the bottom lip with his thumb and forefinger and showed Jamie how to handle it. After he had secured it, he showed her how to hook it on the leader line to keep it from getting away.

She planted a loving kiss on his lips. "You're such a good fisherman, Sweetheart."

"I haven't caught one yet," he chuckled.

"You know what I mean," she said, smiling softly at him. Her admiration for Tim was growing every day. *He is always so patient and kind to me.* The thought rested in her mind like a warm security blanket of love.

"Hey, get the camera and take a picture of me and Buddy fishing!" he said, untying Buddy from his branch.

Tim sat down on the bank and held Buddy up on his lap. Putting the fishing pole between his legs, he placed Buddy's paws around the handle for the benefit of the camera.

"It would look really cute if we put a weed in his mouth like Huckleberry Finn," Jamie suggested.

"Hey! That's a great idea!" he agreed. Jamie walked over to the river's edge and pulled up a strand of wild wheat.

Tim dried the inside of Buddy's lip and stuck it between his cheek and gum behind his canine. Once he'd finished, Tim started gurgling with uncontrollable laughter into the back of Buddy's neck. It lasted so long that his face turned almost purple.

Jamie was giggling extremely hard, as she peered through the lens—so hard, in fact, that she could barely keep the camera from shaking. Buddy sat patiently with his wheat in his mouth, waiting for her to finish with his photo session.

She framed him perfectly so that it looked like he was holding the pole all by himself. She took five pictures before she felt confident that at least one of them would turn out right.

They took turns holding Buddy's leash as they cast their lines out once more. They sat on the bank together and Buddy rested in Tim's lap.

Jamie lay her head on Tim's shoulder. It was undeniably a hot, lazy summer afternoon. Tim kicked his white tennis shoes off and stuffed his socks down inside them.

"Your toenails need to be trimmed, Tim," Jamie noticed. Tim looked at them and chuckled.

"What's so funny?" she asked.

"I remember one time when Jerry was sitting on the couch with Uncle Roy watching television—I was sitting in the recliner. Somehow or other, Jerry shifted in his seat and scratched Uncle Roy's leg with his toenails. Roy grabbed his leg and hollered in pain—there were four huge scratches. When he looked down at Jerry's feet, I did too. They were so long that they curled over his toes, Jamie!" Tim started snickering.

Jamie raised her head up, knowing that he was about to reveal the punch-line to the story.

Tim accidentally snorted, trying to regain his senses and finish the tale. "He got mad and grabbed Jerry by the shoulder, and led him to the bathroom. I could hear him scrounging around in the medicine cabinet for something—it turned out to be the toenail clippers."

"Get those talons clipped right now! If you ever let them get that long again, I'll make you hang upside down and sleep like a bat!"

Jamie started laughing as Tim's line bowed over—he had finally caught a fish of his own.

Buddy started barking when Tim reeled it in. He began jumping and nipping at it as it dangled and flopped around. Tim contorted his face and exclaimed, "Lookey there, Barn! He's still a-smackin' his lips!" The voice was pure Andy Griffith.

Jamie giggled as he put the fish on the leader line with hers. She watched the fish disappear into the murky green water as he dropped the line back into the river.

Jamie sighed in total contentment. "Tim, I think it's so kind of your mom and dad to give us some of their land to build our home on," she said, totally at ease.

"It really is. What kind of house would you like to put out there?"

She thought for a moment. "I would *love* to have a log home, Sweetheart. It's so beautiful and green out there. It gives me the feeling of being in an enchanted forest. What about you?"

"I want whatever makes you happy, Jamie," he said, sweetly. "I would live in a cardboard box as long as I have you to put my arms around every night." He kissed her on the head as she snuggled up against him.

"I think I'll plant a weeping willow in the backyard when we have it built. That's my favorite tree in the whole world because they're so majestic, yet, they look so lonely."

Jamie didn't say anything. She snuggled even closer to him and listened to his soothing voice as it caressed her ears with its poetic rhythm.

"...got another one, Baby!" Jamie was jolted from tranquility as she felt the exciting tug on her line once more.

She was still halfway between sleep and reality as she stood up. Remembering what Tim had taught her, she let her prey play with the bait for a few seconds, then tugged. Her fish was a real fighter this time. It was dragging her line ferociously back and forth across the water as she reeled it in. Its strength forced Jamie to take a step forward.

"Gosh, Kitten! You were *asleep* and caught this one!" Tim shouted in awe. "That's simply amazing! I think you've found your calling! I believe we could live out here forever and never go hungry!" Tim was beside himself with excitement. He helped her to reel her fish in and put it on the leader line with the others.

"That's a whopper, Jamie! Let me take a picture of you with it, that way people will believe you when you tell them how big it was!"

Jamie smiled proudly with her bangs in her face as Tim snapped her picture. She stood on the bank with her fishing pole in her left hand, and she held all three of the fish up with her right. It was *clearly* visible that her fish dwarfed the others considerably.

Tim tried for a couple of hours to catch some bass with lures and flies from his tackle box, but he had no luck. But before he day was over, Jamie caught two more and Tim caught one.

Dusk was approaching quickly. The temperature had dropped a few degrees in the last hour and it was finally tolerable to be out from underneath the shade. There was a mutual silence between them as a breath of honeysuckle whispered across their faces, even Buddy stood still. Tim breathed it in deeply and closed his eyes.

When he opened them back up, Jamie smiled. She completely knew him now and softly whispered—"*Honeysuckle.*"

21

Tuesday morning, Jamie sat at the kitchen table and drank a cup of coffee with Vickie as Tim showered and got dressed. Ed had already left for work over two hours ago.

Tim emerged from the hallway dressed in a royal blue dress shirt and black slacks. *My, you look handsome,* Jamie thought, but only smiled.

He poured himself a cup of coffee, sat down at the table, and put a mere four spoonfuls of sugar in it. He stirred it for a while then tasted. He got up from the table, opened the refrigerator and drew out the milk, filling his cup up the rest of the way.

After putting the milk back, he reclaimed his seat at the table. Then, tasting it for a second time, he shrugged his shoulders and lit a *Marlboro*. Jamie thought he could have made an acceptable skit for *Saturday Night Live* with his morning coffee ritual.

"Are you excited?" Vickie asked.

"Mostly nervous," he muttered.

"I don't see why you'd be nervous, Tim. You already have the job, you're just going to fill out the application," Jamie reminded him.

Tim checked his watch—it was already seven-forty. "Sam will be here shortly," he said, taking a drag from his cigarette and exhaling the smoke. Suddenly he noticed that his family's eyes were all upon him.

"I know, but anything could happen, they may

decide I'm not qualified or something," he concluded. He looked at his cigarette and twirled it between his thumb and fingers.

"Don't go borrowing trouble, Tim," Vickie said. She took a drag of her own vice and sipped her coffee. She exhaled her smoke in the cup as she drank. Jamie thought it looked like a miniature cauldron of witch's brew.

"You're such a worry wart!" Vickie told him after she swallowed her coffee.

Tim blew a perfect smoke ring. It floated across the table, drifted past Jamie's face and burst silently on Vickie's cheek.

Tim and Jamie started laughing. Vickie smirked. "You know, you're still not too big for me to give you a whipping, Tim. I don't care if you *are* a soldier; I'm *still* your mother."

Jamie cupped her hand over her mouth and tried to stop laughing.

"I'm sorry, Mom, but it was still funny," he said, succeeding at his attempt to claim the last word.

Buddy ran to the front door and watched Sam tear the driveway up with his Mustang. Even with the windows closed, they could still feel the vibration from Sam's mighty subwoofer.

Tim crushed out his cigarette as Sam opened the front door and came bolting in. Buddy looked up at him and wagged his tail.

"Good morning!" everyone said in unison. Sam reached down and petted Buddy on the head.

"I wore a *cup* today in case you get any wild ideas,"

Sam said, pointing sternly at Buddy.

The pup raised his ears and cocked his head at his feigned enemy. Everyone started giggling.

Sam walked over to the table, twirling his car keys around his index finger. "So, are you excited?" he asked Tim. Buddy was getting keyed up, and began doing the *Dance of the Deer.*

"What in the world is he doing?" Sam asked. Then Buddy started speaking in German.

"He hears your car keys, Sam. He does that little dance whenever he hears keys jingling because he knows he's going somewhere," Tim explained. Sam looked down at Buddy and shook the keys violently in the air.

"Oh Re-e-a-l-l-y?" Sam cackled wickedly. Jamie could see the imaginary horns starting to protrude from his forehead, as Sam glanced at his watch. "We've got enough time—watch this, Tim." Sam picked Buddy up and headed out the front door with him.

"What are you gonna do with him, Sam?" Tim asked; worry filled his voice. Rising from the table, he followed his brother out the front door.

"You'll see," Sam laughed. Everyone's curiosity was piqued at this point, and they all stood on the porch to see what Sam was planning to do.

Starting the car, he turned it around in the driveway, rolling down the window so everyone could see. He placed Buddy's paws on the steering wheel and drove slowly down the driveway.

"Watch where you're going, Dude!" Sam hollered at him. Buddy immediately took his gaze off Tim and looked out the windshield. Everyone was laughing at him. It seemed as if he were actually trying to do a good job of driving.

Tim was in hysterics at that point.

Jamie ran into the house, grabbed the camera and hurried back out. She knew Tim would ask her to get it anyway. She snapped several pictures of the spectacle, as Sam turned around at the end of the driveway and let Buddy drive back to the house.

"Can you let him drive once more so Jamie can get some good pictures of him?" Tim begged.

Sam started laughing. Buddy was still standing on the steering wheel.

"I think he actually likes it!" Jamie remarked in amazement.

Sam reached into the console, brought out his sunglasses and placed them gently on Buddy's face—his ears were cocked and the handles sat perfectly on them. Again, everyone laughed wildly, as Jamie snapped picture after picture, hoping that one of them would turn out to be a classic.

Sam let Buddy drive his beautiful Mustang once more down the driveway. He concentrated on the road ahead, peering through his sunglasses. Sam helped correct him if he got a bit off course.

At the end of the driveway, Sam turned the car back around and pointed it toward the house. The car rocked back and forth ferociously as the engine raced.

Buddy was looking out the windshield intently with his sunglasses on. Sam accelerated and Buddy raced the Mustang toward them. Tim laughed so hard that the blood rushed to the surface of his skin on his usually-pale face.

Sam put the brakes on and brought the car to a slow halt. He placed Buddy's paws on the horn and helped him honk it. Putting his sunglasses back in the console, he got out of the car and handed the hero back to Tim. Everyone was still laughing and Buddy wagged his tail in thanks.

"For a Dachshund, his driving wasn't too bad!" Sam said mischievously.

As Tim held Buddy, he could tell that his brother had made him a very happy dog.

Sam looked at his watch. "I guess we should go, Tim. I didn't get much sleep last night and I want to take a nap when we get back."

"Sure." He handed Buddy to Jamie and kissed her. "I'll see you later, Sweetheart, I love you."

She smiled at him and he kissed Buddy on the head.

"Will you pick me up a pack of *Salem's* on your way back, Tim?" Vickie asked. "I've only got about half a pack left."

"Sure, Mom," he said. He kissed his mother on the cheek, then he and Sam got into the Mustang, tearing down the driveway as Jamie and Vickie went back inside to finish their coffee.

"Sam is such a clown," Vickie said.

"He's a gremlin, alright," Jamie added.

They both sat down, as Buddy jumped on the sofa in the living room and lay on Ed's pillow cushion. He sighed as he curled up and dreamt about driving Sam's Mustang.

"Those two used to fight like cats and dogs when

they were younger," Vickie remarked.

"Really?" Jamie asked, stunned. "They seem like they're the best of friends. I never would have thought that."

Vickie nodded as she took a sip of coffee. "They grew up," she shrugged. "I guess Sam's really missed him since he's been away... we *all* have." She started giggling.

Jamie smiled. "What's so funny?"

"Sam used to aggravate Tim all the time. He was quite a bit shorter than Tim back then and they had to share a bedroom.

"Tim was *always* listening to his records. The house we rented was very old, and when you walked into Tim and Sam's room, everything teetered and tottered.

"Anyway, Tim had just bought this Buddy Holly album, and was listening to it when Sam came into the bedroom. Tim asked him if he could please be careful not to roughhouse in there because it might cause the needle to jump and scratch his record. I was listening to them from the living room.

"Sam didn't say anything. He just walked over to the door and jumped as high as he could and stomped the floor with both feet. The needle raked across the whole side of the record. Jamie, I thought Tim was going to have a heart attack!"

"What did he do?" she asked, interested in hearing more about her husband's tempestuous childhood.

Vickie took another sip of coffee. "He was fuming. He grabbed Sam by the hair and hurled him face first onto the floor. Sam screamed *bloody murder!* I ran in there and blood was gushing out of Sam's nose so bad that I thought he was going to bleed to death."

Jamie sipped her coffee.

"Ed tore him up with the belt that night when he got home from work."

Jamie froze. Suddenly, all of the things that Tim had told her on the drive up came back. She tightened her grip on the coffee cup handle as rage filled her bright eyes. She stared dangerously at Vickie. One word came tumbling from her shaky lips, *"Why?"*

"What?" Vickie asked, still ignorant that angry eyes were upon her.

"I *said*...Why? *Why* did Ed whip him?" Jamie repeated the question...*slowly*. She didn't move, and she didn't flinch.

Vickie finally looked up and saw the abhorrence in her eyes, suddenly growing uneasy. She was totally caught off guard at this point as she tried to think of a feasible response. "Well, because he lost his temper and hurt him," she said, hoping the answer would suffice.

Jamie slowly shook her head. "You just sat there and told me that Sam was *always* aggravating Tim, didn't you?"

"Yes, but..."

Jamie interrupted her. She realized that she clearly had the upper hand in this discussion. "That leads me to believe that he did it because he knew he could '*always*' get away with it," she said, making quotation marks with her fingers when she said *always*.

"Did Sam get punished for destroying Tim's record?" She pushed further, insistent on getting an answer for Vickie's definition of *fair* justice.

Vickie bowed her head in shame. "No."

For the first time, Jamie saw her 'hang dog' look. It was exactly as Tim had described it and she felt like slapping it off of her face. "That's what I thought," she said, gritting her teeth.

"Jamie," Vickie said softly. "I don't understand why you're so angry about it. That happened a long time ago."

Jamie's eyes began to fill with tears as they stared at each other. She wiped them away with her hand then went in for the *kill.* "There's a lot of things that happened to Tim 'a long time ago'...aren't there, Vickie?"

Her mouth dropped open in shock.

Jamie was trembling. The words were tumbling around in her mind like the balls in a bingo cage.

"I've never broken a promise to Tim, Vickie, but in this case I believe it's warranted. He told me *everything.* Do you know what I'm talking about?"

Lightning shot from her emerald green eyes as she continued to stare her mother-in-law down.

Vickie nodded slowly. She didn't dare say a single word.

Adrenaline pulsed through Jamie's body as she tried to control her temper. "He didn't tell me because he wanted to, he told me because I *made* him. When I told him I was pregnant a few days ago, he shut himself off completely from me. I was *devastated* because I am so in love with him. It was as if all the lights were still on but nobody was home. I'm so ashamed to admit this, but I honestly thought it was because he didn't want his own children.

"But it wasn't that at all, Vickie. *Again,* I

misinterpreted Tim. It was the other way around—he thought that his own children wouldn't want *him!*

"I have never in my *life* heard of locking a ***baby*** in a roasting attic for over a month because he couldn't eat a piece of cornbread!"

Vickie swallowed hard.

"And it gets better! Just when I thought the poor little thing was finally going to get his first morsel of food in over a month, *you* sat there with that same look you have on your face right now and participated in making him eat rancid, rotting food that even *Adolph Hitler wouldn't feed to the Jews!*

"And for the main *course*, Vickie—if his poor, empty stomach couldn't handle it, it's okay—he can eat his own ***vomit!***" She screamed so loudly that Buddy raised his head from the pillow.

Jamie's chest was heaving, as she paused for a brief intermission to catch her breath. She was hyperventilating.

Vickie sat in shame; tears streamed down her cheeks as she listened to Jamie pass judgment.

"My Daddy's dead now, but I can never recall a single time when he dangled me in the air and beat me within an inch of my life, or throw me into a wall, simply because I desperately needed his love and attention...and *now* I see the saga continues—as you sit there and laugh about all of his years of persecution! What kind of person *are* you to let someone do such evil, demonic things to your own son? Are you a sadist?

"Sheesh! It's a wonder he doesn't have multiple personalities!" She paused briefly, rolled her eyes and sighed. "Although, I have to admit he does do some pretty impressive impersonations. Maybe that's what comes when you have so much *alone* time to work with." She shook her head and returned to the conversation at hand.

"You're going to be a grandmother whether you like it or not. As a matter of fact, I don't *care* if you like it or not! But I'm going to tell you one thing, I'll sit in a ditch and hope for the best before I let *you* or anyone else lay a finger on one of my little ones, do you understand me?"

Vickie nodded; the tears covered her face.

Jamie took a bit of compassion on her and got a paper towel from the roller next to the stove. "Tim loves you so much, Vickie...because you're his mother. No matter what you've done to him, no matter who you've let hurt him, and no matter how many times he's needed your protection—and you've *never* given it—he *still* loves you—*unconditionally*. I never understood the full meaning of that word until I met Tim. And *no one*, not even *I*, can pull him away from the love he feels for you. The *only* reason I respect you at all is because of his love for you.

"I'm not going to sit here and threaten you, Vickie. You've been very kind to me, and if you still want us to stay with you, I'll be kind in return. You can even tell Ed and Tim we had this conversation if you want—or, we can be ladies and keep it between ourselves. It really doesn't matter to me."

She took a deep breath. "But as long as Tim is my husband, I'm going to spend the rest of my life making up for all of the bad things that *you* and the rest of the world have dished out to him. I will love that man with all of my heart...*until I draw my very last breath.*" By this time,

Jamie was panting feverishly.

"Can I please say something?" Vickie asked, gently. She looked at her with sorrowful eyes. She waited for Jamie to answer.

"Go ahead," she said, sarcastically after a few moments.

Vickie sighed. "You're absolutely right," she began. "And I told you the other day that there were things in my life that I can never change or take back. There is *no* excuse I can give you for letting those things happen to him."

"Then why *did* you? Why didn't you scratch their eyes out or call someone for help—*anything?*"

Vickie looked down and shook her head in confusion. "I was young and scared. I was in the same boat as Tim."

"I don't believe that! *You* had a choice, *he* didn't. Why didn't you go back up to Minnesota and live with his grandparents?"

Vickie blew her nose into the crumpled paper towel. "The reason I left them in the first place was because Tim started calling them *Mommy* and *Daddy*. I got jealous because no matter how hard I tried to break him from it, he wouldn't stop.

"*That* was a very stupid and dangerous mistake on my part. After I saw how much James hated him I thought about going back, but I was afraid that I would lose Tim forever to them, and he would never recognize me as his mother. After James left us, I just panicked. I was too ashamed to call his parents and ask for help.

"I thought if I could stay with my parents, find a

job, and work just long enough to save some money for a place of my own, Tim and I could live happily ever after, and I would be able to give him the love and security he needed. I *honestly* wanted to do that, but my father forced me to work with him at his frame shop. He paid me little or nothing every week because he was supporting us.

"After what happened to Tim in the attic, I wanted to die." She started crying again. "There was no way out for us, Jamie—so I chose the lesser of two evils. I got in touch with James. After I told him what was happening, I think even *he* was in shock. I promised him that if he would help me just that one time I would never bother him again—I *begged* him!

"I packed what clothes we had, and he picked us up and took us to Jackson, Mississippi. He was a disc jockey at one of the radio stations there. He let us stay with him for a while, and he drove me around so that I could find a job. That was the kindest thing he ever did for me." She wiped at her eyes with the paper towel. It was falling apart, so Jamie got her another one.

"Thank you," she said.

"Did he make Tim stay in his room all that time?" Jamie asked.

Vickie looked down and nodded her head. "Yes, but he took him with us when I was looking for work. I finally got a job at a *McDonald's* downtown.

"He let me save about three paychecks and helped me to find a place in walking distance to work. It was a little two-room shack with a small kitchen, a shower off the end of it, and a bedroom. It was falling apart, but it was all I could afford.

"We lived there for about a year. That's when I met Ed. He *loved* Tim. We saw each other for about a year and a half and he proposed. The last time I ever saw James was at the courthouse where Ed adopted Tim. The first and *only* words that came out of his mouth were:

'Where do I sign?' After that, I never saw him again.

Jamie looked down, shook her head, and sighed deeply. "Vickie," she said, pausing to find the right words. "Why didn't you at least *try* and fight back, or take a stand against them? Were there ever *any* times that you could have reasoned with *any* of them and let them know how cruel they were being?"

Vickie looked at her blankly. She was exhausted. "I couldn't fight back, Jamie."

Déjà vu struck her like a brick in the face as she asked her final question: "Do you mean you couldn't, or you wouldn't?"

Vickie bit down hard on her bottom lip to keep it from trembling. Tears welled up in her eyes and she felt as if she were caught between a rock and a hard place.

Jamie's heart sank deep within her soul, for she already knew the answer without having to be told: Vickie had been abused too. Everything had come full circle now—there were no more missing pieces to the puzzle.

"For the love of God, Vickie, where...*are*...those horrible people?"

"The last time I saw any of them, we were living with my brother, Roy, in Donelson. They were living in a house on Percy Priest Lake in Mt. Juliet. I haven't seen them in years, and I don't really care to ever see them again," Vickie said. Jamie nodded. They both had found closure.

22

Vickie made them both a bologna sandwich and a pitcher of tea for lunch.

"Do you still want us to stay?" Jamie asked, ambivalent about the answer she'd receive.

Vickie nodded. "Of course I do. I was even thinking that you might consider staying behind while Tim finishes up his last few weeks with the Air Force. It would give us the time to renovate, and you could have everything done by the time Tim comes home. He could just start work and not have to worry about any of it." Vickie continued, "We can pick up a stove and refrigerator and put it in for you, and you'll have your own privacy back there. What do you think?"

She cocked her eyebrows as she chewed her sandwich. In a strange way, it all made sense.

Vickie kept talking, "Besides, you *did* say you loved it here, and by staying you'll be able to see it every day. You can even take a walk in the woods and pick out a place to build your home."

Jamie nodded slowly. "I think it's a great idea, Vickie."

"Sure it is! I don't think Tim would mind very much. I mean, he only has five or six weeks left. I think he would understand if he knows you'll be getting his home in order. I know you have to talk with him about it, but surely he can survive *that* long without you," Vickie suggested.

Jamie smiled and pointed at Buddy. "It's not me he can't survive without," she said, chuckling.

Buddy could sense that he was being talked about. Raising his head from Ed's pillow, his left eye was still glued shut with sleep.

Deep thunder rumbled in the background and the rain began to fall. The window fan in the kitchen slowed a bit as the wind pushed against it. Jamie and Vickie walked to the front door and looked out. The rain smelled refreshing, and seemed to represent a pristine new start...for both of them.

"That certainly came up quickly," Vickie remarked. The sunlit afternoon had been replaced by grey and cloudy skies. Jamie observed the hummingbird feeders swinging back and forth on the porch. The wind was moving quickly, and a bright bolt of lightning flashed across the sky.

A few seconds later, a crack of thunder shook the house and sent Buddy scrambling under the bed.

"I think I'm going to lie down for a while," Jamie said, studying the weather.

"Me too," Vickie said sharply. "The boys will be back in a little while." Both women were emotionally exhausted.

Jamie whistled softly for Buddy as she lay down on the bed. She could hear him jingling underneath her as he tugged and scratched his way out. He bumped his head on the bed frame and yelped, making Jamie giggle. Turning around three times, he snuggled tightly up against her—she loved the feel of protection that his warm body gave.

As she stared up at the ceiling, Jamie pondered all the tragic things she had learned about in the last few days. She tried to imagine what it must feel like to live in constant fear and shame of someone. How can a parent be so cruel to their own children and spend their whole life torturing them, and how could someone *hate* their own grandchild?

Would I have done the same thing? She wondered. Putting herself in Vickie's shoes, Jamie thought long and hard, trying to imagine herself in similar circumstances.

No way, she concluded. *I'm a fighter! I wouldn't have let those things happen to my son—I would die before I let that happen. If there* is *a hell, surely those people will be in it, and I want a front row seat so I can roast marshmallows over them while they're burning!* she thought, fuming.

Her anger was starting to flame once more. She huffed, and flung herself over on her side, trying her best to concentrate on happier thoughts.

The oscillating fan was turned to *low*, as Tim stood over Jamie and watched her sleep. He could hear her slow, rhythmic breathing, and it made him smile.

The bedroom was dark and gloomy, and he bent down and kissed her on the forehead. Buddy started to jingle and Tim reached over to pet him.

Buddy rolled over on his back wanting him to rub his tummy, but Tim lay down beside Jamie and gently put his arm around her instead.

A few hours later Tim awoke to soft angel kisses all

over his face.

“Rise and shine, Porcupine!” came Jamie’s sweet voice as if from far, far away. He woke from a deep slumber and stared into the beautiful, green eyes gazing down at him.

“What time is it?” he asked, sleepily.

“It’s time for you to get up!” She whacked him with her pillow. Buddy started rubbing his neck on Tim’s face, almost smothering him.

“I think your son has to go to the bathroom,” she said.

“Did it ever quit raining?” He sat up.

“Yep!”

Buddy jumped off the bed and started in with his ever-famous dance. Tim sighed. He looked at his watch—it was 7:45 P.M. “I must have been really tired, I can’t believe I slept that long!” He slipped his shoes on.

“I have something I want to talk to you about when you come back in,” she said.

Tim nodded, and went into the kitchen in search of Buddy’s leash. Vickie picked it up from the table and rattled it at Tim. Once he’d headed for the outdoors, Jamie sat down at the table.

“I’d like to discuss this in front of everyone when he comes back in,” Jamie said. Vickie had already pitched the idea to Ed.

“I’m going to let *the evil one* sleep awhile longer,” Vickie said, sarcastically, “I don’t know how Tim is going to feel about Jamie wanting to stay, but I don’t want Sam getting him all worked up over it.”

Ed nodded in agreement as he sipped his tea. Tim

wiped his feet and took off his shoes when he came back in. The storm door whispered and clicked against the catch behind him.

Buddy shook the moisture from his coat and proceeded to pounce on the couch with all fours. Everyone hollered before Tim realized that his paws were still muddy. Lurching forward, he grabbed Buddy by his hips. “Sorry about that.”

“There are some towels in the hallway closet,” Vickie said.

Carrying Buddy underneath his arm like a football, Tim walked down the hallway and fumbled with the doorknob, trying not to wake his brother. He finally got it open, pulled out a blue towel, and dried Buddy off.

“I was thinking about homemade pizza for supper tonight,” Vickie said, when Tim got back into the kitchen.

“I’d love that!” he exclaimed, then looked over at Jamie. “Mom uses *Bisquick* for the crust and it’s delicious!” His mouth was already watering.

Tim sat down at the table and watched Buddy jump on the couch again, taking his place on Ed’s pillow. Vickie started pulling bowls and ingredients from the cabinets.

“So how did it go today?” Jamie asked.

Tim casually lit a *Marlboro*, leaving her temporarily hanging. “Great!” he finally said. “Petie took me for a tour of the plant and showed me where I was going to be working. I’ll be running three machines that roll and cut the gift-wrap. After I filled out my application, he told me that I would be making ten dollars an hour!”

“Hey! That’s pretty good money, Sweetheart!”

Jamie cooed.

Tim suddenly realized that a veil of silence had fallen over the kitchen. “What’s going on?”

Jamie and Vickie looked at each other.

“Tim, your mother and I were talking this afternoon about the possibility of me staying here while you finish up in Lubbock.”

“What for?” He frowned, as if someone had just asked him for a million dollars but hadn’t told him anything about the investment.

“Well…we were thinking that we could get the back end of the house fixed up and get everything finished and in place by the time you get back home.” Jamie explained.

Tim’s heart shrank. “I don’t know, Jamie,” he said, hesitantly, “that’s an awfully long time.”

“It’s only six weeks, Honey. That’s three paychecks if you want to look at it that way. It’s not long at all and you won’t have to do all this stuff when you *do* get back home,” she clarified.

Tim meditated a moment before answering. “What about all of your clothes?” he said, trying to make up a legitimate excuse to keep her by his side.

“You can pack them up and send them by UPS. I’ll get them in about three days,” she rationalized.

“There’s a thrift store in town too, Tim. We can get her a few extra clothes and pick up anything else she might need from *Wal-Mart*,” Vickie interjected.

Tim looked over at his father. “What do *you* think, Dad?” he asked.

Ed shrugged. He knew that he was outnumbered, and it was probably a useless waste of breath to argue with two insistent women—one of whom was pregnant. "It's up to you, Son, but you should give it some thought. If she stays, we can get this stuff done a whole lot quicker."

"Come on, Tim! It'll give me something constructive to do," Jamie pointed out.

"What about Buddy?"

"I'll tell you what," Ed began. "Tim, why don't you let her stay and help out, and I'll build a pen for Buddy."

Then Jamie made her closing argument. "Sweetheart, I know how close you are to Rusty, and it may be a very long time before you get to see him again—if *ever.* This way, you'll have an opportunity to spend the rest of your time playing music with him without having to worry about me being lonely. The time will pass quickly and we can talk on the phone whenever you want."

Tim could see that she really wanted to stay pretty badly. Reluctantly, he agreed.

Jamie jumped up and gave him her best teddy bear hug, and a tender kiss.

On Wednesday Tim, Jamie, and Buddy spent the entire day together. He had to use Thursday for packing everything up, and then get a good night's rest before leaving at daybreak on Friday morning.

Already he was dreading having to be away from his beloved wife, for Jamie had become his entire world. Six weeks would be an eternity without her.

"Please take me for a walk in the woods, Sweetheart," she pleaded, sweetly, clasping her hands over her heart. "Your mom said we could pick out a place to build our home."

Tim smiled weakly. "Okay." His heart was heavy and he wanted to take his thoughts off of leaving. He took her hand as Buddy blindly led the way.

She could see the depression in his eyes as they walked together. "Tim, *please* don't be sad. Let's spend the day being happy together. Let's find a beautiful spot back here to raise our children and take pleasure in knowing that they're going to have the security, love and happiness that you never did.

"It's going to be different with them, you know? You have a chance to put all of those horrible things behind you and give *them* a fresh, new heritage."

Tim listened to her as they walked. He held her hand firmly in his. It was so small and dainty, and its warmth sent shivers up his spine.

"Do you know what we have in our marriage that so many others are lacking, Tim?" she asked.

He shook his head.

"Passion! We have passion. I haven't seen any at all with your mother and father. I thought I saw a little in that picture of them on the dresser, but I haven't seen them kiss, hold hands, or even hug each other since we've been here.

"I *never* see anyone in the stores holding hands or looking at each other the way we do. We have a very special *thing,* you and me. And I don't think we're ever going to lose that, because we don't *just* love each other, we're *in love* with each other. I think there's a big difference."

Her voice was so gentle and kind. Tim loved it whenever she opened up her heart to him. It was a very intimate sensation that rushed between them. Tim loved Jamie with all of his being, and he knew every facet of her beautiful heart.

She stepped in front of him and cupped his face with her hands. "Tim, you're the most wonderful husband a woman could ever have. I'm so happy that I have you, and you *are* going to be a wonderful Daddy.

"Just think about all the funny things you do with Buddy and how much you love him, cuddle with him, and spend time with him—now pretend that he's a human being."

Tim gave her a startled look.

"That's right, just think of Buddy as sort of a practice run. Tim, you've made me laugh so hard with that dog sometimes that I've almost wet my pants!" They both giggled.

"The point is, I can't *wait* to find out what you have in store for these two!" She pointed at her tummy. "If they're anything like *you*, and I hope with all my heart they will be *exactly* like you," she rolled her eyes heavenwards and held her hands over her heart. "Then I have a feeling that I'm going to be laughing for the rest of my life!"

She smiled wide, as she continued, "It's hard enough to keep from laughing to death with just one of you, but now there's going to be *three!*

"Growing old with you is going to be a wonderful thing for me, and I hope we have tons of grandchildren to carry on our name. We'll spoil them and love them so much! And it will even be okay when we die, Sweetheart, because we'll never be forgotten."

A tear trickled down her cheek. "I'm so happy right now, Tim! I'm happy because you've *made* me happy. You're everything I've ever dreamed a *Prince Charming* should and could be." She winked. "*Because you're the Kang uh mah heart, Baby'*," she said, trying to sound like Tim.

Tim chuckled because he wondered if that was the way Lisa Marie sounded when *she* talked.

"*Stop* laughing at me and *kiss* me, you silly angel!" Jamie embraced him, as they shared an incredibly *passionate* kiss.

As they walked further into the woods, Buddy had finally stopped darting from bush to bush and walked calmly beside Tim.

"In a way, I think all of the things that happened to me have made me a better person. It certainly has taught me what *not* to be like," he said finally.

"I think it's given you a heightened sense of awareness, Tim."

"What do you mean?" he asked, looking down and listening intently to her as they strolled onward.

"Have you ever heard of people who are impaired having stronger senses? For example, a person who is blind may have a stronger sense of hearing, touch, and smell?" she explained.

"Yes, but I'm not impaired."

She thought for a moment and searched for the right words. "No, not like *that*, but for the lack of love you received...and all of the desperate loneliness you experienced...I think somehow your heart and emotions have compensated for that. I think it's a wonderful gift you've been given," she said, matter-of-factly.

"I don't know about any of that. I just know that I don't seem to fit in anywhere else in the world but with you," he confessed.

She gazed at him, flashing him a sweet smile. "You fit in with Rusty, Tim, and they *all* fit in with you...Heck, *Lubbock* fits in with you," she pointed out.

Tim sighed deeply. "You're right. And now I'm going to have my heart broken twice, Sweetheart. Once when I have to leave you and Buddy on Friday, and again when I have to leave Lubbock in a few weeks." He shook his head in sorrow. "I would give anything to stay there for the rest of my life. It will forever be my *true* home.

"Even Mac Davis wrote a cool song about it. He's one of my favorite singers, too, and I have all of his albums," he said.

"What song did he write?" she asked, curiously.

"Happiness is Lubbock, Texas in my rearview mirror," he replied.

"Oh yeah, I remember that song," she said. She stopped abruptly and her mouth dropped open.

"What's the matter?" he asked.

They were standing in a small glade. She looked around, her face beaming with joy. "*Oh* Tim!" she exclaimed. "Isn't this beautiful?"

Tim stood still and stared at the large oak and maple trees that encircled them. It was cool and shady in the pleasant grove, yet vivid rays of sunlight shone through the verdant tree tops. "It really is," he whispered.

He watched Jamie start to glow, focusing on the twinkle in her eyes.

"This is the place, Tim," she said, resolved in the sight that she beheld.

He continued to admire her beauty as hints of her *Ciara* whispered to him in the breeze. He closed his eyes...God, he was going to miss her *so* much. *"Okay,"* he said tenderly.

After supper they all sat on the porch and basked in the peaceful sunset.

"Tim, will you get your guitar and sing for me?" Jamie asked. They were swaying slowly together on the quaint porch swing. "It's going to be a while before I get to hear you sing my songs again, and I want to keep them fresh in my heart until you come home to me."

Tim lazily rose from the swing and went inside the house. He returned with *Mr. Midnight,* sat back down, and gently plucked the strings to ensure that they were perfectly in tune.

He softly sang a few of the songs composed especially for her. Even the birds seemed to huddle in their nests, completely quiet, as if being lulled to sleep by his enchanting voice.

Buddy was dead to the world, sprawled out and lying on his back between them. His head was hanging over the seat cushion and the whites of his eyes gleamed from behind half-opened eyelids. At least an inch of his pink tongue was hanging out from the front of his lips.

Ed and Vickie had not even realized that they were so completely entranced by Tim's powerful lyrics and vocals.

When he had finished, all that could be heard was the creaking of the porch swing as Jamie gently pushed them both with her foot.

Tim grinned and elected to change the mood. He gave Jamie an impish look and started singing, *Brown Eyed Handsome Man.* When he came to the verse about Milo Venus, he replaced the words and sang instead:

♫ *"Jamie Cunningham was a beautiful lass, she hat the worlt in the palm of her hand!*

But she loss bofe her arms in a wrasslin' match to win a 'fo-eye-dit-ret-neck' man!

She fought and won herself a 'fo-eye-dit-ret-neck' man!" ♫

Jamie laughed loudly, and playfully slapped him on the shoulder as he continued on with his twisted lyrics. Soon, all of them were laughing at Tim's rendition of Buddy Holly's classic song.

Tim got so tickled at picturing Jamie being armless, trying to reach the pancake mix in the cabinet, that he couldn't even finish the song. He laughed so hard that his face turned red. "I guess if you *really* were armless, I could call you *Flipper*, Honey!"

"Tim!" Jamie gasped. He got tickled again and almost dropped his guitar trying to catch his breath.

"Oh—my—goodness!" he said in between gulps of air. "I hope I don't have that thought come into my head the next time I have to perform!"

Setting his guitar against the storm door, Tim lit a cigarette and sat back on the swing with Jamie. They were all still chuckling. Jamie propped her head on her hand and rested her arm on the railing, tousling Tim's hair.

"I've been looking forward to this for so long, Tim," Vickie said. "We're going to have such a wonderful time when you get back home."

He smiled. "I sure hope that Rusty will understand about everything," he said. "And I hope that we'll be able to play enough to last a lifetime. He's about the best friend I've ever had, and so is Acie. He always has this smile on his face like he's about to say something funny. Most of the time, he does.

"The way we harmonize together, you'd think we were born Siamese twins or something. *I* think we sound *better* than the Everly Brothers, and *that's* a bold statement!"

Tim started chuckling and choked on his cigarette smoke. "He told me this joke one time when we were setting up all of the equipment:

'This man was driving down a country road one day when he saw a sign that said: TALKING DOG FOR SALE. He drove a little farther down the road and pulled into the driveway of an old farmhouse. The farmer and his wife came out the front door and greeted him.

"Can I help you?" The farmer asked.

"Do you *really* have a talking dog?" the man asked, not believing the sign.

"Yep! He never shuts up!" he replied. The man stared at him in disbelief.

"Do you mind if I take a look at him?"

"Sure," the farmer said, and pointed behind the house. "He's out in the back yard, help yourself."

The man walked behind the house and, sure enough, there was this sad, old dog chained up and laying inside his dog house.

"Ahem!" The man cleared his throat. "Can you really talk?" he asked, politely.

The dog cocked his ears, sat up and said, "Yes, I can."

The man was bewildered. "That's amazing! How is it that you came to be here?"

The dog sighed deeply. "Well, many years ago I was on the police force. I was in a special K-9 unit and I sniffed out drugs. I helped to catch many drug smugglers.

"After that, I worked with the CIA for a while and won the Congressional Medal of Honor for infiltrating enemy spy networks, and I helped put an end to many terrorist groups.

"I retired a few years ago and these people were nice enough to give me a comfortable home."

The man was simply amazed. He could see dollar signs and imagined all the money he could make off of him.

"I'll be right back," the man said. He ran around to the front of the house and knocked on the door. When the farmer came out, the man said, "How much do you want for him?"

The farmer thought for a moment and said, "I guess I could take twenty-five dollars for him."

The man was speechless. "Only *twenty-five?* If you don't mind me asking, why are you selling him so cheap? I just had an illuminating conversation with him and he's a national hero!"

The farmer shook his head and said, "Because that's all he does is lie! He ain't never done a single one of them things he told you he's done!"

Everyone burst out laughing. They sat talking in the dark until, one by one, they all started yawning.

"I hope you've had a nice time, Son. I know you wish the night would go on forever because you've got to go to bed pretty early tomorrow," Ed told him.

Tim sighed. "I know, I wanted to spend as much time with you as I could tonight, but I think it's time for bed."

Ed patted him on the leg as he got up to go inside the house. Tim picked his guitar up as his father opened the storm door, and Jamie retrieved Buddy from the swing; he was as limp as a wet noodle.

"I'll worry about the dishes tomorrow," Vickie decided.

Saying goodnight, they all went to bed to dream about the brilliant future ahead.

23

Jamie rose early the next morning and began washing Tim's clothes, gathering his things together to be packed.

She covered his face with angel kisses at 9:30 A.M.

"You better get up and spend some time with me, Sweetheart," she crooned happily.

He sat up on the side of the bed to collect his thoughts.

"I'll make you a cup of coffee while you get dressed—I already took Buddy out this morning," she said.

Vickie and Jamie were sitting at the table when Tim came in. The scrumptious coffee smell got his attention in a hurry. Pulling a chair out from the table, scraping it along the floor like chalk on a blackboard, Tim sat down, sighed, and lit a cigarette.

"Good morning, Sunshine!" Vickie beamed. Tim offered a smile and took a sip of his coffee.

"Sam's coming over to say goodbye to you. Would you like some eggs and bacon?" she asked.

"Sure," he said, taking a drag from his cigarette.

Jamie started giggling. "Tim, your hair is plastered down to your scalp on both sides and it looks like the dorsal fin of a shark on top," she informed him with a grin.

He reached up and fluffed it out. "Yeah, I need to get the ole' squirrel fur trimmed up, I guess," he said, forgetting that it was a private joke. Jamie laughed even harder.

Tim's stomach growled as he smelled the bacon sizzling in his mother's cast iron skillet. The toaster popped loudly and produced two dark pieces of toast. Vickie buttered them, cut them diagonally, and placed the pieces upside down on each other so the butter would melt faster. Tim loved his mother's way of making toast, because she made them taste like they came straight from the *Waffle House.*

"I suppose hash browns covered in chili and jalapeños are out of the question this morning, huh?" he chuckled, imagining his mother wearing an apron with a book of guest receipts shoved in the pocket.

"Yuck! How can you eat things like that first thing in the morning?" Jamie grimaced. "You must have sulfuric acid running through your veins!"

Tim was starting to come alive as he finished his first cup of coffee. Jamie loved it when he was jovial in the mornings. It always set her days on a happy course thinking of the hilarious things he would say to her before he left for work.

Tim ran his arm up the bottom of his shirt and pretended that an alien had burst from his chest. His fist "looked" around the room, screeched loudly, and lurched at Jamie. She and Vickie both laughed and shook their heads.

Sam tore up the driveway as Tim and Buddy were finishing up his breakfast. Vickie had made a one-time exception and allowed them to share their last meal together since Ed wasn't home.

"Hey, Tim, come out here for a minute," Sam said, peeking his head through the storm door. Tim put Buddy on the floor and went outside.

Jamie and Vickie continued to talk at the table when Tim rushed back in, grinning from ear-to-ear. He snatched Buddy up and darted back outside.

They gave each other a puzzled look.

"I wonder what that was all about," Vickie said. They could hear Tim and Sam rolling with laughter outside and they got up and stared out the door.

Sam had brought a battery-operated motorized jeep with him, and Buddy was standing up in the seat driving it through the yard. Jamie and Vickie were in hysterics as they stepped out on the porch.

"Where in the world did you get that, Sam?" Vickie asked.

"My neighbor at the apartment complex sold it to me," he grinned. "His son outgrew it a long time ago and he didn't want it anymore."

Sam continued to laugh, as Buddy hit a bump and fell out of the jeep.

Tim sprinted over, picked him up and chased after the moving toy.

"Isn't it supposed to stop when you let off the pedal?" Jamie asked.

"I had to duct tape it down to the floor because he can't reach it," Sam answered. "I thought it would be a funny going-away present for Tim."

Jamie looked at Sam and admired him—not only for his sense of humor, but also for the thoughtfulness that he constantly showed his brother.

Tim bent over, turned the jeep around and walked beside it as it headed back toward the house. After he had placed Buddy's paws back on the steering wheel, Buddy wagged his tail and concentrated on his driving skills.

Jamie rushed inside the house and quickly grabbed the camera, managing to capture quite a few pictures of the event.

Buddy drove his jeep until the battery ran down. The dog's face was priceless, like a teenager who'd just been told they had to wait longer for their license.

Tim tucked him under his arm and followed Sam to his Mustang to get the charger.

"We can keep it in Dad's shed. I think he's got an outlet by his workbench," Sam said.

"Thanks, Sam." Tim gave his brother a hug.

"No problem," he said, hugging him back. "Just hurry up and come back home!"

After they had plugged Buddy's jeep in, Sam grabbed his *Mountain Dew* from the console inside his car and went in the house to cool off. "I'm probably gonna crash out here until it's time for work, Mom...if you don't mind," Sam said, as Buddy jumped into his lap.

"You *traitor!*" Tim hollered.

Sam started laughing. *"Who's your Daddy? Who's your Daddy?"* Sam hissed, taunting Buddy and trying to get a rise out of Tim.

Buddy started barking. *"That's right, Boy!"* he exclaimed in delight. *"Uncle Sammy! Uncle Sammy! All Hail, Uncle Sammy!"* Buddy barked in unison with him as he chanted his own name.

"Uncle Sammy bought you your very first car!" he

said in baby lingo.

Jamie covered her mouth with her hands, as she noticed that on Tim's smiling face there was also a look of aggravation beaming in his eyes.

Vickie lit a cigarette. "Okay, Sam, that's enough."

He put Buddy down and yawned. "I'm going to lie down and get some sleep, Mom. Will you wake me up at 8:30? I want to say goodbye to Tim before I leave for work."

"I will," she said, exhaling her smoke.

Sam decided to head for his room, as the rest of the family spent the day talking and laughing. Vickie baked a chicken with mashed potatoes and homemade gravy for dinner, and Jamie set the table; all waited for Ed to come home from work.

As Ed arrived and dinner began, Tim started watching the clock. The minutes were passing like seconds.

"What time are you going to get up?" Ed asked.

"5:30," Tim answered.

"That's about the time I get up. I'll drink some coffee with you in the morning, Son."

"That would be nice, Dad. This is going to be so hard," he said, looking at Jamie.

She leaned over and kissed him on the cheek. "It's going to be fine, Sweetheart."

Tim looked at the kitchen clock, then down at his watch, hoping that somehow they were both wrong, but it was time for bed.

Vickie woke Sam up. He stumbled down the hallway rubbing his eyes, and accidentally bumped into the wall as he made his way to the kitchen. Tim was on the verge of tears and Sam felt sorry for him.

"I love you, Tim," he said. He embraced his brother tightly. "You have a safe trip and we'll have a lot of fun when you get back."

Tim tried to nod, but Sam was holding him too tightly. "I love you, too, Sam. Thanks for everything," he said, fighting the urge to cry. Sam patted him on the back several times before letting him go.

"I saved you a plate, Sam," Vickie said. "It's in the oven." He went over to pull his plate out as Tim said his goodnights to everyone.

"I'll be there in a few minutes, Tim," Jamie said. "I want to lay down with you."

Jamie waited to hear the bedroom door close and the fan start up. "Vickie, could I talk to you for a minute?"

The women stepped outside and stood on the porch. Insects were swarming all around them.

Ed and Sam were chatting at the table. Jamie could hear them laughing as Sam recounted the tale of Buddy's driving adventure.

"He looked just like this," Sam said, laughing devilishly. He contorted his face and tried to make it look as though his nose were as long as Buddy's. Holding his imaginary paws on the steering wheel, he squinted his eyes, and Ed laughed heartily as he took another sip of tea.

The storm door opened and Jamie followed Vickie back into the house. "I think I have something you can use back here in the bedroom. Let's take a look," Vickie said, walking in that direction. Jamie followed.

She searched through her jewelry box and found what she was looking for, handing it to Jamie.

"It's perfect!" Jamie breathed. "I *really* appreciate this, Vickie." Heading to the bathroom, she smiled at her image in the mirror. She had found a way to be with Tim *after* all.

———

Five-thirty came quickly…too quickly.

Tim fumbled around and smacked the "off" button on the alarm clock. Jamie woke up, took Buddy outside, and started a pot of coffee while Tim showered.

Vickie emerged in her nightgown when she smelled it brewing. She already had a cigarette lit as she entered the kitchen. "Did you give it to him?" she whispered.

"Not yet," Jamie replied. "I want to wait until he goes back into the bedroom. He'll be awake by then."

Vickie chuckled. "I think it'll give him a little security while he's gone—that was a good idea."

Jamie made Tim a cup of coffee. Finishing with the ritual stirring, Jamie tasted the sugary substance and headed to Tim.

"Good morning!" she said, cheerfully, setting the mug on the dresser. "I made you some coffee, Sweetheart." She smiled gently and watched him brush his short, wet hair.

"Thanks," he smiled.

"Tim, I have something for you. It's not much, but I wanted to give you something to remind you of me—maybe you won't be so lonely that way," she said. "Now, close your eyes. I want it to be a surprise." (She checked to see if he was peeking.)

"Now, hold out your hand," she said, gently placing her gift in the palm of his hand.

"Okay, you can look now." She was smiling.

Tim opened his hand and returned the smile. He was staring at a silver locket about the size of a pocket watch.

"Open it," she said, happily.

Tim pulled the tiny latch with his fingernail, and stared at the thick lock of her lovely, dark brown hair. He put it up to his nose and sniffed it. Closing his eyes, he breathed in the delightful aroma of her *Ciara* perfume.

"It's heavenly—it's *you*," he whispered softly to her. He melted her heart with the look on his face, and a tear floated slowly down his cheek.

"I took it outside last night and sprayed a ton of it on there so it would soak in really well. Maybe it will stay fresh if you keep it in the locket," she suggested, wiping his tear with her hand.

He kissed her softly. "I'll keep it there forever, Jamie."

She grabbed him and hugged him tightly. "I love you so much, Tim. You *are* an angel whether you want to admit it or not."

When they went back into the kitchen, Ed had joined Vickie for a cup of coffee. Tim relished the smell of fresh morning dew coming through the fan in the kitchen. Pouring another cup of coffee, he chatted with his father before he left for work.

"You have a safe trip, Son" Ed said, standing up from the table. "Call your mother and let her know where you are when you stop, and call once you get home. I love you," Ed said.

Tim watched his father back out of the driveway. Once he was gone, he loaded up his luggage and guitar into the trunk. Taking a deep breath, Tim looked up at the house, gazing at Jamie through the storm door. Her arms were crossed and she wore a look of pure sadness on her face.

Slowly he walked back to the house. Buddy grunted as Tim picked him up from Ed's pillow cushion on the sofa and hugged him close.

Buddy woke briefly and placed his chin in the cleft of Tim's neck. He knew something was wrong, as Tim kissed him behind his velvet ears and whispered, "Goodbye, Son. I love you." Tim's heart was breaking as he rocked him back and forth.

Tim walked over and kissed his mother on the cheek. "Goodbye, I love you," he said. "I had a really nice visit."

Vickie kissed him on his neck. "I love you, too. Be careful and Godspeed."

He and Jamie stared at each other briefly. She smiled and fought hard not to erupt in tears. "Come on, Sweetheart, I'll walk you out to the car."

As they went outside, Buddy jumped off the couch. He scurried to the door, stood up against the window and looked out. Then...he began to whimper. He suddenly knew he wanted to be with his Daddy.

"Thanks' for letting me stay, Tim. It really means a lot. I'm going to make us a beautiful home while you're gone. It may not be spacious, but it will be filled with love," she said.

"Keep me in your heart and thoughts, as I'll keep you in mine, and call me whenever you want. I'll be here for you."

She choked on her tears. "You tell Rusty, Acie, Marty, and Spider that I love them and I'm going to miss them all very much, and tell them to keep you busy so you don't get lonely."

Tim had his head lowered to the ground. Finally, he looked up at her with heartbroken eyes.

"I love you with all of my heart, Tim!" She grabbed him and they kissed passionately. Holding each other as if it were the last day of their lives, they said their heart wrenching goodbyes.

As he opened the car door to get in, he glanced at the front door and saw Buddy looking out. As Tim stood there and slowly waved goodbye to his best friend, Buddy howled; his shrill barks of terror caused Vickie to cover her ears.

Jamie stood outside and watched Tim back down the driveway. They waved at each other as he pulled into the street and drove out of sight. Then, she turned and walked back to the house and sat down at the table with Vickie.

Buddy stood at the door and watched to see if Tim was coming back. His ears were cocked. He stared out of the window for several minutes and waited for him to return...but he never did. The fur around his eyes was soaked in tears as he turned and looked at Jamie. When she didn't say anything to him, he hung his head in sorrow and slowly walked past them and into the bedroom.

Walking over to the fan in the corner of the room, he looked down; his eyes were still moist with tears. Then, he turned around three times and nested in the middle of Tim's T-shirt that had accidentally been left on the floor; the soft whimpering came from the depths of his soul.

24

It was a long drive back to Lubbock and the weather had not been kind in the least. Storms had pursued Tim like an evil specter the entire trip, and torrents of violent rain had caused him to pull over several times.

He had planned to drive straight through, but with the heavy depression of having to leave Jamie and Buddy behind, and the barometric pressure bottoming out, his senses had gotten the best of him. Several times he had started to doze off behind the wheel as the slapping windshield wipers lulled him to the brink of sleep.

I can just close my eyes for a second. The possibility of a tragic end overwhelmed him. He had veered from the shoulder onto the zipper lane a couple of times, jarring him awake, narrowly averting death.

Cars honked furiously as he swerved the Toyota back into place on the saturated interstate. He was having difficulty seeing, and the headlights from travelers on the other side were causing him to view the road as an endless black mirror.

The water was pouring over the windshield so heavily that the wipers were really no use at all. He had long since gulped down the last of the coffee he had bought earlier in the morning, and he had smoked about all of the cigarettes he could stand.

There was nothing much to listen to on the radio either. It seemed like only boring talk shows with political rhetoric owned the airwaves.

The defroster was quickly becoming his arch-enemy, and the air conditioner wouldn't work right. Every single time he pushed the illuminated AC button, cool air would pour out for about thirty seconds before turning stale and musty. He struggled for several miles to reach some type of reasonable balance between opening the window and using the AC/defroster, but settled for wiping his side of the windshield with one of Jamie's socks that he'd found in the floorboard.

He looked up at the afternoon sky as he drove. It was so dark and grey that he felt like it was eight o'clock in the evening, but it was only three.

As his gaze returned to the road ahead, blurry red tail lights were approaching fast, and Tim practically stood up on the brakes. He shot a quick glance in the side mirror and tried not to fishtail. There was nowhere to go and traffic was too heavy in the left-hand lane to merge.

Were it not for the car ahead of him being able to creep forward a couple of feet before stopping again, Tim would have had a collision. His heart was racing. He could feel the adrenaline burning through his veins like fuel in a high-performance combustion engine.

That woke me up! he thought, gasping in horror. A bead of sweat rolled from his forehead and he wiped it away. Growing even more flustered, Tim decided it was safer to just give up and get a room. He began to watch for billboards advertising the cheapest rates.

Super 8 and *Motel 6* were supposed to be the least expensive, but he found that they were just as costly as some of the others.

That Tom Bodette is full of it, he thought, as he looked in the rearview mirror, *as if the old-time country music in the background of all his corny commercials could make the rates any cheaper! He and his family will* never *have to pay for another motel room in* two *lifetimes!* Tim was suddenly getting jealous of Tom Bodette.

This is insane. I'm condemning a man for doing a radio commercial when I'd do the very same thing if someone offered me a free motel room for life, only I would say, 'Me and Buddy'll leave the light on for ya'.

Tim's stomach screamed for food. He chuckled, remembering an old George Carlin record. George was talking about having to sit in a doctor's office with a bunch of people around, and his stomach was grumbling.

"We-e-r-e po-o-o-r," his stomach groaned, stretching out the words.

There was a motel five miles up the road. Tim decided it was time to pull over and get a room—there were also several restaurants. *Long John Silver's* would be receiving his patronage shortly, he decided.

And it certainly did. He ate his two-piece *Fish and More* meal in silence in his room. He missed not being able to share his supper with Buddy that evening, and there was nothing to watch on television. Tim put his arms behind his neck as he stretched out on the bed, closed his eyes, and became engrossed in his thoughts.

He first reflected on Jamie and Buddy, but his nose was pointed toward Lubbock, and his thoughts soon turned to Rusty and the guys. Tim hoped to see Tinker again; he wanted to keep his promise and give him one of his records, and hopefully play music with him one last time.

I wish I was with Rusty now, he thought. *I'm going to take him to Alpha's tomorrow night and buy him a beer.* Tim could see the smile on Rusty's face as Maggie set a cold one in front of him

Jamie's right, I'm going to spend the rest of my time playing music with him. He reached over and set the alarm clock for 5:00 A.M. If he could make good time the rest of the way, he and Rusty would be sharing a drink by five or six tomorrow night.

As Tim listened to the humming of the air conditioner, his eyelids grew heavy. His stomach was full and he was content, as he drifted into dreamland.

When the alarm clock sounded, Tim instinctively reached for the snooze button. When he kept trying and couldn't find it he shook his head, looked around, and remembered that he was alone in the motel room.

He knew he had no choice. Forcing his body out of bed, Tim took a shower and brushed his teeth. After he had dressed, he ambled to the office to check out. He sighed deeply as he perused the continental breakfast bar.

Tim had always pictured a *continent* as being a huge geographical location—like Asia, or something. Somehow, he didn't think a dozen doughnuts and ketchup holders for coffee cups in a small, isolated corner of a foreign-owned establishment fit his definition of the word.

He stopped at a gas station near the interstate to fill up the tank and check the oil. The *extra* large insulated cup of coffee he purchased was piping hot and looked delicious as he stirred in his cream and sugar.

Morning talk shows flooded the radio. Tim grew

irritated at the constant and ridiculous yammering of all the announcers who were talking just to make noise. Some of the topics really insulted his intelligence, so he drove in silence and focused on the stunning sunrise.

It rained in several places as his journey edged on, but nothing like the travesty of the previous day. By the time he made it to Amarillo, the beloved sun was starting to blaze. He looked at his watch. At this new rate, he would be home by 2:00 P.M.

He smiled as the familiar Texas heat filled his face and nostrils. He was filled with the pleasure that being back home brought to him, and the irritation and grumpiness dissipated under the Texas sun.

He reached down, turned the radio on and was thrilled that he didn't have to tune in a station. Clint Black greeted him immediately with *Killin' Time.* Tim smiled and tapped out the rhythm on the steering wheel as he sang along, eager to be *'killin' time'* at Alpha's talking to Rusty.

When he reached the apartment, a new wave of loneliness struck him when he opened the door and peered around the empty living room. There were no sounds of laughter, no jingling of Buddy's collar as he ran to greet him, and no beat of music from the radio in the kitchen as Jamie prepared *Hamburger Helper* for supper. There was only solitude.

Tim sighed as he turned the air conditioner on to rid the place of stale air. It felt like a crypt without Jamie and Buddy there—a house, perhaps, but not a home.

After he had unloaded his belongings from the trunk, he called Rusty.

"So did you have a nice time visiting with your folks?" he asked.

"I did, but it's good to be back home," Tim replied, honestly.

"I started on a job yesterday," Rusty explained. "But it's turned out to be a little more complicated than I had expected, and I have to get it done by this evening. I'll get cleaned up and meet you up there around 8:00."

"Thanks, Rusty...I really missed you when I was gone," Tim said.

"I've missed you too, Son, glad you had a safe trip back."

Tim hung up and started unpacking. After he put his guitar in the bedroom, he began putting his clothes away in the dresser drawers; they smelled fresh and he could detect a trace of Jamie's perfume.

He remembered the locket that she had given to him before he left, and he pulled it from his pocket. He slowly unlocked it and breathed her scent in deeply, softly stroking the lock of hair with his finger.

He gently closed it and stuck it back inside his pocket. After he finished putting his clothes away, he called her to let her know that he had made it home safely.

"How was your trip?" Jamie asked. He could tell right away that she was excited to hear from him.

"It rained most of the way down and I had to stop and get a room last night because it was raining so hard," he explained.

"We've been trying to figure out where to start with the rooms. And your dad is going to build Buddy's pen next weekend," she said.

Tim's heart beat quickly. "How's Buddy doing?" he asked her, anxiously.

"Uh, he's pretty depressed Tim. He's made a blanket out of one of your shirts and I can't keep him off it. After you left he just curled up on it and went to sleep. He really misses you.

"He stood at the door several times today and looked for you, then went and laid back down when he saw you weren't coming."

Tim's heart sank. "Please let him have the shirt, Jamie, and give him a kiss for me."

"I will. I felt sorry for him so I put it on the bed for him last night to sleep on. Don't worry, Tim. He'll be okay in a couple of days. What do you have planned for tonight?"

"I'm meeting Rusty at *Alpha's.* I really miss him and I don't feel like being alone, plus I want to tell him what's going on," he said.

"That sounds nice. I don't want you to be lonesome, so you have a good time and tell him I said hello."

"I will," he promised. "I'll get your clothes packed tomorrow and ship them out Monday. Is there anything in particular you want me to send?"

"Send everything in the top two dresser drawers, and just pick out some T-shirts from the others. You can send all my jeans too; they're hanging in the closet. I already have all of my makeup and toiletries, so that should do it."

"Okay, I'm going to lay down for a while. I'm pretty

whipped from the trip. I'll call you tomorrow. I love you," he said.

"I love you, too! Have a nice evening with Rusty."

Tim set the alarm clock for 6:00P.M., and took a nap.

"Well, howdy, Stranger! Where have you been hiding these days?" Maggie Tilton hollered.

Tim walked over to the jukebox and deposited his customary quarter. "I just got back from Tennessee," he said, as he punched in his selection: *My Heart Skips a Beat* by Buck Owens.

She wiped off the section of the bar where he sat down, and brought him a *Bud Light.* She started giggling and put her right hand on her hip, leaning against the bar. Maggie *really* knew how to tell a good joke, and always seemed to have one on the tip of her tongue whenever Tim stopped in.

Tim grinned at her. "Uh-oh, this one must be a *doosie*," he said, snickering.

"Have you heard the one about the nun and the cabbie?" Maggie asked. She chuckled and laid the wet rag on the counter top.

Tim lit a cigarette. "Nope. Go for it!."

"A cab driver stops and picks up a nun. She gets in the cab and notices that he keeps staring at her in the rearview mirror.

'Why do you keep staring at me?' the nun asks.

"The cab driver says, 'I have a question to ask you but I'm afraid I'll offend you.'

"She says, 'My son, there's nothing that you can say or do that will offend me. When you're as old as I am and have been a nun for as long as have, you get a chance to see and hear just about everything. I'm sure that there's nothing you could ask that I would find offensive. Speak, my son.'

'Well, I've always fantasized about kissing a nun.'

"The nun replies, 'Well, let's see what we can do about that. First, you have to be single and, second, you *must* be a Catholic.'

"The cab driver gets excited and says, 'That's perfect! I'm single *and* I'm a Catholic!

'Okay,' the nun says. 'Pull into the alley over there.'

"The nun fulfills his fantasy and kisses him as if they were on their wedding night, but when they get back on the road, the cab driver starts crying.

"'My son,' says the nun. 'Why are you crying?'

"The cab driver wipes his eyes and says, 'Please forgive me, Sister, but I've sinned. I lied to you and I have to confess—I'm married and I'm Jewish.'

"The nun says, 'That's okay. My name is really Kevin and I'm on my way to a Halloween party.'"

Tim choked on his cigarette smoke and almost fell off the barstool laughing. He was holding his sides as if they were going to explode, as he fought for breath. There were only two other customers in the bar and they stopped talking and stared at him like he was crazy.

Maggie was like a big sister to Tim. She had been friendly to him from the very start. The first time he ever came to *Alpha's* he didn't say much and she could tell that he was extremely shy. Needless to say, for Maggie, that simply wouldn't do. His first beer had been on the house.

Maggie was in her mid-thirties and had been bartending most of her life, so she *knew* people. She was quite an attractive woman with light brown, curly hair that flowed past her shoulders. Her eyes were dark but kind, and she always wore a sweet smile. She was a delightful person to be around and Tim immediately felt comfortable with her, and he *adored* her sense of humor.

It wasn't long before she had pulled Tim out of his shell. Once he started talking about music—*that was all she wrote.*

Maggie lived in a house behind *Alpha's* with her husband, Dalton, and her two children. That first night she called and had her daughter bring her guitar over so she could hear Tim play and sing. With the exception of his shyness, she had actually been quite impressed with him.

Tim handed the guitar back over the counter to her and took a sip of beer.

She stared at him momentarily then crammed the towel she was holding into the back pocket of her blue jeans. When she stepped out from behind the bar with her guitar, she walked over and sat down on a stool next to him—Maggie could sing, *too.*

She looked softly at Tim, perhaps sensing his loneliness as she gently strummed the strings. She sang a beautiful oldie to him by Dickey Lee called, *Patches.* It was her favorite song in the whole world.

Tim listened intently to the words of the song as she sang about a rich boy who was in love with a poor girl who lived in the shanties. His parents refused to let him court her so she committed suicide.

The words broke Tim's heart and a tear fell from his eye as she ended the song with the young man also taking his own life over the loss of his true love.

She performed the song with such intensity that Tim was speechless afterwards. She reminded him of the singer, Bobby Gentry, who sang *Ode to Billy Joe*. The *likeness* of her voice was uncanny, he thought.

All of a sudden, the world didn't seem so desolate and lonely anymore. He had found his new best friend. At this moment, she was his *only* friend.

Tim's mind raced back to the things he liked most about Maggie. One was the fact that she was also a very talented cartoonist. Every year without fail she had drawn him a giant birthday card made from poster board.

He thought about the one she had drawn for him the previous year. It was a picture of a drunken man wearing a cowboy hat in the bathtub with his feet hanging over the end. He was dangling a gallon jug of moonshine with three X's on it in his hand, and bubbles were all around his head indicating his intoxication.

Balloons were tied on the faucets and the card read: "YOU'RE NOT TOO DRUNK IF YOU CAN STILL HOLD ON TO THE FLOOR!"

Maggie's kindness is unreal, Tim thought. *Twice,* Steve had let her hold a benefit and auction for people who had lost their homes to a fire. One couple was elderly and had no insurance to cover their losses. To Tim, Maggie *was* the definition of Lubbock hospitality.

"So what's been going on?" she asked.

Tim looked down and sighed, trying to brush away

the memories and concentrate on the here-and-now. "Maggie...Jamie's pregnant...with twins," he said.

Maggie let out a whistle, managing to get a tongue-in-cheek grin from him. "So what's the problem?" she asked.

Tim lit up another cigarette and exhaled slowly.

"Jamie wanted to stay behind; she fell in love with Tennessee. I've tried to think of every option and every way to stay here, but I've come up with nothing. I have to go where the work is, Maggie, especially now, with Jamie expecting and all.

"I have to tell Rusty, but I'm afraid he's going to be mad at me because he's invested so much time and money into our music. He's like a father *and* a brother to me, and I don't think I could bear losing his friendship.

"If we could have had just a little more time, I honestly think we could have made it. He's been so happy and excited about all of this, I feel like I'm about to ruin his life."

Tim took a sip of beer and inhaled a long drag from his cigarette.

Maggie observed him for a moment. She patted his hand, seeing the discouragement on his face. "Tim, I don't think Rusty's that kind of a person. Some things just can't be helped, you know?" She said kindly. Tim sat in silence and Maggie felt it best to change the subject.

"I want you to look at something," she said.

Reaching beneath the counter, she pulled out a copy of *TIME* magazine. She licked her finger and thumbed through the pages until she found the article she was looking for. "Do you recognize this person?" She pointed at a man in the picture, tapping it twice. Tim studied the photograph and shook his head.

"Look really close." She kept her finger just above the man's head, but Tim still had no recollection.

"It's Dalton," she said, firmly.

Tim's mouth dropped open in shock as he slowly fixed his gaze on Maggie. He looked back down at the photo. It *was* Dalton. He was running furiously beside several other soldiers out of a jungle in Vietnam. Hell was being unleashed behind them as napalm sent everything up in flames. He had a savage war face that sent chills up Tim's spine. One of the men was carrying a body over his shoulder as they scrambled for safety. Tim couldn't tell if he was wounded or dead.

Arnold Schwarzenegger was nothing compared to what Dalton looked like in *his* picture. There were no Hollywood special effects; he was the picture of *raw* masculinity built with solid muscle.

Like Spider, Dalton was a man of very few words. Tim had almost surmised that Clint Eastwood had gotten his character roles from *him*. If Dalton *had* to speak, someone *better* get four coffins ready.

One evening before he was married, Tim was sitting at the bar chatting with Maggie. Dalton was seated at one of the nearby tables eating his dinner; his children were running around the table laughing and playing. At one point, they started becoming a little rowdy.

Dalton stood up, grabbed his belt buckle, and the children disappeared into thin air. He did that without saying a word or batting an eyelash. He looked at Tim and Maggie with his piercing, deadly, gunslinger eyes, then had sat back down and finished his meal.

25

About that time long, lanky arms wrapped around Tim's shoulders—it was Rusty. Tim stood up and gave him a hug.

"Maggie, can I buy Rusty a beer, please?" Tim asked.

"Sure." She walked over to the cooler, took one out and opened it, as Tim reached into his back pocket for his wallet.

Rusty plopped down on the stool at the corner of the bar and lit a cigarette. When Maggie returned with his beer, Rusty held it up to Tim. "I appreciate it, Son," he said.

They both took a sip and Tim began to unburden his soul. After he finished, he lowered his eyes, expecting the worst.

Rusty leaned on the bar, resting his head in the palm of his hand.

Tim looked back up and saw that he was grinning. "I thought you'd be mad at me," Tim said.

Rusty exhaled his smoke and shook his head. "Don't go around beatin' yourself up about this, Tim. This is something I was *hoping* for, not *counting* on. I'm a *little* disappointed, but not with you...but because it just wasn't meant to be." He took a long pause, and then leaned in towards Tim.

"I want to tell you something, Son. I've been playing music all my life. Some make it and some *don't,* and that's a *fact*—but you made it. You may not think you did, but you *did*. The people will put you where they want you and Lubbock's about the best place in the world for that to happen, because we care for one another here. It's not about contracts and millions of dollars, Tim. It's about music, plain and simple.

"We made a good record together and it's on the air. *We* made it—with *your* songs! Buddy Holly would've been proud of you. For Pete's sake, you wrote my song on a bank slip!"

He took the last draw off his cigarette and crushed it in the ashtray, exhaling the smoke. Rusty sighed and shook his head. "Music is an instinct for people like us, Son—it runs in our blood, through and through. Like a master artist with a paintbrush, it's just who and what we are." He grinned. "And it's already cost me *two* marriages."

Tim stared in amazement. "You have *got* to be kidding me."

Rusty shook his head. "Nope. And that's not all. Marty's been divorced for five years, and Acie's wife ran off with some other musician—he came home from work one night and all of her stuff was gone! He hasn't seen or heard from her since.

"And Spider—well...Spider is just Spider—*'nuff* said. It takes a special person to be able to put up with the likes of us. Once all the excitement wears off, the wives get bored. They get tired of the repetition and they stop going to your gigs. Along with that, you have three demons that are constantly tugging at you: booze, pills—and *women*," he said, counting them down on his fingers.

"You've got a very special lady, Tim. And you

wouldn't want to lose a fine lookin' woman like that. I think you should cash in your chips and quit while you're ahead."

Tim gave him a startled look.

Rusty pushed his hat up with his thumb and hollered, "Let's ride in this rodeo til' it's over and have fun, fun, fun, till our daddy takes the T-bird away!" He crossed himself as he said it, and threw an imaginary key over his shoulder.

Tim and Maggie simply smiled. There were some people who just simply knew what they were, and how to live life to the fullest.

It was actually Tuesday before Tim could ship Jamie's things to her because there were no boxes to be found.

Rusty decided to do something very special for Tim. He spent most of the day on Monday contacting people and making arrangements, and Maggie put an ad in the *Avalanche Journal.*

Monday evening came round and Rusty invited Tim and the rest of *The Sucker-rods* over for drinks...and a proposition. Tim grew excited as Rusty began to tell them all about it.

"That Mickey Jarvis fella is having a 'goat roast' out at his place next weekend for Labor Day, and he wants us to play. He's putting six of 'em in the ground," Rusty announced.

"I've never had goat meat, what does it taste like?" Tim asked.

"It tastes pretty darned good if it's cooked right," Rusty said, chuckling. "So what do you say?" Rusty asked.

Everyone was in agreement and they spent the rest of the week rehearsing.

Tim rode with Rusty out to Mickey's goat roast on Saturday afternoon. The rest of the band drove behind them with all of the equipment loaded in their pickup trucks.

Tim's mouth fell open as Rusty pulled into the open, thirty acre field. Billy's flatbed was parked beside a barn, and a huge banner hung above it.

Maggie had spent a great deal of the week painting it for him. It read, in huge red, white and blue letters: "SAYONARA TIM, LUBBOCK WILL MISS YOU!"

They spent the next hour and a half setting up and doing sound checks. The goat pits were about a football field's length away from the stage.

"I've had these rascals in the ground since Thursday!" Mickey said proudly, as they walked over to the pits. "They should be nice and tender when we take them out tonight," he concluded.

The fire was burning on top of huge sheets of aluminum. Mickey threw more wood on the fire, and Tim had to step back as the intense heat licked at his face. A cold beer sure sounded good to him right now.

People started to arrive around 6:00 P.M., along with a couple of news crews. Everyone had brought their own beer and liquor with them. The strip had almost sold completely out of everything for Labor Day.

Mickey rented a dumpster and had it placed on the opposite side of the barn, so everyone could discard their beer cans and waste.

As dusk approached and various individuals lit tiki torches around the barn, a few of Mickey's neighbors chipped in and furnished generators to power the equipment and lights around the stage.

Several familiar people, including Maggie, stood at the end of the flatbed. Tim shook hands with them all, but he gave Maggie a big hug and thanked her for all the hard work she had done on his banner.

The Sucker-rods climbed the rickety ladder and took the stage. Tim looked out over the vast crowd and they all began to cheer.

Rusty tapped on his microphone a couple of times to make sure it was on, and addressed the crowd. "Folks, we'd like to thank all of you for showing up on such a beautiful Labor Day weekend."

Rusty looked over at Tim as he continued to talk, "We're here to say goodbye to this nice, young fella, as he bids a kind farewell to Lubbock and embarks on a new life's journey in Tennessee." A hush fell over the crowd.

Maggie stepped onto the flatbed and walked over to Tim. She carried a giant Styrofoam key that had been spray-painted in gold metal flake and had a giant, white ribbon tied around it. She smiled as she presented it to him and kissed his cheek. "Tim, we can't give you the key to the city, Son." The masses let out a laugh.

"But we *can* give you the key to our hearts. Lubbock will be a sadder place without you, and we hope that you can find your way back to our fair city one day and take your place among us."

Rusty began to get choked up and he cleared his

throat. "I think I can speak for everyone here when I say that you are one fine gentleman—but one *helluva* singer!"

The crowd went wild. Cheers, whistles, and applause mixed together like the roar of a fierce ocean wave.

"We love you, Tim! Now let's play some music for these nice folks and let 'em dance till their stockin's are hot and ravelin'!"

Rusty counted off and Tim sent electricity bolting through the multitude with *Brown Eyed Handsome Man.* Tim got cold chills up and down his spine as Acie's dog-house bass thundered across the field.

Rusty really got into the song when Tim started the first verse. "*Aw yeah!* Sing it like ya wrote it, Son!" he hollered.

Afterwards, a woman held up a plastic cup full of beer. Perspiration was starting to saturate his black shirt, and Tim gratefully bent down and took it from her. He was parched, so he guzzled the golden nectar like it was ice-cold water, as he wiped the sweat from his scorching brow.

Rusty sang *Sugartime* by Johnny Cash next, and nailed the shrillness of the guitar break in the middle. He was really on his game tonight.

Tim guzzled another beer after the song was over. His shirt was becoming soaked with sweat.

Several songs and several beers later, they took a much-needed break. Tim had become a tad bit intoxicated.

Someone handed him another beer as he stepped down from the stage. Many of the people gathered around him to shake his hand, offer compliments, and wish him good luck. He was so humbled, and he talked and joked with them.

The news crew from *KLBK* made their way through the crowd and caught up with him.

"Mr. Cunningham? I'm Melanie Foxx from *KLBK*. I was wondering if I could have a brief interview with you?"

Tim felt honored. Melanie was an *extremely* gorgeous young woman. The long, golden blonde hair and deep, blue eyes set her apart from the other women. Her perfume smelled heavenly, and her well-shaped form was wrapped in a pair of tight blue jeans and a V-neck shirt.

Tim could sense that she was nervous as she talked with him. Taking another sip of beer, Tim studied her briefly—she was giving him "the look" and staring at him with ardent desire.

A crowd was gathered around them in a circle as the news crew stood by, holding their cameras. Rusty was leaning against the front of the trailer with his arms crossed, puffing on a cigarette...keeping an eye on his friend.

"You sure can," Tim said, teetering a bit.

"Uh, if you could please put your drink down for a moment—we can't have alcohol in the picture," she asked politely, apparently afraid that Tim would be offended.

He stretched his neck, loosening the wet grip that his collar had on it, and handed his cup to a bystander that was standing next to him.

The cameramen got ready as Melanie primped her hair and tried hard to attract Tim's attention.

"In *three*, two, one," the director rang out, pointing

to Melanie.

"We're here with Tim Cunningham. The citizens of Lubbock are hosting a Labor Day party to say farewell to this unique young man who has given such entertainment, and captured the hearts of many people in the Lubbock area during his enlistment in the United States Air Force.

"Tim, how do you feel about your stay here in Lubbock?" She aimed the microphone at his lips.

"Melanie, I've been stationed here for seven years, and I have to say that I've never met a kinder bunch of folks in my entire life," he said, humbly.

"Do you plan on pursuing your music career in Tennessee?" Melanie asked.

Tim looked around and saw Rusty smiling at him. "No, Ma'am. I don't." He looked straight into the camera. "Our group has a very distinctive sound that I find irreplaceable. We have a strong kindred bond between us, and I can't imagine playing music with *anyone else but them*."

Melanie shuddered when he made that statement. She had heard him sing Ricky Nelson's *Anyone Else but You*, and he enunciated the last sentence exactly like he sang the song, in his rich, velvety voice—she stalled.

Tim grinned at her and picked up the empty pause. "You see, Melanie...it's not about contracts and millions of dollars, it's about music— plain and simple," he reiterated Rusty's profound words.

"Do you ever plan on returning to us—I mean, Lubbock?" she asked.

Tim stared sadly at her and sighed deeply. "I

certainly hope so, and I mean that with all my heart."

"One last question, Tim. Are you enjoying yourself tonight? Are you having a good time?" Her hands shook as she again aimed the microphone at his lips.

"That's actually two questions, Melanie." Everyone chuckled, including Tim. "But, yes, I'm having a fantastic time tonight. We're gonna play some more music here shortly, and then I plan on having some ghost meat later on."

Melanie giggled at him and lost her composure. One of the cameramen doubled over with laughter and almost dropped his camera.

"What's so funny?" Tim asked.

"You said *ghost meat*," Melanie smiled. She touched his arm.

"I meant to say 'goat meat'," he laughed.

Melanie was waiting for the rest of the news crew to leave. *They're taking forever!* she exclaimed in her head. When they *finally* turned and left her alone, Tim reached for his beer.

Melanie gazed at him as he took a sip. "I love you, Tim," she said, tenderly.

Tim knew what she wanted...*now.* All eyes were on him, including Rusty's. Leaning over he placed a kiss on Melanie's cheek. "Thank you, Sweetheart, I love you too," he said. A few people *cooed* as Tim turned around and made his way back to the trailer.

"That was a close one," Tim said, blowing air through his pursed lips.

"Boy, Howdy!" Rusty exclaimed, shaking his head. He pushed his hat up with his thumb and watched as Tim

drank his beer. He knew that Tim missed his wife and little dog; he also knew that loneliness could tempt a man into doing many stupid things.

"Tim, why don't you just stay with me for the next few weeks?" he suggested.

"I—I couldn't impose on you like that, Rusty," Tim said, shaking his head.

"But I insist," Rusty stated firmly. He was wearing a stern, fatherly expression on his face.

"Yes, sir," he said, quickly.

"Attaboy!" Rusty exclaimed, slapping him on the back. "I want to get as much music outta you as I possibly can, Son! You're gonna feel like a rung-out sponge by the time you leave Lubbock!" Rusty chuckled.

"Lord knows if we'll ever get to see each other again, but we need to part ways with nothing but good memories under our hats and no regrets."

No matter what, Rusty sure had a keen way of putting things into perspective.

It was a brisk and chilly October morning at the *Walk of Fame.* Tim sat silently on the hood of the Toyota and patiently waited for the sunrise.

He shivered, and thrust his hands deeply into the pockets of his windbreaker. It was quiet and calm. He loved this place; he could think here—he dreamed here.

Reminiscing over the last seven years of his life, Tim's mind was full of images and feelings. A great deal had happened. He remembered the many walks with Jamie through this beloved place. He missed her very much and his heart longed to be with her again.

Buddy would be thrilled to see him, too. Tim would never be without his loved ones ever again, he decided. It was just too difficult.

Rusty kept him busy, just as Jamie had predicted—he also kept him out of trouble. He had been a true friend, and Tim would cherish and love him all the days of his life.

The sun began to peek shyly over the horizon. The night gently stole away as the morning tenderly revealed herself. Tim slid off the hood of the car and strolled slowly up the sidewalk. He lingered at the monuments. One by one he visited with them, touched them, and read them one last time.

Finally, he stood before Buddy's statue. He stared up at his distant friend and said goodbye. Putting his arms around it, Tim pressed his face against the concrete pedestal. Closing his eyes, he thanked Buddy for sharing his legacy with him.

It started to sprinkle. He didn't want to leave. The rain began to fall harder...

The autumn leaves stirred bitterly around him. Some of them were clinging to his pant legs as if they were begging him to stay.

The wind howled sadly as Lubbock *wept* in her early morning rain—for already she was mourning over the loss of her second... *native* son.

Epilogue

Ladies and Gentlemen,

It's been many years since I performed in Lubbock, but I remember them as if they were yesterday.

I've always thought if I could touch just one heart with my music, it would be worth more than all the gold and money in the world.

I still take my strolls down the Walk of Fame through the many pictures I have, and I visit it often.

I twirl my cigarette between my thumb and fingers the way Rusty did; although, I had to switch from Marlboro to Doral Lights; they became too harsh for me, and I reminisce over my photos.

Jamie grows more beautiful with each passing day; her beauty is ageless and timeless.

I still drag my old, black Alvarez from the closet and play the songs I wrote for her whenever she asks me to, and she still melts my heart with her shimmering, emerald green eyes, as I sing to her.

Our twins have long since been grown and gone; Sarah is a veterinarian and Golden is a truck driver.

Our third child died at birth; I named him, Vincent Andrew. He was a beautiful child; he looked like Jamie.

It was the most heart breaking experience of my life, but I respect the Lord's decision and I'm honored to know my son is with him; I can't wait to see him again.

Buddy died several years ago; words cannot describe how much I miss him.

He was blind and deaf, and he couldn't speak in German anymore.

He was lying on a blanket on the kitchen floor one morning; I picked him up gently, and cradled him in my arms like an infant.

I kissed his soft, velvet ears and whispered to him, "I love you, Buddy;" then, I rocked him back and forth.

He was panting so hard; he didn't want to leave me, and I was reminded of a beautiful song I once heard when I was a little boy; I sang the last verse of the song to him and he wagged his tail.

"... but if dogs have a heaven, there's one thing I know; Old Shep has a won...der...ful home..."

He went Limp in my arms and I cried for hours; he had not only been my best friend, he had been a son.

I buried him beneath a Large weeping willow tree behind our home, and I visit with Buddy... 'Everyday.'

Your Friend,
"Tim"

www.ingramcontent.com/pod-product-compliance
Lightning Source LLC
LaVergne TN
LVHW040827090826
845145LV00001BA/253

* 9 7 8 1 9 3 5 7 8 6 1 2 2 *